Anthony Burgess was born in Manchester in 1917 and studied English at the university there. He was drafted into the army upon graduation in 1940 and spent six years in the Education Corps. After demobilization, he worked first as a college lecturer in speech and drama and then as a grammar school master. From 1954 to 1960 he was an education officer in the Colonial Service, stationed in Malaya and Borneo, and it was while he was there that he started writing *The Malayan Trilogy* (published in Penguin as *The Long Day Wanes*). In 1959 Burgess was diagnosed as having an inoperable brain tumour and was given less than a year to live. He then became a full-time writer and, proving the doctors wrong, went on to write at least one book a year and hundreds of book reviews right up to his death in 1993.

A late starter in the art of fiction, Anthony Burgess had previously spent much creative energy on music, and in his lifetime he composed many full-scale works for orchestra and other media. His Third Symphony was performed in the USA in 1975 and *Blooms of Dublin*, his musical version of Joyce's *Ulysses*, was presented in 1982. He believed that with the fusion of the musical and literary forms lay a possible future for the novel. His many other works include *Inside Mr Enderby, Enderby Outside, The Clockwork Testament, Enderby's Dark Lady, Tremor of Intent; Honey for the Bears; Urgent Copy; Nothing Like the Sun; Man of Nazareth*, the basis of his successful TV script *Jesus of Nazareth; Earthly Powers*, which was voted the best foreign novel of 1980 in France; *The End of the World News; The Kingdom of the Wicked*, winner of the Prix Europa in Geneva; *The Piano Players; Any Old Iron; A Mouthful of Air; Home to QWERTYUIOP*, an anthology of his reviews and journalism; and two volumes of autobiography: *Little Wilson and Big God*, which was awarded the J. R. Ackerley Prize for 1988, and *You've Had Your Time. A Clockwork Orange* was made into a film classic by Stanley Kubrick and was dramatized by the RSC in 1990. His last novel, published in the spring of 1993, was *A Dead Man in Deptford*, based around the murder of Christopher Marlowe.

Anthony Burgess died in November 1993. *The Times* described him as 'one of the cleverest and most original writers of his generation', and among the many people who paid tribute to him were David Lodge, who considered him 'an inspiration and example to other writers', and John Updike, who believed that 'The literary world seems much more sparsely populated with Anthony Burgess gone. He had the energy and the wide-ranging interests of a dozen writers ... [and] seemed not only a prodigious intellect, but an affectionate spirit, whose mind, like Ariel's, circled the globe in a few seconds.'

Gilbert Adair is a novelist, screenwriter and critic. His most recently published novels were *Buenas Noches Buenos Aires* and *The Dreamers*, the latter of which was filmed by Bernardo Bertolucci. He lives in London.

Anthony Burgess

M/F

PENGUIN BOOKS

PENGUIN BOOKS

Published by the Penguin Group
Penguin Books Ltd, 80 Strand, London WC2R ORL, England
Penguin Group (USA), Inc., 375 Hudson Street, New York, New York 10014, USA
Penguin Books Australia Ltd, 250 Camberwell Road, Camberwell, Victoria 3124, Australia
Penguin Books Canada Ltd, 10 Alcorn Avenue, Toronto, Ontario, Canada M4V 3B2
Penguin Books India (P) Ltd, 11 Community Centre, Panchsheel Park, New Delhi – 110 017, India
Penguin Group (NZ), cnr Airborne and Rosedale Roads, Albany, Auckland 1310, New Zealand
Penguin Books (South Africa) (Pty) Ltd, 24 Sturdee Avenue, Rosebank 2196, South Africa

Penguin Books Ltd, Registered Offices: 80 Strand, London WC2R ORL, England

www.penguin.com

Published by Jonathan Cape 1971
Published in Penguin Books 1973
Published in Penguin Classics 2004
007

Copyright © Anthony Burgess, 1971
Introduction copyright © Gilbert Adair, 2004
All rights reserved

The moral right of the author has been asserted

Printed in England by Clays Ltd, St Ives plc

ISBN-13: 978–0–141–18780–8

www.greenpenguin.co.uk

MIX
Paper from
responsible sources
FSC® C018179

Penguin Books is committed to a sustainable
future for our business, our readers and our planet
This book is made from Forest Stewardship
Council™ certified paper.

Introduction

In 'Oedipus Wrecks', one of the eleven essays that make up *This Man and Music*, an eclectic anthology of writings on musical composition and culture, Anthony Burgess offers a lengthy, comprehensive gloss on the intricate web of references embedded in the narrative of *M/F*. His justification for this critical apparatus, a justification inscribed within the essay itself, is that it was important for him, in a period of ruthlessly remaindered and/or pulped novels, that some significant trace remain of what was presumably one of his, if few other people's, personal favourites. Or, putting it bluntly, Burgess, who in his day reviewed innumerable books for the British press, elected to write a review of one of his own books, the kind of densely analytical review he himself patently believed it deserved but never received (except for a lonely rave from Frank Kermode).

The Burgess of 'Oedipus Wrecks' (which was, interestingly, also a title used by Woody Allen) is very much the writer as back-seat driver, steering the reader towards the completest possible appreciation of his work like somebody lending unsolicited assistance at a game of solitaire. ('Black eight on the red nine.') The most *Irish* of English writers, he prefers to flaunt his learning rather than wear it lightly or simply let it be. Hence we learn that the plotline of *M/F*, combining two immemorial literary themes, incest and the double (or incest and what one might whimsically call 'twincest'), derives essentially from a legend told by the Algonquin tribe of North American Indians – which is why, in its opening chapter, the protagonist, Miles Faber, one of the novel's several M/F referents, along with *male/female*, *motherfucker*, *mezzo-forte* and so forth, is staying at what is still perhaps the best-known Manhattan hotel, the Algonquin. We learn that he, Burgess, first encountered this legend via a lecture given in Paris by the doyen of structuralist anthropologists, Claude Lévi-Strauss – a source reflected in the rigorous structural underpinning of *M/F*'s ostensibly corkscrewy storyline as also, more trivially, in its allusions to jeans (Lévi) and Viennese waltzes (Strauss). We learn that one character's name, Feteki, comes from the Sanskrit word for 'riddle' (*M/F* is not only stuffed with riddles but is one itself); another's, Fonanta, from Zoon Fonanta, Greek for 'talking animal' (virtually all its characters are metaphorised as animals); and a third's, Aderyn, from the Welsh for 'bird' (she, for it's a she, trains exotic birds for a circus act). Burgess even mischievously directs our attention to a handful of proper names which have no referential significance whatever, inevitably making us wonder fretfully if there might be a meaning in the very absence of meaning.

'Oedipus Wrecks', if read *after M/F*, will certainly provide the novel's readers with all the exegesis they are ever going to want, and then some; if, on the other hand, read *before M/F*, it will just as certainly prove counterproductive. What, the pre-*M/F* reader will be tempted to ask, is the point of Burgess genning up (as even he, famously erudite as he was, must have had to do) on all this arcane linguistico-cultural lore, encoding it into his narrative then blithely supplying us with a master key permitting us to decode it at the other end? The impression would be of a futile and claustrophobic indulgence.

Yet, for the lucky reader who comes to *M/F* without either preconceptions or foreknowledge, that isn't at all the case. And, to explain why, I submit the following superficially paradoxical theory: that the experience of reading *M/F*, a magically virtuosic fable of a young American whose every endeavour to avoid copulation with his own sister brings him ever closer to committing the Oedipal sin, is not merely not diminished but actually *enhanced* by ignorance of the multi-layered referential grid which would appear to be its primary *raison d'être*.

Consider this string of examples, all of them taken from the novel's earliest pages. Burgess's hero – Miles Faber, as I say – is determined to quite New York and fly down to Grencijta, capital of the Caribbean island Castita, in one of whose streets, Indovinella, is located a house containing the literary and artistic remains of his idol, the late poet and painter Sib Legeru; he is, however, repeatedly prevented from doing so by two cartoonishly sinister characters, Loewe and Pardaleos, both lawyers, along with a weird posse of thugs and perverts. I might add that, while still marooned in Manhattan, Faber dreamily overhears the waitresses of a restaurant barking out his fellow diners' orders: 'Indiana (or Illinois) nutbake. Chuffed eggs. Saffron toast. Whiting in tarragon, hot. Michigan (or Missouri) oyster-stew. Tenderloin. Hash, eggs. Ribs'.

Now – what the reader of 'Oedipus Wrecks' discovers (either before or after the event) is that Grencijta means 'Big Town' and Castita 'Chastity', which one might just have been capable of guessing on one's own; that 'siblegeru' was the term coined by an Anglo-Saxon bishop, Wulfstan, for incest or 'lying with one's sib', something absolutely nobody could conceivably have guessed on his own; that 'loewe' is German for 'lion' (and, of course, 'ewe' is also lurking in there) and 'pardaleos' Greek for 'leopard'. Of 'Indovinella' Burgess cavalierly remarks, 'I need not translate.' As for that lovingly detailed menu – which, as it happens, is spread over three pages of *M/F* as though to render solving the puzzle an even trickier challenge – it turns out, naturally, to be an acrostic. How could the reader have failed to notice, one imagines Burgess thinking, that the initial letters of each of these dishes spell out INCEST WITH MOTHER?

That is, to be sure, all very enlightening, but it's also a little like being given a crossword clue just as you are about to hit on it yourself. And I think of G. K. Chesterton's comment when confronted for the first time with Times Square's gaudily neon-lit advertising billboards.

'How beautiful they are!' he exclaimed; only to add, 'If only one didn't know how to read!'

Similarly with *M/F*. If one doesn't know how to read them ('read', that is, in the sense of 'interpret'), how self-sufficiently beautiful are Burgess's character- and place-names. Sib Legeru, let's say, might be one of Tolkien's goblins. Z. Fonanta, Professor Feteki, Llew Aderyn all sound like enigmatic eccentrics out of Kafka or Borges. And one would not be too surprised to come across Castita in one of Stevenson's pirate romances. For an 'innocent' reader, *M/F* in its entirety bristles with meaning, meaning all the more potent, the more subtle and insidious, for being uncaptioned, for one is constantly aware of the hum of implied meaning even if one doesn't always know, on a casual conscious level, precisely what that meaning means. Yet, though one may not instantly understand why the author chose this or that specific name, this or that turn of plot, one nevertheless cannot help feeling, as one hacks one's way through the novel's lexical thickets, that this is how it had to be, this way and no other. By thus burying its complex network of symbols and references deep in the textures and trappings of the text, so deep that no reader, realistically, will be capable of extricating them without the author's aid, Burgess is not just flourishing his fabled cleverclogs erudition; it is, supremely, a device by which he was allowed to mine his way to the indelible and indivisible 'thisness' of myth.

If Frank Kermode is to be believed, Burgess himself, notwithstanding his own self-exegesis, was ultimately alert to the implications of having what theorists of language call the 'deep structure' of his novel, a novel with as many concealed layers as a smuggler's suitcase, laid too bare. According to Kermode, he became persuaded not just that it was unnecessary for a reader's enjoyment of *M/F* that its riddles be answered in advance but also that any instinctive hunger, on the part of that reader, 'for an alembicated moral', as he characteristically put it, was a form of cowardice. Magic must be left intact. A riddle is more potent when it remains unanswered and a solved puzzle is as dispiriting as it is momentarily gratifying. Like incest itself, as Kermode pithily proposes, 'it brings together elements that ought to stay separate'.

The novel, in any case, offers the motivated reader such a cornucopia of less latent inventions and ingenuities that one soon forgets the itch to apply the author's decoding key. The real pleasures of *M/F* are those familiar from all of Burgess's fiction. There is his deft story-telling skill; this mastery of dialogue; his very Irish way with a pun; his brilliance as both an aphorist and a metaphorist (of a limo, he writes that it was 'a vehicle polished like a shoe'; of a rancid cut of meat, that 'the beef was as alive as a telephone exchange'); his monstrous climactic twist (one which he reveals in 'Oedipus Wrecks' but which I refuse to reveal here); and, as Nabokov phrased it in the last, lyrical sentence of *Ada*, much, much more.

Per Liana

Donna valente,
la mia vita
per voi, più gente,
è ismarita.

In his *Linguistic Atlas of the United States and Canada* Hans
Kurath recognizes no isogloss coincident with the political
border along Latitude 49°N.

S. Potter

C'est embêtant, dit Dieu. Quand il n'y aura plus ces Français,
Il y a des choses que je fais, il n'y a aura plus personne pour les
comprendre.

Charles Péguy

Enter Prine, Leonato, Claudio, and Jacke Wilson
Much Ado About Nothing (First Folio)

I

– Totally naked, for God's sake?

All this happened a long time ago. I had not yet come of age, and I'm imposing the postures and language of what I call maturity on that callow weakling in the Algonquin bedroom. I do not think, for instance, that I really replied:

– Functionally naked, call it. All the operative zones exposed.

– And in broad daylight?

– Moonlight. Chaste Massachusetts moonlight.

Loewe's sadness lay between us, unappeased. Believe that I said what follows. Believe everything.

– It was mainly her idea. She said it could be regarded as a mode of protest. Not that she herself, being well past student age, was qualified to protest. It was meant to be, in the British locution, *my shew*. Shameless public copulation as a means of expressing outrage. Against tyrannical democracies, wars in the name of peace, students forced to study –

– You admit the shamelessness?

– Skeletal Indian children eating dog's excrement when they're lucky enough to find any.

– I asked if you ad––

– There was no shame at all. It was outside the F. Jannatu Memorial Library. The assistant librarian, Miss F. Carica, was just locking up for the night. I distinctly saw her snake-bangle as she turned the key.

Part of my brain was engaged in riddling *Loewe*. I'd arrived at:

> Behold the sheep form side by side
> A Teuton roarer of the pride.

*

9

Loewe the lawman sat sadly on the chair while I lay un-
repentant on the bed. I was naked, though not totally. He
wore a discreetly iridescent suit of singalin for the New York
heat which raved, cruel as winter, outside. He was leonine
to look at only in the hairiness of his paws, but that, after all,
was, is, a generic property of animals. His name, though, had
bidden me see it as non-human hairiness, and, seeing it, I felt
an inexplicable throb of warning in my perineum. I had
known a similar throb, though located then in the liver, when
Professor Keteki had presented the problem of that entry in
Fenwick's diary, May 2nd, 1596. I drew in the last of my
cigarette and stubbed it among the other stubs. Loewe
snuffed the smoke like a beast. Throb. He said:
  – Is that, er, hallucinogenic?
  – No. Sinjantin. A product of the Office of Monopoly of
the Republic of Korea.
  I read that out from the white and greengold pack, adding:
  – I first came across them at the Montreal Expo. It was
there too that I first got this feeling of the evil of divisions. I
had crossed a border, but I was still in North America.
  Loewe sighed, and it was (throb) like a miniature im-
ploded roar. His glasses flashed with reflections of burning
West 44th Street.
  – I needn't say, he needn't have said, how shocked your
father would have been. Thrown out of college for a shameful, shameless –
  – My fellow-students are agitating for my reinstatement.
Firearms flashing on the campus. Books burned at sundown –
reactionary Whitman, fascist Shakespeare, filthy bourgeois
Marx, Webster with his too many words. A student has a
right to fuck in public.
  I took another Sinjantin out of its pack and then reinstated
it. I must watch my health. I was thin and not strong. I had
had cardiac rheumatism, various kinds of asthma, colitis,
nervous eczema, spermatorrhea. I was, I recognized, men-
tally ill-balanced. I was given to sexual exhibitionism despite
my low physical energy. My brain loved to be crammed with
the fracted crackers of useless data. If a fact was useless, I
homed unerringly on it. But I was determined to reform. I

was going to find out more about the work of Sib Legeru. Useless really, though, for who would care, who would want to know, how many knew even the name? And Sib Legeru's work was exciting to me because of its elevation of the useless, unviable, unclassifiable into –

– How, for God's sake, could you be so crazy?

– There was this lecture given by Professor Keteki. Early Elizabethan drama.

– But I understood you were supposed to be studying Business Management.

– It didn't work. I was advised to transfer to something useless. I was appalled by the lack of oceanic mysteries in Business Management. But, when you come to think of it, Elizabethan drama can teach you a lot about business. Intrigues, stabs in the dark, fraternal treachery, poisoned banquets –

– Oh, for God's sake –

– There was this matter of the entry in Fenwick's diary. He was recording the wonders of London life to savour in provincial or foreign exile. He'd seen a play at the Rose play-house on the Bankside in the summer of 1596. All he said of it was: *Gold gold and even titularly so.* Professor Keteki was drunk that morning. His wife had given birth to a son, their first. You could smell the Scotch from the third row. Keteki, crane-like in body, owl-headed, ululating a mostly unintelligible lecture, with the smell of Scotch as a kind of gloss.

I couldn't, I suppose, really have said that last bit. But I really said:

– He was quite intelligible, however, when he offered twenty dollars to anyone who could say what play Fenwick had seen.

– Look, I have a client at –

– It came in a flash. I'd been dating a Maltese girl from Toronto, a student of her native literature. She'd shown me one of her texts, and I was struck by the word JEW, pronounced *jew*. She said it meant *or*, the conjunction. But *or* in French and heraldry is gold. She'd also said once that I was as randy as a *fenech*, meaning rabbit. So this Fenwick might have been Fenech – a common enough Maltese surname, I gathered – and an English-speaking Maltese agent of the English chapter of the Knights. The play he'd seen had to be Marlowe's *Jew of Malta*. I'd got the twenty dollars out of Keteki before he'd wiped the chalk off his fingers. I drank the money.

– Ah.

– There's a Chinese restaurant in Riverhead called the Pu Kow Tow. Riverhead, as you may know, was named for Lord Jeffrey Amherst's birthplace. A great hero up there, Amherst. He did for the French and made North America free to revolt against the British. His nephew, William Pitt Amherst, was sent to China as British ambassador. He messed up the job by refusing to grovel before the Emperor.

– Look, this client's coming at five.

– Aren't I a client too?

He looked foxily at me. He said:

– What precisely is it you want?

– First, to complete the story. I meant to eat there, but I got drinking instead. There was this very gay and game lady, also drinking. She taught them to mix a cocktail called a Clubfoot. Very brutal, with Bacardi and bourbon and double cream. She was just passing through, she said, on her way to Albany. She had this very game idea.

Looking down at my hand, I discovered that I'd been smoking another Sinjantin in total automatism. But I was determined to reform. I was nearly twenty-one, and time was slipping away.

– You realize, Loewe said, I can do nothing for you till you come of age.

– I know, I said, all about what's due to me in due time. At the moment I'm still concerned with my education. I want to pay a visit to Castita.

– *Where*, for God's sake?

– Latitude 15, south of Hispaniola. Three hundred miles west of the Leewards. A one-time British protectorate. Capital, Grencijta. Population –

– I know where it is. I know all about the damn place. What I don't understand is –

– *Why* is simple. Professor Keteki got me interested in a

man called Sib Legeru, a Castitan poet and painter. Very
obscure, very talented. You've never heard of him, nor has
anyone else. His writings are unpublished and his paintings
mouldering away unseen. I read a xeroxed manuscript.
Astonishing. There was a colonial administrator who did his
best for Legeru's work when Legeru died. A certain Sir
James Pismire. He fixed up a sort of Legeru museum on
Castita, an unvisited house with the key hanging up in a
tobacconist's. I'm curious. I want to pay it a visit.

Loewe did another imploded roar. He said:

— I refuse to be superstitious. Your poor father met his
death in the Caribbean, as you know.

— I'd forgotten.

— Never mind. The position is this. You come of age in, let
me see, when is it —

— December. Christmas Eve. Two minutes to midnight.

— I know, I know. You're aware, of course, of the condition
of inheritance.

— A totally stupid condition.

— That's not, shall I say, a very filial attitude. Your father
had the cause of miscegenation very much at heart.

— When I marry, it will be for love.

— Oh, Loewe said, that's very much a young man's notion.
If everybody married for love it would be one hell of a world.
Love is something you learn along with the other duties of
marriage. All the rest is for poets. I hope to God, he went on,
worried, that the Ang family don't find out about your,
your —

— If you tell me where they are I'll drop them a note.

— No, no, no, no, no.

— The *Riverhead Star* didn't carry anything. The college
authorities saw to that. Something may get through to the
more responsible organs, but there'll be no name mentioned. Protesting students possess only a collective existence.
Identity swallowed in purpose or ritual. Slogans at the point
of orgasm. Guitars and bongo drums and a brotherhood-of-
man song. Glossy young beards opening to cheer us on to a
dead heat.

— The young lady, Miss Ang, is a very estimable young

13

lady. Her photographs don't do her justice. And very strictly brought up. These old Cantonese families. Moral, very moral.

– Moral, indeed. A dynastic marriage. A device for getting money. Otherwise that combine in Salt Lake City –

– Well, Loewe said irrelevantly, you can't imagine anybody in Salt Lake City doing what you did. I mean, the reliability of a product is tied up with the morality of the producers.

– Utter nonsense.

– As for you going to Castita – I can't for the moment see anything – There may be something in a subsidiary file – I'll see when I get back to the –

– Did you bring the money?

– Your call sounded very confused. Were you still tight?

– It was a bad line. A thousand dollars?

– There's a clause about reasonable sums being doled out in respect of your education. *Education*, indeed.

– It's a very wide term.

– I had Miss Castorino get five hundred from the bank. A thousand's much too much. Five hundred should keep you going very adequately till your birthday.

Loewe suddenly smiled with horrible saccharinity. He said:

– You're a crossword man, yes?

From among the papers, all about me, he dug out a puzzle torn from some newspaper or other. I now throbbed from prepuce to anus.

– A difficult clue. Listen.

He read out, or seemed to:

– Up, I am a rolling river;
Down, a scent-and-colour-giver.

The answer was obvious: *flower*. But the throb told me not to give Loewe the answer. Why not? I'd been quick enough with that answer to Keteki. Then I knew why not. Loewe was being, for some reason, deceitful. The *up* and *down* of his clue referred to the respective tongue-positions that started off the diphthongs of *flow* and *flower*. No crossword, except in a linguistics journal, would have so learned a clue, and linguistics journals did not go in for crosswords. Loewe smiled, saccholactically.

– Well?

– Sorry, too tough for me.

The throb went. Loewe seemed to shrink and become less hirsute. He nodded, seeming pleased, and said:

– I take it you'll be back here in plenty of time for your birthday.

– I'm not sure that I want to inherit. Let Salt Lake City take over. I like to feel I'm a free man.

– Oh, for God's sake, Loewe scoffed. Nobody's free. I mean, choice is limited by inbuilt structures and predetermined genetic patterns and all the rest of it.

He blushed minimally and added:

– So I'm told.

– By the *Reader's Digest*?

He had recovered from his embarrassment and went on boldly:

– Nobody can help thinking these things these days. The French started all that. Not a very abstract people, despite their boasts about being the big rational nation. Philosophy can only come to life in the bedchamber or over the *coq au vin* or before the firing squad.

– The existential marinade.

– That's a good phrase. Where did you pick up that phrase?

– Not in the *Reader's Digest*.

Loewe looked fattish and fifty and unlionlike. He said:

– As for freedom, you're not free not to eat and sleep. You're free to cease to exist, of course, but then freedom has no more meaning. It's just silence and emptiness.

What I said now I hadn't, I think, really thought of before. I said:

– Only if you're thinking in terms of structures. Perhaps you can get beyond structure and cohesion and find that it's not quite silent and empty. Words and colours totally free because totally meaningless. That's what I expect to find in the work of Sib Legeru.

15

– And, Loewe said, not listening, on top of necessity there's duty. Your very name implies duty. That's its meaning.

– *My* name?

– It means a soldier. You were enrolled before birth in the regiment of your family name. Miles in the service of the Fabers.

– The hell with the Fabers.

– Yes? But your father wanted the Fabers to embrace everybody. You marry Miss Ang and your son marries Miss Makarere and his son marries Maimunah binte Abdullah, and so on for ever. Creative miscegenation, he called it. The only hope, he said.

– There's no hope.

– For God's sake. Today's youth. Is that all your moonlit campus frolic meant? Nihilism. I thought you were supposed to be protesting about something.

Generous in victory, he handed over four bills of a hundred and five twenties. I crushed the stern presidential faces together in my hand that held yet another burning Sinjantin. I said:

– I have no duty to an abstraction. I mean the abstraction called Faber. My father cared nothing for me. He even refused to see me when I –

– You have to make allowances. When your mother was drowned he changed terribly.

A cold death. New Dorp Beach. Terribly young.

– To see you would have reminded him of her. But he provided. He'll go on providing.

– Miss Emmett was no real substitute for a parent. Where is Miss Emmett, by the way?

– There are a number of charities. He goes on providing. I don't see the whole picture. Your father employed various legal advisers. There's one in Florida, another in the state of Washington –

– I could contest that marriage clause, couldn't I?

– You'll learn a lot between now and your birthday. An arranged marriage is nothing very terrible. French civilization is based on arranged marriages.

– I claim the right to choose.

– That's right, Loewe said indulgently, packing me away in his paperholder. You go right on claiming. But not in that terribly immoral way any more. It was a very shameful thing to do.

– Shameless.

– And also shameless.

When Loewe had gone, I telephoned Air Carib and booked my one-way flight to Grencijta. The next one left from Kennedy at 22.00. There'd been no need, then, for Loewe to book this room at the Algonquin, for which I would have to pay out of the five hundred dollars (I'd need every cent). We could have conferred at Grand Central, whither I'd come on the filthy train from Springfield, Mass. Or at his office. Still, being here, I'd get some of my moneysworth. I showered, then dug out a clean shirt and the summerweight green pants from my grip. Transferring coins and matches and pocket-knife from the summerweight blue, I found a crumpled slip of paper. It was a note in felt-pen. *A yummy piece of protest. Hope we'll protest some more some place some time. A small small world. Remember Carlotta.* How had she managed to slip that slip in? Of course, yes, there'd been one hell of a scuffle between our student abettors and the armed Burns men who were our campus police. We'd sheltered in the tent of the crowd, covering with speed the functional nakedness that was our badge of criminal identity. She'd taken me back to her room at the Lord Cumberland Inn and ordered sandwiches and coffee. Then the Clubfoot had risen on me and I'd been sick in the toilet. My nakedness, I kept thinking while I threw and threw, was still capering out there. My act, like a rousing sermon, was being broadcast by the idiot protestants. Faber, you're out. No, no, I quit.

Showered and dressed, I looked for the television set. As this was the Algonquin, it was concealed in a mahogany sideboard. Strong literary tradition, Ross, blind Thurber, fat Woolcott, Dorothy Parker who knocked everything. I tried channel after channel, but they were all dull, as if for the benefit of those literary ghosts. A pop group wailed, scruffy in checkered shirts and levis. There was an old

movie with a funeral in it, wreaths being laid sobbingly on
the coffin to music that sounded like *Death and Transfigura-
tion*. An untrustworthy young man in black spoke to the
frail weeded widow:

– Don't cry, ma. He lives on, I guess, in his work and our
memories.

The living-on bit was true of my own dead father, though
there was no fatherly image in what he had made, and even
my physical memories were quite unreliable. I just couldn't
see any face. He lived on in his will, so rightly named. And
then I remembered the manner of his death. An aircraft –
Air Carib? – hijacked and diverted to Havana, there to dis-
integrate on landing. Where had he been going? Business,
something to do with business, investigating openings in
Kingston or Ciudad Trujillo, perhaps even Grencijta. Anna
Sewell Products, my conditional inheritance.

I tried another channel, and it was slow-motion trampo-
line stuff, athletes dreamily levitating to waltz-music –
Artist's Life, Morning Papers, Vienna Blood, one of those. Then
another channel, and a Red Indian in a smart suit and
hexagonal glasses was a guest on a show, and he was talking
about the Weskerini and Nipissing tribes that now, alas,
lived on only in the names of certain pseudo-Indian curios
manufactured in Wisconsin. Those were, I remembered,
members of the great Algonquin family: exquisite coincidence. West 44th Street was Indian territory; a few doors
away stood the Iroquois, named for the traditional enemies
of the Algonquin nation. Dozing off, I asked myself why the
Algonquin and Iroquois were like birds. Nothing to do with
the feathers they wore; wait, wait – pigeons. I'd seen a
documentary movie of the Berlin Wall, and the commentator
had commented, rather movingly, on the pigeons that for-
aged to and fro, east and west, over it, perching and nesting
in blessed ignorance of the bitter ideology that cut a city in
half. The border between Canada and the rebellious Union
had meant only transitory foreign alliances to the Iroquois
and the Algonquin. The Moon of Bright Nights came, and
the Moon of Leaves followed, and the long hunting year
died in the Moon of Snowshoes, and the opechee and

owaissa returned in their season, and the dahinda croaked, and Gitche Gumee, Big-Sea Water, Lake Superior, endured the lash of Mudjekeewis, and the wawa or wild goose flapped wawa wawa over it. And all white men resolved at length into palefaces, French or English, royalist or republican, and all their tongues were ultimately forked.

In my dream a munching toothless squaw appeared, feeling her way in near-blindness, and a chief boomed, plumed as long as a keyboard: *It is she of the koko-koho.* Owls flurried about her in a gale that was a broth of their feathers, twitting away. One owl perched on her left shoulder, rocked, settled, then owled me in the eyes and spoke. *Esa esa,* it twitted. I fought my way up through burst featherbeds to waking. I lay and panted, tasting salt on my upper lip as though I'd drunk tequila. On my palate the stale Sinjantin smoke lay like dirt. The long day was declining. An after-image of birds or angels gyrated. It was the television, some programme about hunting in Maine. Then a commercial broke in, something earnest about stomach acid and ulcers. I looked at my watch, but it had stopped at 19.17. I dialled ULCERSS but got no reply. ULCERSS, I remembered, led astray by the commercial, was for Los Angeles; in New York it was NERVOUS. Time, north or south, was as painful as a *Mauer* or a parallel or a taxonomy. NERVOUS told me it was time for dinner.

2

– Indiana (or Illinois) nutbake.
  – Chuffed eggs.
  – Saffron toast.

Something like that, anyway. Dreams, I was thinking, foretell (when they prophesy at all) only trivialities. In the cheap bright eathouse on the Avenue of the Americas I ordered, with my hot beef sandwich, a soft drink new to me – Coco-Coho, confected in Shawnee, Michigan. The bottle was owl-shaped – the potter's first crude moulding, though in green glass – and the label showed what considerations of economy and packing forbade to be sculpted – stare, ears, beak. The drink was green and frothy with a faint bite of angostura under the saccharine. It amused me to take my revenge upon that hisser of my dream by drinking his likeness off, hiss and all.

– Whiting in tarragon, hot.

I ate my hot beef sandwich in the European manner, with knife as well as fork. Although I was an American, and had a passport to prove it, I had lived as a child so long outside America that many aspects of its life still struck me strangely. Why, for instance, cut everything first, in the manner of the nursery, in order to fork in everything after? Infantilism, mom standing fondly by to approve the hungry tining of the mom-cut morsels? A relic of the Union's urgent need to be educated, a Noah Webster spelling-book gripped in the left hand? Or perhaps the left hand had once gripped the fork, the right ready for the holster. Chew your meat and your enemy simultaneously. Or perhaps once, in this still violent country, your knife had been removed as soon as possible by the cautious frontier waiter, lest, after cutting meat, you thought of cutting throats. There was an American thing against knives. At breakfast you were allowed only one knife, so that ham-fat flavoured the strawberry jelly. A vestigial something or other.

I am imposing again, obviously.

And then there was this business of the hot beef sandwich – a virtual Sunday dinner for one dollar fifty. The British, with whom I'd had my earlier education, were supposed to be the great understating race, but to call a Sunday dinner a sandwich was the litotic, or something, end. Under the thick slab of steer, mashed potatoes, tomato-wheel, peas, obligatory fluted cup of coleslaw (signature, only marginally esculent, of the Spirit of American Short Order Cookery), there indeed lay a gravylogged shive of white bread, pored like a sponge, but that was a mere etymology, no more.

– Synchronic metaphor of the diachronic. An instant soup, as here, symbolizing the New World's rejection of history, but in France there are still kitchens where soup has simmered for all of four centuries.

France again. The voice had a French accent and was rapid. I couldn't see its owner, for this was a place in which, if you didn't wish to eat in enstaged dramatic public at the huge half-wheel of the counter, you had to be nooked between wooden partitions. I was so nooked, and so was the speaker.

– Thus, a good meat broth set bubbling about the time of the League of Cambrai, bits of sausage added while Gaston de Foix was fighting in Italy, cabbage shredded in while the Guises were shredding the Huguenots, a few new beef bones to celebrate the Aristocratic Fronde, fresh pork scraps for the Peace of Aix-la-Chapelle –

Masochism? A teacher of French too discursive for our utilitarian classrooms, hence poor and driven to instant soup?

– End of neck for the Jacobins, chitterlings Code Napoléon, bitter herbs for Elba.

Able, very, evidently, but this was no country for such mushy fantasy. His interlocutor seemed to reply in Yiddish – *Shmegegge, chaver* or something – but that was perhaps somebody else's interlocutor. What was a Yiddish-speaker doing in a non-kosher noshery? It was time to drain my coffee and go.

- Michigan (or Missouri) oyster-stew.
- Tenderloin.
- Hash, egg.
- Ribs.

The French-accented speaker, I found, was speaking his English into a miniature Imoto tape-recorder.

- Douse the fire, cool the broth, and history dissolves into that amorphous and malodorous brewis which is termed the economy of nature –

He was plumpish, bright-eyed, probably not mad, about sixty-five, totally bald, in an expensive summer suit the colour of cassia honey, and, if by a Frenchman we mean Voltaire, Clemenceau and Jean-Paul Sartre, then he was not a Frenchman. A pair of crutches sat with him. His left hand appeared to be artificial: the fingers moved, but they had a ceramic look, dollish, or like cheap religious statuary. His bowl of soup lay quite cold on the pink formica tabletop, a faint film of grease mantling its surface. He looked at me and nodded in a kind of shy confidence. I frowned, puffing out Sinjantin smoke. The face was not unfamiliar. This did not necessarily mean that we had met before; his assumption seemed rather to be that I had seen him as a public image, or that I might be expected to have done so. Had I, in fact, glimpsed the face and caught the accent on one of those offpeak television shows that give the eccentric their brief say – flat-earthers, scrymen, royal-jellyites, mole-readers? As the maw of television must soon, if its twenty-four-hour and twenty-four-channel appetite were to be satisfied, swallow every face in the United States, so the Electronic Village would become a reality, there would be no strangers, performer would greet presumed viewer in acknowledgement of electronic contact, and there would be no onesidedness, since viewer and performer were readily interchangeable. So I smiled faintly back, noting that he had a small black case with magnetic tape cartons in it, and that on the case was embossed in fading gold-leaf what seemed to be his name, though surely an impossible one – Z. Fonanta.

The Yiddish-speaker was, I saw now, Japanese, and his listener had a Malayalam look: no riddle there. Many a monoglot immigrant was taken on as a kosher waiter in New York and gladly learned Yiddish believing it to be English, undisillusioned by the cunning proprietor.

– *A nechtiger tog!*

It was, rather, a dayish night in hot tiffanied Manhattan, jewelled codpiece now but tomorrow a bare penis in blue underpants, ejaculating into Buttermilk Channel (fanciful, very, perhaps not mature imposition) or catheterized by Brooklyn Bridge. Living dildo, rather, if you saw Harlem River as of the isolating order of Hudson and East, a slim knife cutting off your manhood, white boy. Rikers Island somewhere to the right as I walked north, a tiny floating ballock with, appropriately, a Correctional Institute for Men on it. I strolled towards 44th Street, admiring the upward thrust of the masonry which pushed back the night to the limit, the new broom of the Partington Building especially, with the stubbier Penhallow Center and Shillaber Tower flanking it. I admired also the vast induced consumer appetite of this civilization, expressed in its windows and skysigns. It was safer to be bombarded by pleas to eat, drive, play or wash hair with Goldbow than put Madison Avenue and its tributaries in the service of the ideology of the ruling power. A free society.

The freedom was perhaps expressed in the act of robbery being performed, somewhere near 39th Street, by three shag-haired youths on an old man who had a rabbi-beard. There was no violence, only the urgent frisking for notes and small change of boys desperate for a fix. No kicks from mugging, no leisure to hurt save where resistance was offered. The old man knelt, crying. Some few passers-by watched with little curiosity: this was daily soap-opera of the streets. On the wall behind someone had chalked SCREW MAILER; an indifferent workman up a ladder was chipping out a smashed window in tinkles.

I have to set down my, really his, thoughts and feelings, such as they were, thus:

Hooked, and then getting fixes fulltime job, therefore work impossible even if wormholed wasted carcase, capable of coming to full life only for robbery, handing fixbread over, filling spitter, seeking skinpatch as yet unholed, were acceptable to employer. No charitable grants, state or private, for buying fixes. Robbery only way, therefore cruel, even when prudent, to interfere. Their need greater than, however needy the victim. Succour to victim after departure of thieves who fell on him? Again imprudent. Belated appearance of police or fuzz, taking in, questioning, suspicious of youth making any kind of social gesture to aged. What you have seen is a show as on television. It is an aspect of the Electronic Village. Emotions not to be engaged. We must school ourselves to new modes of feeling, unfeeling rather. It is the only way to survive. Besides, I must hurry. I have to catch that helicopter to Kennedy. It is later than I realized. The Good Samaritan was able to be good because he had time as well as money. He was travelling neither by air, nor rail, nor freeway. Amen.

So I arrived back at the Algonquin. I had left my gladstone in my room, rather than with the porter, being childishly determined to get my moneysworth. Childishly also, I intended to micturate up there without flushing the bowl, like a cat asserting its rights through smell. My urine had always been strongly aromatic. I went up; the elevatorman, a neckless Ukrainian, was frowning over baseball results in the evening paper, muttering:

– Been in centre field his throw-in'd've nipped dat runner at de plate.

When I unlocked the door of my room I found Loewe sitting on the bed, an arm round my gladstone as if it were a dog. Sitting on the chair was a presumed member of Loewe's staff, though he did not look legal, rather the opposite. He wore neither jacket nor tie, and he was making loud love to a ripe peach. Splurch, imploded (not roar, which was for Loewe) wilmshpl. He had a paper bag richly juice-soaked on his lap, and peachstones lay around his sandalled feet. He nodded pleasantly enough at me, a youngish bald large man with eyes set very wide apart, like the quadrantal spheres of a binnacle. I half-smiled back, being, in a mad minor chamber of my brain, vaguely pleased that the room had not been wholly wasted in my absence. But I said to Loewe:

– How and why?

Loewe wore a white tuxedo and, a fashion too young for him, a black silk shirt with a ruched collar. He was smoking a panatella and, from his tone, seemed to be rehearsing the urbane rhythms of after-dinner conversation. He said:

– Not to cause trouble at the desk, or meet it for that matter, Charlie here opened up with a Schirmer. An instrument with an aura not merely of respectability but of positive virtue. It is in common use in the C.I.A. and the F.B.I. and other agencies of national security.

Charlie, his simple act thus ennobled, flashed teeth and peach-juice at me.

– As for why, Loewe went on, it's to tell you that you're not going to Castita. Not just yet, that is. I mean, one takes it that there's no hurry. And yet your bag is packed, as if you were hotfoot and urgent. Your mention of Castita this afternoon rang a muffled bell. I called Pardaleos in Miami. Pardaleos confirmed what had been presented to me as a mere, a mere –

– Mere susurrus of something?

Loewe ignored that, though Charlie paused in his peach-worrying to be impressed. Loewe said:

– Certain things have to be done, certain adjustments made, before you can safely voyage to the Caribbean. Trust me. Two or three days, say. Stay here. Charlie will stay with you: he has no objection to keeping awake and alert indefinitely in the service of a valued client. I'll arrange for the bill to be sent to my office. And now, to be on the safe side, would you be good enough to hand back that money? I made a mistake, I freely admit it. A few more days, and it will be yours again.

– Look, I said, you have to freely admit that this is most unlawyerlike.

All the time, God help me, I was riddling *Paradaleos* and was already as far as:

> Crack back, valley, and be shown
> A Roman mouth, a Roman bone.

– Look, Loewe countersaid, I've put myself *in loco parentis*. Charlie here will be only too happy to be *in loco fratris*.

– I want to know more, I said.

– For God's sake, Loewe said tiredly, I've had a tiring day and the day itself, you'll admit, has been tiring. It's a long story to tell, and it's rather an upsetting story. Do what I say, there's a good boy. There'll be time enough to explain later. I'm late for my dinner engagement. Do hand that money over.

It was not, I knew, uncommon for lawyers to have thugs on the payroll. It was Dickensian, really. Save man from gallows and he responds with slavering lifelong devotion. Puts criminal skills or criminal violence in service of the *right*, which means getting people off, guilty or innocent. Weak as I was, I had to attack now. I said:

– The money's in that bag. Safer there, I thought. Mugging and so on. Allow me to –

And I moved to the bed. To my surprise, Loewe made no objection. Charlie smiled, tilted his chair back so that the front legs hovered high above his peachstones, and then took a large mushy globe, maculate with ripeness, from the bag. Loewe was near the end of his panatella and was suddenly stabbed by the bitterness of the tar accumulated in the stub. He put it out in what was still my ashtray, making a lemony face. Charlie's face, on the other hand, was moronically entranced by his rosary of sweetness (he'd told nearly a decade, judging from the stones). I stood above Charlie now. His new peach was at his mouth. I pushed it so that it squelched all over his muzzle. The push, weak as it was, was enough to send him and his chair (*yields tender as a pushed peach* – G.M.H. How exquisitely appositely a line of verse will sometimes enter the mind) over. He thudded, made a noise like ghurr, then bicycled at the air vigorously, at the same time scooping peachpie filling from his face into his mouth, as if primarily to the end of keeping the carpet unstained. I grabbed my gladstone. Loewe made no protest, either in countergrab or loud words. He merely laughed. I froze an instant in apprehension. Then I made for the door. Loewe called quite cheerfully:

– You had due warning, boy. We did our best, for God's sake. Now you must take wh –

I slammed the door and froze another instant, this time in a kind of sickness, my eyes riveted to a framed Thurber drawing of a myopic curate admonishing a walrus. Then I started off down the stairs with my bag handy as a thrusting weapon: there might be more Loewe thugs below. As for behind me – But nobody followed.

The vestibule was crowded with people greeting each other, thumping, not seen for years (is Margie okay? Sure sure), reunion of some kind, the very best dentures that dollars could buy. A young man in levis politely pushed through, carrying a floral tribute to somebody. At the desk I said:

– My Loewe, Mr Lawyer, will be down. My name's Faber. He'll pay my bill.

The clerk nodded somewhat crossly, as though the paying of room-bills was a distraction from major business. At the telephone between the reception desk and the Blue Bar there was a man on crutches, talking with speed and cheerfulness. Then a woman in a floral tribute hat and with Eleanor Roosevelt teeth got in the way, saying My my my to somebody, and I couldn't see, nor did I particularly want to see, whether it was the history soup man (I got a stupid unbidden image of alphabet pasta ready-formed into HASTINGS and WATERLOO, dissolving in broth-heat) or not. What had he got to do with anything anyway? Anyway, I had to get to Kennedy, very quick. A loud slurred voice in the bar was saying to somebody:

– And so, like I told him, Alvin slipped this disc. In Kissimmee Park it was. Know where that is?

The one addressed didn't know, but I did; I knew far too many things like that. Outside on hot West 44th Street I stood hesitant among people wanting taxis. I couldn't afford a taxi but I'd have to afford one. It was getting late and I wasn't sure how often these helicopters helixed up from that roof, whichever it was. I never knew the things that were necessary. The doorman had his back to us all. He was bending to the driver of a vehicle polished like a shoe and as long as a hearse, though much squatter. The doorman then turned his soft mottled face to us and cried at a point well behind me:

– Limousine for Kennedy. Air Carib, Udara Indonesia and Loftsax.

Strange companions for my airline, but I was delighted. God bless this syndicate that gave service. The driver even got out, a dark sad dwarf with large shoulders, and slung my gladstone, light to him as a peachstone, into the baggage-trunk at the rear. It was dark inside, and there were only two other passengers. More, perhaps, would be collected at other hotels. These were two young men in open shirts, not at all dressed as for an air journey, and they were indifferent to me and to each other. The driver swung his great shoulders and his vehicle out into the traffic.

In less than five minutes I was uneasy. Every man to his own trade, but this did not seem at all a reasonable route for reaching Kennedy Airport. First, as I remembered, you had to get out of Manhattan on to the big land-slab called Queens by crossing the East River, by Queensboro or Williamsburg Bridge, I thought, or go under the river by the Midtown Tunnel. This man was driving north. Surely that was Central Park to the right. And surely this was Broadway. I had to call, nervously:

– Far be it from me to tell another man his job –

The driver ignored me but the two other passengers now became communicative. One of them even left his seat to sit next to me, breathing a kind of anchovy-sauced pizza odour as he confided:

– That's good and right. Far far far from you, like you said.

He smiled from an open and untrustworthy saint's face. I felt new apprehension and then turned it into shame that I'd spoken: this driver surely knew what he was doing, surely. I mumbled:

– I know there's Triborough Bridge but that's for La Guardia and I thought –

The other young man was now in the seat just in front, twisting to look at me, his arms folded on the seatback. Take the septum as a radius, then his nostrils were about fifteen degrees higher than normal. He said:

– Talk nabout bridges, I got this bridge, see, but it don't fit none too good.

He opened his mouth, and four top front teeth dropped in a single comic wedge. He sucked them up again, simulating relish. The driver called, without taking his eyes off 96th Street, it must be, just ahead:

– I want those seats kept nice and clean, fellers.

– Now will be fine, Jack, said the saint-faced boy. Right here.

The limousine pulled in to the sidewalk. I said bitterly:

– From Loewe, are you?

They waved me courteously out. The bridge-boy swung my bag from the boot. They waved the driver courteously on. We stood there on Broadway by a cinema showing a film called *La Forma de la Espada*. There were a lot of Mediterranean types about, scuttling in the garish lights. The bridge-boy courteously handed my bag to me. I took it then, as expected, swung it towards the stomach of his companion. They were delighted. I had initiated violence. The first thing they did was to wrest the bag from me, open it up, then start distributing odd articles of clothing to the dago poor. The carton of Sinjantin they split among themselves. I got very mad, as expected, and tried to belabour both of them. They laughed. The saint-faced one said:

– There's a lot of ways out of Manhattan. Like this.

Then they started on me, while people passed indifferently by, many of them speaking Spanish. One on the Throgs Neck and another in the Robert Moses Causeway and a good crack on the Tappan Zee, two for luck on the Goethals and a final flourish on Hell Gate. That was all a prelude to taking my money. Bridge held me in a painful lock while Saint Face, as if wishing to play pocket-billiards with my balls, thrust his hands in from the rear and pulled out nearly the whole of five hundred dollars. He kissed the little bundle a big smack as if it were some precious relic, then, Bridge swinging my bag jocularly through a knot of Latin children, they made off without so much as a backward jeer.

They had not hurt me much. They had been playing on a dummy keyboard, performing a ritual obligatory before robbery, little more. Now what the hell was I to do? I counted the small change they had left in the pit of my pocket. Three dimes, four or five nickels, two quarters, several pennies and (though this had an aura of unspendability around it, like a holy medallion) a Kennedy half-dollar. There was a bar just by *La Forma de la Espada*. I went in and up to the long dirty counter. A man was ordering a stein.

– Yes, friend? said the bartender.
– A stein, I said.

There was a large blonde woman in a tight psychedelic-patterned summer dress, ample patches of sweat under her oxters. She stood by the counter with an empty glass that seemed to have contained an Alexandra cocktail. She looked boldly at me and said:

– You get roughed a little or sumpn?
– That's right. Robbed and rumpled.
– Tough titty, she said with little sympathy. I moved my stein and myself nearer to her. I had to get some money somehow.

3

She took me to her elfin grot, which was a third-floor apartment on Riverside Drive, but only after a long long session at a smeared table in a dark unsavoury corner of that bar. Her autobiography: a young and promising life smeared by dark unsavoury-cornered men. She was willing enough to buy many drinks for me, matching the many she bought for herself – mostly powerful mixtures like vodka and green chartreuse; rum, gin and grenadine; benedictine and cognac. She was well known to the management here: the bar's more exotic stock was evidently laid in for her only. As for me, whom she called a pretty boy, it was not drink I wanted: I wanted to get in, on, in, out, off, out, off, with some of those high-denomination bills she had in her handbag. Loewe, or it might after all be key-carrying chance, had delayed me, but I did not propose to be delayed beyond the next available flight, which, I thought and would check soon, was at dawn. Dawn was, at that season, not really all that far off. Stupid Loewe, by hinting at a mystery and asserting a lack of urgency, had made the solving of the mystery very urgent. I could not delay finding out why delay, if enforced, was being enforced. I nearly forgot about Sib Legeru: he had become the mere oyster crab in a shell made margaric by Loewe. The point at present was: how much in hard cash would my little portion of hard manhood seem worth to this woman?

Whose name was Irma.

– So he said: *Irma, you're a tramp*. That made me cry cos he knew it wasn't true, you still listening?

I was still listening. The men in her life were all swine before whom she'd cast the margaric treasures of her mind and body, and she had artistic talent, everybody had said so, she could stick things together as good as that guy Rauschenberg, and she had been thwarted by men. The connection was not clear. She had been married three times and they'd all been a shitty lot of bastards and now she was living off alimony (fat alimony I could tell) and still she was thwarted. There there, poor poor Irma.

– And now there's Chester and he's *good* and he *wants* to love me but he can't, you know what I mean?

Yes, I knew: thwarted. She was about the same age as yummy-bit-of-protest Carlotta but brassy, fleshy, not at all tough-tittied. The tang of sweat from her was, in this phase of preamation, not unexciting – a sort of subdued dual growl.

– Thwarted, that's the word. His mother's fault, a thwarted childhood, and now when he wants to do it, you know, normal, you still listening?

– Try and stop me listening.

– Something kind of gets in the way.

She did not in the least stagger, despite her burden of spirit. We walked very steadily to Riverside Drive. In the little elevator she embraced me, as it were, functionally and said again that I was a pretty boy. When we entered her apartment she had to telephone and the telephone was in her bedroom. Those were her pictures on the wall, she said, you look at them and see the thwarted talent while I make this call. The talent, I thought in my uncompassionate youthful way, had been thwarted in the egg. She had stuck bits of old magazines on to canvas, chiefly photographs of astronauts, flexing beefcake, soldiers in First World War gasmasks, politicians and the like, and she had blended these elements with streaks of crimson and cartoon shouts (zoom and zowie and so on) done bold with a Giant Jumbo Marker. But to my astonishment.

But to my astonishment one of her cut-outs was a page of the book section from an issue of *Seee*, there though presumably not for the one column of letterpress but for the advertisement for Cherry Heering (on the rocks breaks the ice), and at the head of the one column was a photograph of the yummy protest woman herself, demure in sweater and pearls, with the legends CARLOTTA TUKANG (what

nationality was that for God's sake?) and *An Upward Shift*.
I read:

seems to be that, the human sex-urge taking fright as the population
explosion reverberates westward, the center or centers of erotic
gratification may become exclusively mammary. Novelist Tukang's
bathycolpous heroine Letitia is well endowed to cope with such an
upward shift. It is a pity that the prose is no match for her sharply
supported uberty. Swinging but slack, it lacks both point and con-
tour. However fetching in conception or contraception, stylisti-
cally *Bub Boy* must be rated a flop repeat flop.

That was all. The beginning might be on the other side,
which was stuck to the canvas. The rest of the page started
off an equally waspish review of *The President's Nephews*
(652 pages. Einbruch. $9.95), a book in which Author
Blutschande had a hard long bang at, as the title indicated,
nepotism in the state. It was not possible to tell how old the
issue of *Seee* was, but Carlotta had looked that night much
as she looked here, bathycolpous too. To have indulged in an
act of sexual protest with a real woman novelist whose
picture had been in *Seee* – well, I was awed, proud, uplifted.
And she had not been a bit like this man said her prose was.
  – When you are.
That was Irma throating from the bedroom while I was
looking at her bookshelves. Michener, Robbins, Mailer,
Henry Morton Robinson, *The Rolled Gold Notebook*, but
nothing by Carlotta Tukang. Well, there was time, I was
young, the world was before me. And so I entered the bedroom and found Irma before me, lying fully clothed on the
bed, a quadruple one. The room had a pleasant mixed smell
of cognac, cocoa-butter, female sweat and Calèche. I
stripped myself totally and then set about stripping Irma. I
know that the reader claims a right to be let in as voyeur of
any sexual encounter required by the action of a story (this
was very much required, since my getting to Castita de-
pended on it), but I have always been shy of, to use Professor
Keteki's heavy whimsy, lambdacizing pubic activities. All I
can do is give you vulgar frigidities of symbolism, debased
Blake, saying that she lay on that bed like Long Island, the
sheets being blue, and that I caressed such areas as Wantagh

and East Norwich till they were flaming with light, and then my calm lapping like the waters of Flanders Bay provoked by a miracle riot in Riverhead. Not, of course, the Amherst Riverhead, but there was a coincidence. Eventually it was her wish more than mine that Manlingamhattan, though keeping its rightful place on the map, should have its isolating rivers sucked away, to be embraced by membranous Jersey City and South Brooklyn. Guns were ready to fire in Battery Park when I became aware that the groans of male joy were not mine, since they emanated from well beyond Irma's feet. Ships in Upper Bay sent up their jubilant flares and boomed multiple thanksgiving, then I swam to land in two strokes to see a naked man coming into the bedroom from the bathroom. Irma flicked my body away with large strength, then held out both her arms to this man. He held out both arms to her. She cried:

– Chester honey. It was so so good.

– Irma my heavengiving little baby.

Then they were squirming and yumyumming in each other's arms on the bed, and I saw how I had been *used*. Chester, so called I thought from the size of his chest, considerable, had entered the apartment with his own key, gone into the dark bathroom by its living-room entrance, and then got down to literal, not literary, voyeurism. His glans glistened wetly in the rose bedside light as he nestled next to Irma and enjoyed the languor of afterlove. Being an exhibitionist, I had to fight against being gratified in order to feel properly angry. I had been a dildo; I had been one of those complicated Japanese sex-robots that cost so much; I had been Chester's expendable emanation, sexed but nameless. I would have hit both of them, lying there only marginally aware of me as though I were something on the Late Late Show, had not Chester been so large and muscled, though bald and not young. As it was, I had at least the right to cry:

– Money, I want money.

Chester was appalled. He looked up at me from large dark eyes, his arms round Irma, and cried back:

– You'd desecrate? You'd make our love all dirty? You'd be a desecrating dirty little male prostitute?

Despite the fine rhetoric and the high sentiment, there was an endearing low touch in that *dirty*, which he pronounced almost, but not quite, as *doidy*. I said:

– Ah, balls, if you know what those are.

I tucked my own away in their Y-front. I was dressing quickly, dissociating myself from that bare and sentimental squirming. Shut-eyed Irma said, in a superior lazy tone:

– Some men, Chester, do not know what love is.

– I guess you're right at that, honey.

– They deserve our pity.

– So they do, I guess.

– He can have whatever's in my bag. Friday is alimony day.

– I want something out of Chester too, I said. It's only fair. He got plenty out of me.

– I resent that, Chester said unresentfully.

I could see what he thought he ought primarily to be resenting: my familiar use of his name and him not easily able, since he was naked, to put on dignity. He was a mother's boy, despite his bald muscle, and had been brought up on, I could tell, outmoded proprieties. He had not yet learnt social modes appropriate to his sexual needs. He should by rights be speaking very vulgarly to me now. But there was Irma there, and he loved and respected Irma. When I was dressed and ready to go and look for money in the living-room, he hugged Irma in a tightness that was protective, as though I might bring a gun or his mother in.

In Irma's bag I found less than a hundred dollars. Nor were there any odd bills tucked away in drawers or rolled into vases: I searched very carefully, even examining the thwarted collages to see if she'd incorporated the odd tasteful greenback in her vulgar designs. But no. Spitefully I tore off what was detachable of the *Bub Boy* review, and this was mostly, which I wanted, Carlotta's portrait. Why did I want it? Youth, boastfulness, the working out of an epigram about tale and tail. The collage looked all the better for my rip. In Chester's pant-pockets there were only odd dimes and nickels; in his wallet in his jacket there were two fives and a ten, also a Diner's Club card which I toyed with the idea of taking, but I saw that that might lead me into awkward criminality. No, I had to be satisfied with $115.65, not a lot considering how much I'd done for them and their love as they called it. I went back into the bedroom and said:

– Sorry to intrude on your epipsychidionizing, but I must use the telephone.

They were recovering quickly from their languor. They looked up at me with eyes that would soon grow doggy and pleading. They would need my services again, but how could they pay for them? It is a hard world; the facts of economic life are desperately cruel. I sat on the edge of the bed at right-angles to Irma, and, while I looked through the telephone directory, she poked a sly finger in my rump-cleft. I ignored the gesture. I got through to Air Carib at Kennedy, found out that there was indeed a dawn flight, but, when I asked about the fare, learned that I had not nearly enough for a single economy class ticket. This made me tell Irma to take her finger from my ass and snarl at Chester's shortage of cash. But Chester was mild in his response and also helpful. He said:

– You want to get down to Miami and work your passage. There's a lot of nice little millionaire boats there on the keys – Key Largo that they made the Bogart movie on and Pigeon and Lower Matecumbe. They're always glad of some guy that wants to bum a ride to the West Indies if he's willing and respectable. To do galley work, entertain their wives and etcetera.

– You've worked your passage? I asked.

– I've done galley work, Chester said. When I left home I went to Savanna la Mar. Then I came back again because I knew it would break my old lady's heart.

– Well now, Irma said, pumping my thigh with her fingers. How about you getting back there into the bathroom, Chester?

– What you want to do, Chester said, is to call Unum Airlines at La Guardia. They run these very frequent flights to Miami. You could get one, I reckon, about 6.00 a.m. You call them and find out. They have what they call Pluribuses, jimbo jets, not jumbo, not big enough, but cashing in on the name, see. I was involved in that Pluribus. Patriotic, too. I used to help write their publicity.

– That your job? Advertising?

– Pardon me, Irma said old-fashionedly, for living. Shall I move out and then you two boys can be nice and cosy?

– You'll see one of mine in the subway, Chester said. His nakedness and limp prick (love in a man limps well behind vocation) were now properties of the changing-room. It's Folly's Fish Pickle, Chester said. There was the Pickle Mavin, then it was my idea to have Mawinski, Reginald Mavin-Pantiwaist, Van Mavin, O'Mavin and MacMavin, och aye.

– My father would have liked that, I said.

– Yes? Well, now they call me the Mavin mavin.

– Chester, Irma said sharply.

– Yes, honey, Chester said, patting her unseeingly like some monster chihuahua. How about some ham and eggs? All that exercise. Kind of hungry.

He smiled at me and even sketched a wink. It was as if Irma had been the dildo or catalyst or engine for bringing him and me together. A biological urge wanted to be a society-building urge but could only achieve that through being sidetracked to a shameful onanism. These great structural machines throbbing away, those messages in code. Irma presented her aggrieved bottom to us and pretended to sleep. Chester cooked ham and eggs, dressed now and social, and told me about the failure of kosher ham, a synthetic venture that tasted only of cotton-wool and salt. He had not been in on the advertising.

4

Dawn not being for individual acts of violence, only the collective murder of disciplined squadrons, I walked without much fear to the East Side terminal. I tried to step out as briskly as Irma's eventual snores, though I felt tired and was strongly aware of my general fragility. Inside me Chester's decent breakfast settled comfortably enough, picking its teeth. Aurora, aurora, I was, I think, thinking – the right name for the thunder of the raider's dawn, but how did you match in a word this marvel of fragile light over the city? Eolithic, yes – topless towers, rhodochrosite, rhodomel, touched by rhododactyls. A sad E-string must always sound in an early city-walker's brain, knowing this innocent beauty to be as morally meaningless as Christmas and the violence and treachery and vulgarity of the day already to be warming up, or over, like yesterday's cold hot cakes. Ah yes, I thought sadly. I was, you must keep on keeping in mind, very young.

When I boarded the bus for La Guardia I felt that one of the male passengers was more interested in me than was proper for a stranger. Did we perhaps know each other? He wore a black lightweight suit as for a summer funeral; light shimmered from it like corinthians. His face was heavy, so that his jowls shook to the bus in a fractionally delayed sympathy; his eyes were pale and bulging, meniscal water. He sat just across the aisle, and each time I looked warily over he looked boldly down. On his knee was a paperback called *Faggots for the Burning* – a study of irregularities in high American places, significant exposure, very popular at that time. When we arrived at La Guardia he thrust the book in his sidepocket, looked at me somewhat balefully, then got off and got lost. Perhaps his funeral was not mine after all, I thought. Still, I was wary when I boarded the Pluribus jimbo jet for Miami, looking round for him. He was not to be seen: perhaps he had shuttled off to Boston or somewhere.

This jimbo jet did not seem any bigger than any aircraft I had taken before: it just seemed to have more seats in it. But there were not many passengers for Miami, and I had a whole swathe of the economy cabin to myself. I was served my second breakfast – coffee, pineapple juice and a sticky pastry – and then I dozed. Because Loewe had mentioned her in our meeting of the previous day, I dreamed of Miss Emmett. She was tutting as she sponged slopped viscous white soup from a formica tabletop. She was using my pyjama-pants for the job, and even in my dreams I marvelled at the economy of the image. Dear Miss Emmett, with her severely corseted waist from which scissors always dangled, her ginger cat Rufa that, before its only pregnancy, had been called Rufus, her delight in chewing lump sugar and crunching buttocky meringues, her four Honeydew cigarettes a day. In my dream she began to sing her one song, *You will be my summer queen,** as she turned from the cleaning of the mess (why formica? We had had nothing but good tough deal and oak in our house in Highgate) to the packing of my bags for my return to St Polyerge's Preparatory School or Amise's College of God's Deliverance (a Tudor establishment in Redruth, Cornwall). Into the bags she was shovelling loads of hardboiled eggs. The dream was reminding me of her one kitchen fault. She could never, no matter how I complained, serve a softboiled egg for breakfast: she would put the eggs on the stove before she called me, then forget about them. A hardboiled woman herself, a tough old faggot.

Faggot? It seemed to me that a sense of the impropriety of the word, here anyway in America, disturbed me into waking, but the true cause was physical: the breakfast coffee was at its diuretic task. I got up and walked to the rear of the

 *   *etc.*

aircraft. In their galley the two vacuously pretty stewardesses, uniformed in turquoise, scarlet and offwhite, were dealing with refreshment orders: there were so few passengers to the hot South; their work was easy. Still, despite the fewness, one of the toilets had the engaged sign glowing, and it still glowed when I came out from my long piss and quick rejection of myself in the mirror (I must at least buy a razor in Miami: I must not look bummish bumming my trip on the keys). Going back down the aisle I saw on an empty seat a copy of that faggot paperback. I started. But, of course, the book was popular. Still, I was quietly disturbed as I returned to my place, wondering if the blacksuited man was coffined in that toilet, on my tail. An agent of Loewe's, not averse to my getting to the American limit on my pilgrimage to Castita. Was it all perhaps a pre-inheritance test, written into my father's will, of my intelligence and initiative?

I needed to smoke, and I had finished my Sinjantin. Those thieving swine. I rang for a stewardess, and she eventually obliged me with a complimentary pack of four Selim, just enough for Miss Emmett's day had they been Honeydew, watery tasting cigarettes untarred and decarcinogenized by a whole midget factory in the tail. Oral violence at least had been eliminated from modern America.

When the track of the pluribus turned from a parallel to a hypotenuse, I discovered that I had been apprehensive in vain. I had to go back to the toilet (Jupiter Inlet, Juno Beach) and on the way saw that the faggot book was now being read, but not by the summerweight mourner; it was a middleaged woman in lime and pomegranate with huge boiled arms. So that (Lentana, Gulf Stream, Village of Golf) was all right, and that it was so (Boca Raton, Hugh Taylor Birch) seemed confirmed by two glowing *vacant* signs. I thought I would make my piss a sort of gleeful libation, but to my horror blood came along with the water. Why blood? What had I done to myself, what was wrong with my body? I looked at my unshaven horrified face, the lips parted, and it seemed to me that the alignment of the right upper incisor was wrong. I felt the tooth. It was slightly loose; it was curiously twisted in its socket. I was not well.

The *return to seat* sign was on. I shook back and fastened my seatbelt in a tremor. And then the tremor subsided. After all, everybody had something, nobody was one hundred per cent healthy. That blood was nothing: I had overfrotted in my bout with Irma. In the struggle for my bag and money I'd been fisted, though not overhard: that could explain the tooth which, if I massaged the gum, would strengthen again. One could sometimes bless violence, for it worked in the exterior light, you knew where you were with violence. In a sense it was clean and just and as human as music: the very sound of the word suggested music. It was the unjust processes that went on in the dark that had to be feared – teeth dropping (Fort Lauderdale) from mouths sweet with dental floss and mint gargles, ulcers (Hallandale) for milk-drinkers, lung cancer (Ojus, Surfside) for those who abhorred tobacco.

We swooped very low inland over the racetrack at Hialeah, shout of ironic triumph for so many punters, and then it was Miami International Airport in ghastly heavyweight summer. I unclicked my seatbelt as we bumped down and started the long taxiing. And then, how the hell he'd managed the invisibility I just could not figure, something to do with that black? he was solid in the aisle beside me, saying:

– Move over.

– Why the hell, who the hell?

– Ah, come on, move over, I want to explain, see.

I moved over. I was, after all, curious to know what the whole game was. I said:

– From Loewe, is that it?

He had a breathy voice and the not unpleasant falling tune of the Bronx. He said:

– Not Mr Loewe direct. It's more for Mr Pardaleos that I operate. But Mr Loewe, he comes into it. Who you're going to see now is Mr Pardaleos.

He settled himself comfortably for the taxi-ride and began to clean his nails with a toothquill, saying:

– This Riverside Drive one you was with, she called Mr Loewe, but then, see, it was Mr Pardaleos that takes over.

41

– Irma? Irma was in on this?

– She might be Irma or she might be anybody, names not always meaning anything in these kind of operations. Lot of calling last night, you seem to be more important than what you seem to be.

– And you're taking me to see Pardaleos?

– Well, I figure you ought to know my job could have finished at La Guardia when I see you buying the ticket and speaking out where you're going clear and loud. I call Mr Pardaleos as requested, but it's not him personally I talk to as he's asleep, it's early yet at that time, and they say this one word: coincident.

– What, who?

– I say to them I've got this funeral at Cypress Hills, but then they say it's the living comes before the dead. Who do you mean, I tell them. Well, it seems they had this tip from one of the airlines that there's this Guzman that's on the charter flight going back to Ojeda. Guzman, after all these years, what do you think of that? And I don't care much for funerals, even though he was a buddy. Took three bullets straight in the back of the throat, and all those guys just looking on. So all I do is hand you over to Mr Pardaleos who'll be waiting at the breakfast table, real aristocracy he is, and then I pick up Guzman.

– Are you some sort of police officer?

– That's a laugh. Don't you worry none, now, about matters of legality and the such. I'll get Guzman back where he's wanted, no trouble at all.

He nodded seriously at me, stowing the toothquill in his shirt pocket; a man, the nod meant, in whom I could have every confidence. By this time the aircraft had sidled up to its bay, and I knew there was no point in asserting my right to enter the airport as a free man, or boy. This escort in black to an intended purpose not now to be fulfilled –

– You're in mourning for him, that's the important thing.

– Who? I get you. And it's kind of right and proper to pick up Guzman dressed like this.

– The trappings and the suits of woe.

– That's very good, that's very well put, though there's

only the one suit. One black suit's enough for any man. Last him all his life if his weight don't change too much.

Held, I say, my elbow gently as we stepped from the cool aircraft straight into the cool building to which it had glued itself, and he moved me briskly along miles of corridor, past all the boarding areas with their waiting knots of the loud and indulged and sunburnt, to the huge abstract zone of counters and boutiques, where flying was not yet a matter (feared, fascinating, apocalyptical) of moving into the air but a calm easy one of money, kilos, code-numbers. He led me to a restaurant called the Savarin. It was crammed with breakfasters (would breakfast-time never end?) and it reeked of coffee like a Rio warehouse. He said:

– That's him over there, see.

With reverence. He straightened his black tie with one hand, pushing me with a new force with the other. Pardaleos had, despite the crammed breakfasting urgency, a large table to himself, and he was discussing the menu slowly with the Negro waiter, as though it were dinner-time and the name of the restaurant had to be taken seriously. He did not look Greek, not, anyway, dark and stubbled Greek; he was fair and pale, almost albinoid, and wore an exquisite suit of a glistening cranberry colour. He was of the gods, not demos. My escort said:

– This is him you want, Mr Pardaleos, and now I get on with your kind permission with the other job.

Pardaleos nodded him off with a flash of contact lenses, stood to show five and a half well-knit feet, shook hands with me – such a crusty kiss of rings – and courteously indicated that I sit. I sat. My escort patted me shyly and went. Mr Pardaleos said:

– They do a rather good kidney omelette. Shall we say that, preceded by a kirsch-laced *frullato di frutta*?

The voice was totally without accent, the tones of abstract intelligence purged of class and region. He was over forty. I said:

– I've already had two breakfasts.

– You wouldn't think it too early for a pint of champagne?

– Much too early. But what an excellent idea.

43

He smiled an archaic smile and then ordered a breakfast for himself quite different from what he'd proposed for the two of us: trout kedgeree with chilli sauce, cold turkey pie, Virginia ham very thick with a brace of poached eggs, a chilled strawberry soufflé. And, for there was not much choice, a 1963 Bollinger. He drank iced water and black coffee while waiting. He said:

– Faber. A good *making* name. Homo faber.

– I beg your pardon, was that last remark meant to be –

– How sensitive the young are. Nothing about sex, no. But, since you've raised the subject, there's a sexual question I'd like to put to you. What is your view of incest?

– What is my –

– Incest, incest. Keeping sex in the family. Most cultures have pretty rigid taboos on incest. My own ancestral one, for instance. Oedipus, Electra, all that. Some don't care much. England didn't. They didn't bring in their Incest Act till 1908.

– Why do you, why are you – What's all this about anyway?

– You young people are great for smashing the old barriers. Loewe told me what you'd done – very clever, most bold. Would you be prepared to commit incest?

– It's an academic question. I've nobody to commit it with.

– Stall not, my friend. Now when I talk of committing incest I have in mind the whole works: *eiaculatio seminis inter vas naturale mulieris*, and no pills or diaphragms or pessaries. I mean preparedness to risk incestuous conception.

– Look, I think I have a right to know what's going on. I'm trying to get to Castita to fulfil a legitimate educational enterprise. Everybody seems determined to –

– I know all about it. Wait. Now, while I'm eating this kedgeree, I'd like for you to perform a brief act of the imagination. A boy is in bed with his mother, right? They're naked. He, or she, puts out an embracing hand. Take it from there.

– First Loewe has me robbed, now you have me dragged here to talk about –

– Go on. Start imagining. Close your eyes if it helps.

I sighed. Could I, a young man, be blamed for thinking that the old were mad? The champagne was brought in an ice-bucket, and some of the breakfasters stared, though not for long: this was, after all, sybaritic Miami. I closed my eyes and saw what Pardaleos had bidden me see. There was a double bed, the sheets not too clean, and there were flies buzzing. High summer: this was to explain the nakedness. Above the bed hung a photographic reproduction that I could not clearly see: something surrealistic, a red room crammed to the limit with chairs and a sort of fiery paraclete dancing. Then I looked down. The mother had no face, but her body was clearly defined – big breasts, belly, buttocks shining sweatily in the morning light. The son was bony and overeager. Their engagement was urgent, and he came as quickly as a young rooster. Then he lay back, wet and panting, and his face was something like mine.

– Well? said Pardaleos, who had finished his kedgeree.

– It was just sex. If it were a sort of morality cartoon you could stick a shocking label on – SON FUCKS MOTHER. Primal sense isn't revolted, except perhaps aesthetically. It's ideas, words, irrational taboos, pseudo-ethical additives that that –

– Words, eh? Very clever. Right. Send the mother and son packing and bring in a brother and sister. Go on.

– You know, this is really –

But, my eyes on the easing-off of the champagne cork, I left that bed in my mind, the sheets changed and the light changed too – for some reason to winter afternoon light with the sense of an electric fire glowing, to be occupied by a boy and a girl, both lean and comely, and they made love with hunger. Their faces were not clear: they were glued together in a kiss. The cork shot, and the waiter gave the fuming overflow to my flute. I couldn't help grinning. I said:

– Premature ejaculation.

– Very witty. This time what you call primal sense wasn't revolted, right? But think now. Nine months later she has a child. Any comments?

– It wouldn't be fair on the child. Dysgenic. Family weaknesses massively transmitted. An irresponsible act.

– Drink off that champagne before the gas goes. Then have some more. Good. So then, what you're telling me is that incestuous sex is wrong if there's the danger of issue, but it's not out of order if conception is avoided. Right?

I drank off the flute at his bidding. There was an instantaneous firing of the accumulated bad air in my stomach, then bubbles discharged through my nose. One of the pleasures of drinking a fizzy wine is the separation of the nasal exordium of vomiting from the desire to vomit. Pardaleos forked in cold turkey. He chewed, cocking his head at me, waiting. I said, with care:

– Contracepted incest should be a human right. What I mean is, people should be able to claim it as they might want to claim the right to eat shit. But there are better things to eat. Why sleep with your own mother or sister when there's such a world of women to choose from?

– You're very naïve, said Pardaleos. You haven't read much. We condemn incest because it's the negation of social communion. It's like writing a book in which every sentence is a tautology.

– My father, I began to say. ·

– Your father was all against social tautology. But every son is against his father. A young man who protests against the society his father built by copulating with a stranger in the open air might be quite likely to –

– No. Besides, it's totally academic. I couldn't commit incest.

– And you wouldn't even if you could?

– No. I claim the right to, but I wouldn't. There's no contraceptive that's a hundred per cent sure.

– I knew your father very well, said Pardaleos. He was a friend as well as a client. My compassion for him lives beyond the grave. He chose a freedom that not many would choose. Or shall I say he was impelled into that freedom, turning it into a bondage. He committed incest.

I became aware, after five seconds, that my jaw had dropped. After five seconds I became aware that if I continued to grip my flute so tightly the glass would shatter and everyone's attention would be drawn to my dropped jaw.

I took in Pardaleos's inexpressive eyes, glazed with their minuscule lenses; his mouth was calmly busy with turkey pie. This mouth said:

– Well, he's dead now, God rest him. And she's dead too.

I tried to croak out the question but couldn't. I shook down more champagne. It was cold and blessed and sexless. I felt myself madly, in the act of drinking, to be in clean, cold, blessed communion with a ghostly father, not mine, blessing from a great way off. It was champagne's creator, Dom Pérignon. Pardaleos answered the unspeakable:

– His sister, yes. Your aunt-mother, to be Shakespearean. But don't think this was no more than the feeble gesture of a rebel of the last generation. The whole thing was rather Hellenic. He was in love with her, she with him, and they lived as man and wife.

The ham, dead flesh, arrived, along with the blind staring eyes of the poached eggs. I tried to read the plateful like a cryptic message from the underworld. I borrowed the stare. The sickness of my body seemed to be gathering its parts together to sing a diabolic motet to a Father Giver Of All Things. I tried to speak.

– It. So that. You don't.

– Down more champagne, then down the rest of the story. You're a tough young member of this new tough generation, you can ingest anything. Your father's wife-sister was overtaken by terrible remorse after her second confinement.

– Her sec her sec her.

– She was, as you know, but you never knew the reason, found drowned. The body was disfigured but your father identified it.

– Her. You said.

– Yes. You have a sister. Your poor father recognized that some day you would be put in the position of possibly meeting her. The world, as they say, is small. He was obsessed by a fear that if you met her you might conceive, against your will no doubt, undoubtedly against your will, an identical passion of unlawful degree. Hellenic, again. The curse on a house. As flies to wanton boys. Sport of the immortals. Nonsense, I told him. Loewe, I may say, does not know the whole story. Nor does Acheson in Seattle. Nor Schilling in Sacramento. Your father and I were, as I say, pretty close. Anyway, the odds, I told him, are totally against it. I reject all this house of Atreus nonsense along with all the other mythified superstitions of my race.

– A sist.

– A young and, I have seen for myself, charming girl. Not very strong, of course. She needs warmth. She has been living in the Caribbean. If you are to visit the Caribbean we must get her out of the Caribbean. It's merely a matter of antedating her departure for Europe. A finishing school in Nice.

– My. It. I can't.

– More champagne?

– Brandy. Bran.

– I have some here.

He took a silver flask from his sidepocket. It lightninged at me, as slim as a cigarette-case. He poured brandy into my empty champagne-flute, but I could not at once drink it for I was trembling too much and a fat stern bald man in glasses was looking at me. Pardaleos said:

– There's nothing to worry about. Your shock is the shock that attends all new and sudden acquisitions of knowledge. Things go on behind your back, and you resent this. You're reminded that not even youth possesses total awareness of the magnitude, subtlety and horror of life's hidden engines.

He had eaten all his thick-cut ham and both his eggs. There was nothing to read on his plate but a brief message in mustard that I could not decode. Was it perhaps *Homo fuge*? The stern watching fat man attacked a large plate of something mushy and yellowish. Between tremors I got my brandy down. Pardaleos's strawberry soufflé was brought, and also his bill for many dollars. I looked with sick fascination at the pink airy mound, grossly warted with large unsucculent halves of stippled berries. Picking up his spoon, Pardaleos said:

– I've no legal right to keep you here, of course. I hope you'll see things my way. A bit of posthumous humouring. He was, after all, your father.

I felt as though I'd eaten my father, a vast coffined ham with poached eggs for eyes, his brain a soufflé, his fingernails alive and pricking. That was the brandy.

– You'll like my apartment. Leisure City – a pleasant name. Stay till I receive word that they've caught the plane to Paris. It's not really an infraction of your freedom, is it? What is time, after all? You have all the time in the –

– They? They?

– The old lady who looks after her. Believe me, this stupidity won't go on for ever. When you're twenty-one, married, settled down –

He scooped up pink brain-stuff. I said, feeling the well of a powerful nausea that, I knew, was red, an intimation of thick beef-extract at the back of my throat:

– I have to go to the –

– By all means.

He let me go. Leaving the restaurant, I saw two young men in festive shirts and mirror-spectacles get up from their table near the entrance. They were why he let me go. I ran, looking for the room marked MEN, pushing against middleaged women who tutted and their paunched escorts who prepared to say *hey young feller*. One man, I saw, carried skis. Skis? *Skis?* I pushed open the men's room door and saw, thank God, it was crowded, noise of many waters, flyzipping, pudgy forearms being warmly laved. The two followed me in, breathing easily, smiling faintly but kindly. One had middle-parted rusty hair, thick waves tucked behind his ears; the other wore a plaited trilby. Their mouths were soft, unbrutal. I bent double from my middle and coughed a thick rusty gout on to the tiles. There was the expected mixed response: genuine and assumed indifference, distaste, embarrassment, outrage cut short, a very little concern. I cried feebly and cunningly:

– A doctor, take me to a –

Pardaleos's two were only too ready. They sidled up smiling, their hands stiffening slowly to hooks. Less feebly, more cunningly:

– No, no, no, keep them off. They did it, they.

A couple of shirtsleeved executive-types flashed their

glasses at me and then at them, doing sternly their cuffs up. Then the washroom attendant, a tough old black in white with lined grey elephant-skin, took me about the body.

– You want the first-aid, son? Come along a me.

He got me out of there, and Pardaleos's men were curiously slow to follow. Indeed, I saw the one with rusty hair move to a urinal, his thumb ready to shell down, podwise, his fly-zipper. I was out in the great crowded concourse, free but puzzled. Puzzled also about why I didn't want to rest up, a weak boy made weaker by the morning's revelations, in Leisure City. Pardaleos's proposal seemed all very reasonable. If I'd spent twenty years without a younger sister I didn't need a younger sister. Why the rush? Still, I said:

– I'll be all right now, I guess. My plane. Just a temporary –

– You sure? You don't look none too good, son. Where you aiming to get to?

– Castita.

– Castita? Where's that?

I knew why the rush. I hungered for Sib Legeru as for the only sanity in the world. Then I saw that Bronxman, all in black, a memento mori to the gay-attired, a briskly moving warning poster of what, for them all, lay beyond this brief spasm of holiday sun. He had in front of him a small fiercely mouthing moustached brownskin in a fawn suit, swiftly propelled in a hidden armlock. Guzman caught, like he'd said he would be, prevented from returning to – A British bell-ringing towncrier, in tricorn, kneebreeches and machicolated topcoat overlaid with the soundtrack of a Russki yesman: I'd filed that image unknowingly.

– Ojeda, I mean. Charter flight.

For Ojeda was, was it not, some four hundred miles due west of Castita?

– You'll find where the gate is up there on that TV, son. Me, I got to get back to the old waterhole. You sure you going to be okay?

– Thanks, I said, adding: We Guzmans are tough.

5

There I was then, rolling due east a couple of days later in a trim Bermuda cutter called *Zagadka II*, a nice new job about thirty feet on the waterline and ten feet beam. It was owned by a man called Frank Aspinwall, around forty-five, fleshy and brutally bald, like an Oriental monk or torturer, born in Harrisburg, Pennsylvania, retired from minor fashion-designing for women to a life of moody deep-sea cruising. He hated women and would not even, when referring to his boat, pronominate it to *she*. He had a companion, also a misogynist, named Pine Chandeleur, twenty-odd, a poet who, I gathered, would desert Aspinwall periodically in one port or another of the Caribbean but turn up in another port, bruised, starved and repentant.

What, I wondered, was the name of my sister? Anna-maria, Clarinda, Ophelia, Jane, Prudence, Charity, Carlotta? No, not Carlotta. Not that I gave a damn. It was just idle curiosity. On the other hand, would not this sister be my responsibility when I came of age? Let her finish finishing school, then finish her off in marriage. But then I was assuming that I would endue that stiff shroud of head of family. Why should I? Aspinwall and Chandeleur were free, though in desperate sexual bondage to each other. I had learned to take sex as it came or went. I could, like the imagined work of Sib Legeru, be wholly free. Free even of the grumbling and nagging of my body. I was feeling better now, belaboured by all this ozone, the Caribbean sun clinging to my back. It was as if, now knowing the cause of all my small sicknesses, I could assign them to that cause like so much movable property. I willed them all back to my father.

I was, at the moment, preparing the midday meal – a sort of *bouillabaisse* of canned herrings, clams and squid, cooked in

51

instant fish stock with onions and peppers, to be followed by a dessert of peach crescents embedded in caramel cream. My galley was aft of the big forecastle that was used mainly as a sailstore – to port, with the not too well stocked pantry, facing the washroom and heads to starboard. Aft of me at work was the saloon, leather settees on each side, table in the middle, small chart table against the forward bulkhead. Pine Chandeleur was lying on one of the settees, straight blondish hair, pebble glasses, fishlike protruding lips that extruded, in vocal tryout, phrases from the long pseudopoem he was working on: *Scumstewed, stringlimp, equation proved, equalsign* – Nothing about the circumambient sea: all acrid smoky bedsitter sextripe. – *Droops, pipe at rest at last from blowing*. He was in boiled spinach slacks and a shirt that looked at first like an oldfashioned newspaper shirt but turned out, close to, to be patterned with pages from, for some dirty reason or other, mystical writers. Aspinwall was grim at the helm, naked except for his pipe.

Dorothea, Margrit, Frederica, Ricarda, Edwarda. The hell with her, damnable responsibility.

It had been all too easy boarding that charter plane to Ojeda. Such a mixture of boarding colours, for Ojeda was full of races, that I passed as an unremarkable Caribbean. There was no question of having to show a ticket. A brown man with steelgrey curls ticked off names on a checklist, not looking up. Cortex, right. Cortey, right, right, Cortez. Credite. Manducastis. Right, right, right. Guzman, Guzman, Guzman, right. Most of the passengers were right, that is to say tight. They had been holidaying in Florida and were now returning to an island that had, inherited from the English Muslim fathers who had sailed away from English Puritan intolerance in 1647, fairly stringent drink laws. One passenger took me for genuine Guzman, being presbyopic with whisky, and talked of the time we'd had together at Hialeah Park Race Track. Still, to be on the safe side, I spent most of the flight in one of the toilets. There I considered my future seriously.

I would first have a look at the works of Sib Legeru, as planned, and then, somehow, find my way back to the United

States to wheedle money out of the keepers of my father's coffers, enough to sustain me in peaceful frugality for a year or so while I tested myself for creative talent. I would, I decided, be moderately docile when it came to the laying down of prohibited areas, such as the South of France where Nice was and my sister would shortly be. I did not like being tricked, that was all. Tell me all, however unreasonable, and I respond rationally. Sister: I could not get over having a sister. The deceitfulness of it. But it was easy enough switching off the knowledge of having a sister. What did having a sister mean, after all? It meant as little as being – but this was a bond with her, I could not deny that this was a sort of bond – born of an incestuous union. For there were people in the world, thalidomide babies, dwellers in goitrous valleys, oversmokers, cyclamate-drinkers, exhaust-breathers, who had real sicknesses, and I could not say that my body's little caprices rendered me so sick as to be taxonomized as one of life's permanent invalids. The whole of the stupid past is our father, just as the whole world is our hospital. A recitative, that latter, I remembered stupidly, from Bach's Cantata for the Fourteenth Sunday after Trinity. That, of course, was my other kind of sickness.

Let me go, say, to Mexico, to some nice quiet dirty place like Hidalgo or Manzanillo, and there, living on tortillas and tequila, see whether this formless mind of mine, a medieval quarter crammed with junkshops, could make inconsequentiality yield significance. What I had the notion of doing was, in fact, the writing of a play. I recognized in myself a certain histrionic gift, another term for exhibitionism. I could imagine any number of theatrical situations. The working of them out in action, my own, could be thrilling, like that Carlotta business, but it was also wearisome and dangerous. Better to have theatre where it was supposed to belong, namely in the theatre. I had no play-shape stirring in my mind, but I had a lot of situations which could be strung together. There, in the toilet, soothing myself with the airline's toilet-water, I conceived a scene with great distinctness:

GEORGE. Half-regained Cimon the spider-crab.

MABEL. A pelican fish of Herculean proportions. The three
Eusebii in baskets, I mean Basque berets.

GEORGE. Yes yes. The thundering legions.

These words to be spoken on a bed, with copulation proceeding. The significance, of course, would lie in the inconsequentiality. Being so young, I did not realize that this sort
of thing had already been done.

We arrived at Ojida airport, which is just outside Blakes-
lee, the wretched dump they call their capital. What I
needed now was sea-transport, passage-working, to Castita.
I asked in the coffee-bar opposite the town air terminal what
chances there were, and I was directed to the bar of the
Besson Hotel near the Marina. There I met Aspinwall and
Chandeleur, pointed out to me by the bartender as yachts-
men who proposed, for the sake of a change and in default of
something better, taking a trip to Castita for the Senta
Euphorbia *fista*, all statued processions, fireworks, candyfloss, miracles and drinking. Aspinwall and Chandeleur
were not at first too sure whether they wanted me, but when
I said I could cook they said they were sick of their own
cooking and each other's. Urgent, I said. Good, they could
do with the condiment of a little urgency.

Why urgent? Why, for God's sake, urgent? Because
Loewe and Pardaleos had said it was not urgent. Did they
not, then, understand the selfwilledness of youth, that if they
employed weapons on behalf of non-urgency I would turn
urgency itself into a weapon of my own? I said:

– I thought of spending a week there.

– A week will suit us too. You can sleep on board.

– And you?

– Sometimes on board, sometimes not. It all depends on
what comes up.

So now, twin-elemented in frightful fire and turquoise but
surrounded in the saloon by comfortable artefacts, we had
some bourbon and lime juice and then ate lunch. On Pine
Chandeleur's left sleeve I read: *The more God is in all things,
the more He is outside them. The more He is within, the more
without.* Aspinwall spooned through his fish-soup distaste-
fully, looking for some odd solidity that he thought he.

might possibly bring himself conceivably to eat, then said:

– Barometer's two millibars lower than the book says it ought to be.

– Signifying what? Chandeleur asked, showing a grey bolus of chewed fish. He always showed what he was eating while he talked at meals, a bad habit like his verse. *This depth is called the centre, the fund or bottom of the soul.*

– Signifying a bitch of a storm somewhere offstage. Not usual this time of year.

He knew all about the sea, the worst of bitches. I nodded. I'd had an intimation of a remote promise of nausea while in the hot galley. It was not my father, then.

– Put the trysail on her after lunch, I guess.

He did not seem to like his *bouillabaisse.* I brought in the dessert, which wobbled on the table. He dug his dessertspoon in delicately and fished out a sicklemoon peachslice. He examined it as though for flaws. There was a perceptible shaking in the adherent custard. He said:

– Right.

Pine Chandeleur ate heartily, then went back to his pseudo-poem on the settee. Aspinwall and I got the weighty canvas up on deck by way of the forehatch and dragged it aft of the mast. He got down to reeving the lacing and halliard and sheets while I watched him. There was a wind rising, sure enough. He hoisted the sail and I pulled the sheet taut to the cockpit. We got the spinnakers down, he the lee and I the weather, and stowed them. Then he set the storm jib. He said:

– That should do it. It rides well like this. How about some coffee?

I made coffee, instant freezedried perked. Chandeleur lay there on the settee, looking up, his eyes vacant. On his belly: *The Atman is that by which the universe is pervaded, but which nothing pervades; which causes all things to shine, but which all things cannot make to shine.* While I was bringing the coffee-mugs in he said:

– I *hate* storms.

– I thought poets liked them.

– Not this poet. Frank likes them, though. He *loves* them.

It makes him feel all masterful, fighting them. Like the Flying Dutchman or somebody. He can *cope*, you see.

I called that coffee was ready. Aspinwall wanted Chandeleur to take the helm. Chandeleur said:

– I'm not taking the helm. I must lie here. Storms *petrify* me, even in prospect.

So I took the helm while Aspinwall went below for his coffee. The wind was rising steadily and a thin high film of cloud was at work on the sun, lunifying it. I was cold in my slacks and shirt. Soon Aspinwall came up to lock down the forehatch and to fit the weatherboards over the cabin skylight. He said:

– Force six wind, I reckon. Bitch bitch bitch.

Bitch indeed. Aspinwall went below again to dress himself in stormgear. He came up, grimly masterful, took the helm from me and said:

– Get down there and start making a lot of sandwiches. Plenty of mustard in mine, Dijon mustard. Very strong black coffee in the thermoses, laced with brandy. Not the Cordon Bleu, though. Too good for lacing.

– It's going to be pretty bad, is it?

– A bitch.

– And what's your er friend going to do?

– Lie there. Just lie there.

The Inner Light is beyond praise and blame; like space it knows no boundaries.

I made sandwiches with readysliced bread and canned pork-meat, salami and cheese-shives. Chandeleur moaned. I brewed coffee black as a dog, and made it growl and bark with cognac. I took the two big thermoi (?) and kennelled it safely, then I put on my coat and went to the forecastle to look for storm clothing. There was only one set there, and, for that matter, there were only two lifejackets: these were of a sick orange colour. Chandeleur saw me dressing up for tough seamanship and didn't like it.

– How about me?

– You're going to lie there.

– Oh.

Behold but One in all things; it is the second that leads you astray.
I went up to help Aspinwall. The wind was increasing, to
his satisfied grimness. It was not easy to take in a reef on the
trysail. Aspinwall backed the foresail a bit and hove to on the
starboard, or maybe port, I can't remember, tack. The
vessel lay fairly comfortably then, doing two knots or so to
leeward. Then we went below. Chandeleur had brought
sandwiches in from the galley and was wolfing away. He
had a smoking mug of laced coffee. He munched:
— I get hungry when I get frightened.
*If you call God good, or great, or blessed, or wise, or anything else
of this sort, it is included in these words: He is.*
— St Bernard, I said.
— Eh?
— On your right tit.
— Leave him alone, Aspinwall said.
— All I said was —
— Leave him alone.
— Sorry, I said, not wanting trouble, knowing they were
both unbalanced. Chandeleur took another sandwich and
said:
— And how about this just above my navel?
*It is God Who has the treasure and the bride in Him; the God-
head is as void as though it were not.* I said:
— I think it's Meister Eckhart.
— Eckhart, said Aspinwall. Don't mention that name here.
We need all the luck we can get.
— But Eckhart was a great mystic, I said.
— Eckhart was a great son of a bitch. Eckhart was a
chiseller. I wouldn't be where I am now if it wasn't for two-
timing shystering Eckhart.
— And where are you now? Chandeleur asked. Or, I
should say, where are *we* now?
— Wherever it is, it's still some place in the Caribbean.
He lurched over to the chart-table to brood over a chart,
grabbing a sandwich as he went. Brooding, he bit it bitterly
and chewed a while. Then he said:
— Not enough mustard.

– Sorry, I said. Chandeleur said:

– A sort of Godboy, are you? All that about St Bernards snuffling at my right tit.

– You're all dressed up in God, I said. I'd call that a God-shirt. Apotropaic, is it? To ward off storms and other nastiness?

– Shut up about God, cried Aspinwall indistinctly through bread, salami and not enough mustard. We need all the luck we can get.

God, like a dog, hearing his name, leapt in a great slavering joy upon us. The sea cracked and ground at the bones of the bows in a superb accession of appetite. We rode rocking-horse the quaking roof of the waves. Aspinwall cried:

– God Jesus Christ Almighty.

There was an apocalyptical rending above us and then the thudding of wings of a tight and berserk archangel. Aspinwall bounded for the deck, sandwich in hand, and I lurch-followed. Brine spray spume jumped on us ecstatically. He threw his sandwich savagely into the rash smart slogger, which threw it promptly back, as he gaped appalled at the fluttering flagrags of old laundry on the bolt ropes, stormjib eaten alive, trysail sheet-blocks hammering. He had time to look at me with hate before yapping orders that the wind swallowed untasted. A war, a war, or something. No, a warp. But what the hell was a warp? He tottered to the forecastle himself, cursing, while I clung to a rail. Then I saw what a warp was: a sort of towline. He and I, he still going through a silent-movie sequence of heavy cursing, chiefly at me, got the trysail down and then furled it with this warp to the main boom. There was no sail up at all now. The yacht just lolloped moronically in the troughs. It was a complicated torture of an idiot child tossed by one lot of yobs in a cloth, another gang of tearaways singing different songs loudly and pounding him, her, it with icelumps that turned at once to warm water. Night, as they say, fell. At the helm I left Aspinwall, whipped by warm water that broke in heads of frantic snowblooms, and went below, being scared of being washed overboard.

If He is found now, He is found then. If not, we do but go to dwell in the City of Death. Chandeleur was sitting up now, gripping the settee, his feet raised and poised a foot or so above the cabin floor, which was all slopped in bilgewater. He seemed to be reading the bilge, a stupid adenoidal costive lout reading a comic on the floor of the toilet. I said:

– She's filling up.

– Who? What?

– We'd better start pumping.

The cabin lights went down to an orange whisper. Chandeleur first gave a little orgasm scream and then said:

– Jonah.

– Wet's got into the batteries. Who's a Jonah, me?

– We never had this trouble before.

– Screw you, oysterballocked poetaster. Help me get the pump.

– That's not fair. Alfred Kazin liked my poems.

– Screw you just the same, Godshirt.

Everything happened then. The vessel failed to ride, cracked round to starboard, fell on her beamend, plunged down down down. Before the almost no-light fuffed out, every damn thing in the ship came rioting and galloping down the cabin's port side, tins of beef stew, glugging open brandy, caulkers, wrenches, pans, plates, the charlie noble, claw rings, chinkles, chiveys, cheese, kye, dead men, a ditty box, a fanged dog, sextants, bullivant's nippers, splines, whisker poles, whifflows and so on, or perhaps not, me being no seaman. But I remember the noise, human and *chunky* against the swirls of the sea-and-wind's burly. Broached to, broadside on, or something. And absolute swinging drunk dead dark. There was still a candle inside my skull, of course, enough light to show an imagined smirking face, my own, saying: *This is what you wish, no? The death of form and shipwreck of order?* Then something hit me, very sharp, like a table angle, and that inner pilot was doused as I went down into slosh and debris, the belly of Jonadge, black damp whaleboned gamp.

I came to in sickish cold light – dawn and a convalescent sea. The unbelievable fever was burnt out, quite. I was flat on one of the settees, and it squelched like a bathsponge to the ship's rhythm. I was all alone. Chandeleur must be on deck or overboard; Aspinwall, grim and triumphant, at the helm as ever. My stormgear was still on and I did not feel wet. I felt for the pain and found it buried in my hair, a nasty little gash. My probing stiff fingers were answered by stiff dry gory elflocks. The cabin was still a mess of smashed and battered whifflows, but the floor had been pumped to mere moistness. My belly, Jonadge's belly, growled a crass demand: *bub and grub*. My head, I found on waking, did not hurt overmuch. I got up and saw Chandeleur's mystical shirt, damp and unwearable till the sun should be stoked some hours, lying among the debris. I took in a new text like an oyster. Then I went out on deck, ready for a grim meeting.

The mainsail was up. Aspinwall at the helm turned to look at me, still in oilskins, a red scar saltdried on his right cheek, all unspoken reproach. But what the hell had I done wrong, for God's sake? Chandeleur was in a thick sweater that was evidently dry, stowed in one of the high waterproof lockers probably. He had lost his pebble glasses and blinked and blinked in the strengthening light. I said:

– It wasn't my fault I got that crack on the skull.

– Landfall? Chandeleur asked Aspinwall, his eyes screwed up towards the inching sun that was our goal.

Landfall, indeed, a half-note's rest on that grotesque circular leger line. In an hour or two or three I could perhaps be ashore and away, dry, warmed, with no money in my pocket but the Caribbean daytree ahead with fruit for plucking. I didn't feel too bad, all things considered. I would, I knew, no longer be expected to assume that I was welcome to sleep on board, nor would I wish to. On my own, the hell with the two of them, fags, fruits. Chandeleur stroked his fagfruitfriend's oilskin fondly, saying:

– You were wonderful, Frank.

– I know.

– Look, I said, ignored, I did my best, didn't I? That storm wasn't my idea, strange as it may seem. I worked, didn't I? More than can be said for –

– Leave him alone, Aspinwall's back said.

– Aaargh, I began to say, and then I caught the after-image of that text I'd just seen on Chandeleur's shirt: *The fear of solitude is at bottom the fear of the double, the figure which appears one day and always heralds death.* Who'd said that? St Lawrence Nunquam? Cnut of Alexandria? Damn it, I had no fear of solitude. I went below to confirm that I'd actually seen that, but it was not to be found. I picked through the shirt as for lice, but it wasn't there.

6

Senta Euphorbia, martyred under Domitian, jogged along Main Street, or the Strèta Rijal, eight feet high, in meticulously carved soft wood. A sure sign of amateur art is too much detail to compensate for too little life. Eyelashes of blackened hog-bristle were glued to her wooden eyelids, and I could see the pink swell of a tongue in the mouth that was half open in her last pain and first glimpse of the ultimate. Her red robe billowed, all in wood, except where the great phallic spike of her martyrdom had called forth blood to tack the cerement to her body. The blood was there, lovingly painted, though the wound was decently hidden. Her sturdy plinth was fixed to a four-poled litter; she was borne by four men in claret habits with hoods. Her way was cleared by a brass band, the players in dark mufti, whose instruments flashed silver like sudden points of her pain: it played a slow trite march with sentimental harmonies. Behind her ambled priests in surplices, behind them toddled wide-eyed children in a kind of scout costume. Two women near me wept, whether for the saint's agony or for the sweet innocence of the children I could not tell. I was wedged in the middle of a crowd that smelt of clean linen, garlic and musk.

I needed money; I needed somewhere to stay. I had walked the mile or so from Purta, where the Yacht Harbour was, to the centre of Grencijta, having had my passport merely nodded at and my lack of luggage unremarked. The officials on the quay had assumed I was a limb of the *Zagadka II*, meaning that the *Zagadka II* was my warranty of probity, meaning property. Aspinwall and Chandeleur seemed to confirm this. Relieved that I was leaving them, aware that a landed Jonah was harmless as a stranded whale, they were willing to wave me off, but not with the enthusiasm that could be taken for a farewell. They would be seeing me later, they seemed to say. But they would not really, ah no. A real farewell to those two faggots. And so I walked, my headache renewed with the heavy sun, away from the sea and the godowns down a wide road to Grencijta, noting that bunting, holy slogans (*Selvij Senta Euphorbia*) and constellations of light-bulbs had been maimed by that storm, as strong on the coast here as it had been at sea. But now the sky was maria-blue, with not a cloud, and the gulls planed at their ease.

> *Senta Euphorbia,*
> *Vijula vijulata,*
> *Ruza inspijnata*
> *Pir spijna puwntata,*
> *Ura pir nuij.*

A chorus of marriageable girls now appeared, all in white save for a busklike splash of red in the front, chanting that prayer. This was the old language of the Castitans, derived from the Romance dialect spoken by the first settlers, who themselves had gone to settle on the Cantabrian coast from some nameless place in the Mediterranean. They had been enslavers, but that curious wave of British Muslims, that had colonized Ojeda also, had freed the slaves and, becoming lax in their faith under this sun, had been absorbed by the Christianity of the island, though not before they had iglooed the frozen honey of the local stone into mosques. It was to the Dwumu, or great mosque-cathedral, in Fortescue Square that the procession now moved. And who had Fortescue been? A British governor of the time of the British raj or *rigija*, now ended. That rule had left, I discovered, a public works department, the English language, a thicket of laws, but no democracy.

To my surprise, but everybody else's joy, the procession now turned brusquely secular. The enharmonic chord, or chordee, that was responsible for the modulation was a huge wooden phallic spike, painted red seeming to ooze from its crown like the jam of a caramel cream, and this was held in the arms of a Punch-like clown who leered from left to right as he shambled along in his clumsy boots. Behind him came floats with young people's tableaux – The Jazz Age (Eton crops, Oxford bags, Nöel Coward cigarette-holders, a horned gramophone), Prison Reform (lags drinking champagne with silkstockinged wardresses on their knees), Castitan Agriculture (a papier-mâché cornucopia spilling bananas, pomelos, pineapples, corncobs and jackfruit, with plumplimbed girls striking poses in the scanty garments of Ceres), The Fruits of Our Seas (Neptune and court with a huge netted catch, including a still-writhing octopus), Silent Movie Days (megaphoned director in knickerbockers, camera cranking, Valentino, Chaplin, etc.), God Bless His Excellency (blownup photograph of a fat handsome face with clever but insincere eyes, garnished with flags and saluting Ruritanian children), and others I seem to have forgotten. Then came a circus band ripping off a redhot march with glissading trombones. This did not clash with the solemnity of that earlier march, since the subfusc bandsmen had already piled instruments at the entrance to the Dwumu, Senta Euphorbia being within and probably jogging towards the altar. Then elephants.

– Elephants? I said, astonished. Faces turned gleefully to say:

– Elefanta's Circus, Fonanta's Circus, Bonanza's Circus, Atlanta's Circus.

The name was not clear. After the elephants, Jumbo, Alice and a baby with its lithe proboscis clinging to mother's tail, there came tumbling augustes and a couple of joeys banging drums. Then there came two lions in one cage and a tiger and tigress in another, a truck with a pair of performing seals, both balancing striped beachballs, and a lovely flight of white liberty ponies with their waving ballerina mistresses. And then the crowd grew silent.

A gaunt woman in a terracotta robe, her face glowing faintly as with henna, strode alone in a kind of tragic pride. Around her head circled fluttering birds, mynahs, parakeets, starlings, all chattering or screaming human language – fracted words drowned in the band-noise. The aura of the woman seemed numinous or sorcerous; hence the crowd's silence. A speaking bird is a kind of enchanted man. The woman sternly looked into the crowd, first left then right, and it seemed that our eyes met an instant and in hers was a speck of instant and angry recognition. But she strode on, and the moment of quiet and disquiet was exorcized by the open-faced wholesome finale – the Castitan football eleven that had, I was to learn, defeated Venezuela in the Central American Cup Final. They trotted along, as in roadwork, in their orange-and-cream jerseys, their grinning captain bearing the silver trophy aloft like a monstrance. Cheer after cheer after. We had come a long way from Senta Euphorbia.

The watching crowd now flooded on to the road to become the joyful wake of the festal convoy. It was chiefly children with comic hats and false noses, blowing kazoos and rasp-berrying hooters, young guffawing men in jeans with iron crosses or swastikas dangling from their necks, giggling girls in white or yellow or duckegg blue. The older sort smiled and jostled good-humouredly on the sidewalks towards Fortescue Square, or else streamed into the drinkingshops. I was thirsty too. I had just ninety American cents.

The shop I entered was a cavern as long and as narrow as a railway coach. Drinking, on this island of very fierce sun, was always an activity of the dark: the sun in the wine was never acknowledged, on laughing boulevards, to the sun's face. I could hardly see, I groped my way through drinker's noise, stumbling over feet. One man's noise was louder than any other's:

– How did he get where he is, eh? You all know damned well what I'm talking about, and if there's any presidential spy leering in the shadows he can do his worst. Because I'm past caring. Because the truth is the truth and can't be gainsaid not by any amount of state falsification or the jiggerypokery of hirelings.

– Come on now, Jack, said a man in a white apron, a ghost in that dark from the waist down. Finish what you've got there and get out on the job.

– The job. The prostitution of fragmented truth, that's all it is. But nobody asks the right questions ever, oh no. What did our beloved President do with those two little girls on the night of June 10th, 1962, in a house that shall be numberless in a street that shall be nameless? Why did the fleet of Cadillacs appear so soon after the door-to-door collection in aid of the orphans? Why did James Mendoza Callaghan so suddenly and unaccountably disappear in the autumn of 1965? Those questions and questions like them, never, oh no. And I know all the answers, boy, oh yes.

I could see him now, a blubbery wreck of an intellectual in a dark suit complete with waistcoat, sitting alone at a table from which liquor dripped. Customers interrupted him:

– Knock it off, Jack, the police are around. All right, let's have no trouble today of all days. Christ, a man comes in for a quiet drink. Clever, but look where his cleverness is going to land him.

I stood at the counter and ordered a glass of white wine. I asked the aproned man:

– What was all that about the prostitution of fragmented truth he was talking about?

– Eh? Who? Him? Goes round the towns on feasts and marketdays putting on his little show. *Donj Memorija* or Mr Memory.

He then turned on him, still loudly seditious, and addressed him fiercely in the first, or alternative, language of the island:

– *Chijude bucca, stujlt!*

– Explain the unaccountable disappearance also of the editor of the *Stejla d' Grencijta* after a very mildly censorious leading article.

– What sort of a show? I asked.

– Answers them all. *Todij cwéjstijonij.* Shut your big fat black mouth, you troublecauser. Else I shall have to send for the *polijts*.

– Is it a total coincidence that the deputy chief of police was once His Excellency's bumboy?

– *Tacija!* Knock it off! Kick the *idijuta* out!

I fancied, turning around from the counter to look at the protesting faces, that I saw, peering in from the sun, the grinning face of Chandeleur and the stern one of Aspinwall. They were there a second or so only. My headache started throbbing again. Then there stood, much longer, the recog-

nizable silhouette of the law framed on the threshold –
tropical law, with starched shorts and briefsleeved shirt emphasizing the thin wiriness of a body schooled in violence.
Holster, arms akimbo. The assembly, except for Donj
Memorija, grew silent as if to listen seriously to music.

– Ask me a question, anybody, a question relevant to the
sick times and leprous state we live in.

There was a response of frightened shushes. I got in with
something sedative:

– Who was the short apple the father of?

– Eh? Eh eh? If the apple is a pippin, the pippin is Pépin
le Bref, king of the Franks, father of Charlemagne. 714 to 768,
if you want his dates. But that sort of question is as meaningless in these terrible times as as as –

I could see him peering at me with one eye, wondering who
or what the hell I was, his ample hair dirtygrey, a triple
round chin wobbling. The silhouette at the door moved in on
heavy boots, and the features of the policeman began to
emerge, as from a bath of hypo. The policeman said:

– Let's hear more about these terrible times.

– Brutal state lackey, presidential claw, how is the world of
bribes nowadays?

I thought I'd better get out. The policeman was not, as yet,
interested in stopping me. I said to an old chewing man, who
had a mess of bread and crumbling brawn on greased paper
in front of him:

– Where does he do this job? You know, him.

– Dagobert Place where the fair is, said a younger man
with a twitching left arm.

The policeman already had Donj Memorija up, more or
less, on his feet, one hand on his collar, the other bunching
the seat of his pants. I left, hearing:

– When you get back to headquarters ask what they did
with Gubbio, Vittorini and Serafino Starkie. Unpared toenail of bloody repression –

I was out then, wrinkling my blind face in the sun. Dagobert Place? I was thumbjerked towards it or even shown by a
vigorous semaphore signpost yardarming. A helpful people,
with a lot of submerged energy. I went down a cobbled lane

with a shut printingshop, turned into one where men, singing, threw caraway seeds on to round loaves that other men were painting with eggwhite, and then came to an oblong piazza with two playing baroque fountains (writhing stone musculatures in hell gaping and grasping for the tantalizing water), where stalls had been set up for a fair season. They sold the usual things – cutprice children's vests, football boots, candyfloss – and had try-your-luck pennyrollers and gungalleries. Gay people mostly laughed in the faces of the barkers, strolling, licking cones. I saw a fairly quiet corner and claimed it. I needed a sort of platform so begged, in dumbshow because the stallman spoke only Castitan, a loan of three or four sturdy empty Coco-Coho (not so new then: the drink was already in the Caribbean) crates. I mounted my dais and called:

– Mr Memory Junior is here! Any questions! Anyanyanyany questions!

Shy and giggling, a sprinkling of youngsters was soon with me and yet not with me: they might as well be there as anywhere, but none would meet my eye or challenge. Then a middleaged man, not quite sober, called from afar:

– How can I stop my wife nagging me?

– Stop her mouth with kisses, I called back. Exhaust her with love.

There was laughter. The knot grew. A schoolboy tried something the others could not hear. I cried:

– I am asked by this young gentleman to say when television began. If he means the first public showing, the answer is July 13th, 1930, in England, by the Baird process.

The boy's question had, in fact, sought the date of the founding of the multiracial University College in Salisbury, but I did not know the answer to that. Encouraged now, louder-voiced members of the crowd put their questions: the first Morse message? (May 24th, 1844); the Dunkirk evacuation? (June 3rd, 1940, anniversary of the death of Blood Circulation Harvey); the old name of Bulgaria's capital? (Sardica, Triaditza to the Byzantine Greeks); the twelfth wedding anniversary? (Silk and Fine Linen); the autobiographical synthesis of Che Guevara? (born in Argentina,

fought in Cuba, became a revolutionary in Guatemala);
Death in the Afternoon? (champagne and pernod, well
chilled); record for beer-drinking? (Auguste Maffrey, a
Frenchman, downed 24 pints in 52 minutes); Beaufort 8?
(fresh gale: twigs break off trees; progress is impeded); who
said that the English think soap is civilization? (the German
philosopher Treitschke); artemisia? (wormwood or old
man); guanaco? (large species of llama, used as a beast of
burden); International Henry? (= 1·00049 Absolute
Henry); how to treat trypanosomiasis? (with tryparsamide
or Bayer 205); cleaning off soot-stains? (try carbon tetra-
chloride); Edith Sitwell's middle name? (Louisa); Derby
winner of 1958? (Hard Ridden, C. Smirke up).

These may not, of course, be the actual questions that
were asked, but there were certainly many questions, to each
of which the questioner usually knew the answer, which was
his reason for asking. I made a score of about 80 per cent.
And then, to my unease, the questions began to change into
riddles. A giggling plump desirable young matron asked:

– What can you not hold more than a minute, though it is
lighter than a feather?

That was an easy one. Then a lined old woman said:

– A drawing-room with many chairs and a clown dancing
in the middle.

A drawn tubercular youth:

– It's locked up inside you, and yet they can steal it from
you.

The breath grew sour in my mouth, and my heart pumped
hard. Perhaps I needed food. The headache was frightful.
Then someone said, and I could not see him clearly:

> – White bird featherless
> Flew from paradise,
> Pitched on the castle wall;
> Along came Lord Landless,
> Took it up handless,
> And rode away horseless to the King's
> white hall.

– Sun, yes, I said. But how do you know about snow?

And then a scholarlylooking man, in a widebrimmed hat and a selfpropel wheelchair, spoke in a tongue I had not expected to hear in the Caribbean:

> – I have a jelyf of godes sonde,
> Withouten fyt it can stonde.
> It can smytyn and hath not honde.
> Ryde yourself quat it may be.

– Too easy, I said. Too obscene for this mixed assembly. I am now going to take the hat round.

I snatched, smiling acknowledgement of unasked permission, a cap from a schoolboy's head. Some of the crowd began to disperse quickly. But a sudden creature stood out, crying *Wait!*, and I was appalled. Was this distortive headache, sun, hunger? It was the lion face of some grotesque ultimate leprosy, framed in an ironically indulged piebald mane. The body was small and twisted but undeniably human. The arms seemed to yearn forward in an arc to engage the ground as paws. The cheap blue suit was well pressed for a holiday, the collar clean, the tie patterned with dogroses. The creature called in a muffled bark, as though its mouth were furred with carney:

– Answer if you can!

I didn't want to answer, though I didn't know why. I countercalled:

– Today's show is over. Try tomorrow.

But the crowd desisted from its dispersing and cried that I should answer. The creature put up a foreleg arm for silence and then propounded its riddle:

> – Throatdoor, tongueback, nose and teeth
> Spell a heavenblack hell beneath.
> Engage warily, young men,
> Lest it prove a lion's den.

– I know the answer, I said, but I may be arrested for uttering a public obscenity. It's the counterpart of that jelyf riddle. No, no, the show's over. Your contributions, please. My brain may be crammed but my pockets are empty. Give please of your bounty to a poor stranger in your midst.

The lionman shambled off, giving nothing. From what was left of the crowd I collected – in small change save for a whole dollar bill from the jelyf scholar – seven Castitan dollars sixty-five, the Castitan dollar, because of its derivation from the old British demi-pound, being worth somewhat more than its American cousin. Having answered so many questions I felt entitled to ask one of my own: the reader will know what it was. The jelyf man gave me a courteous and prompt response. His accent, I now noticed, was French or Creole. His left hand was gloved in good leather. I thanked him and went off to find a cheap hotel.

7

There was a telephone on the little stand by the main door, and a pretty young girl in a short dress – variegated amethyst and bullock's heart fruit – kept saying into it:

– One one three. One one three. Mr R. J. Wilkinson.

And then she looked at me as though she'd met me before and didn't like me much. I didn't care. I walked up to the desk with my new razor and three new handkerchiefs. I explained my lack of further luggage, and the proprietress tutted in sympathy. The things that go on in New York. The Indies far safer. She drew in her lips till they disappeared, at the same time shaking her head. She was a mocha-coloured woman with purplish hair that a white swathe cut like a road, and she was dressed in a *kebaya*. Three dollars a night did not seem excessive.

– Your name here in the book. Your passport.

Her hotel was called the Batavia, so I took it that she must be from Indonesia, or rather the old Dutch East Indies. One Indies as good as another. Signing, I saw on her desk a near-empty pack of Dji Sam Soe cigarettes, clove-flavoured, made in Surabaya. I suppressed, as with two tough cerebral thumbs, my rage at the loss of my Sinjantin. I growled:

– New York.

– Yes, yes, terrible.

The little lobby was a warm crammed drinking lounge hung, for some reason, with quite ordinary Malaccan work-baskets. Large grey lizards scuttled on the walls, dodging behind pictures of sailing vessels, and they made lipsmacking noises. Some men were playing cards and one, blinking in total inattention, was being humorously berated for cheating. A lone drinker probed his cheek with his tongue, one eye closed, the other on an East Indies looking calendar whose picture showing a young brown couple kissing on the lips while a shocked conservative elder in the background half averted his eyes. *Her* eyes? I can't remember. There was a pleasant smell of cinnamon and camphorwood. A large open door led out to a garden in which a girl shook stiff sheets and a boy cleaned a well by stirring the water with a stick. Some unseen tyro was plonking a sort of lute unhandily – C d F A. It seemed a good place to be in.

I carried my key up the stairs to Number 8, belching on the spiced fish stew I'd eaten in a sleepy restaurant. The window, which was open, so that a sea breeze danced the nylon curtain, looked on to Tholepin Street, which was cheerfully noisy. There was a cobbler's shop, a goldsmith's, a fortune-teller's. A ramshackle cinema was showing *The Day After the Day After Tomorrow*. The seawall lay beyond. Gulls freewheeled. Charming. So was the simple room, air its main furnishing. Water? I went on to the corridor and found a rudimentary washroom – a mere stone floor and a couple of faucets. I washed my shirt with a bar of coarse blue soap, but first, with a hand as cup, I washed down the six aspirins I had bought. The lump on my head was subsiding, but the pain still thrust and beat. I shaved blind, soaping my beard with the naked bar. I would wait to do what I wanted to do, had to do, till tomorrow. Meanwhile, rest. I hung my shirt on the one wire hanger in the breeze, then got between the rough clean sheets. *The Day After the Day After Tomorrow*, said the after-image of the cinema's poster. No, definitely tomorrow. Early.

I could not at first sleep. I lay on my side, taking in for the first time the little bedside cupboard. What was in it? A chamberpot, a Gideon Bible? I opened it and saw a book far too small for a bible. The cover was at an angle like a roof – a sizeable bookmark in there. The bookmark was a heavy bright professional referee's whistle, and the book itself a rulebook for association football. *A player is offside if he is nearer the opponents' goal-line than is the ball unless there are two opponents between him and the goal-line or unless the ball was last played by an opponent.* Very sedative stuff. An absentminded visiting referee had slept here, then. Absentminded or finally disgusted with what the game had become – a pretext for head-crushing or bottle-throwing, the referee's rulings disregarded. I must hand the book and the whistle in downstairs. But, no. It was a handsome whistle and I would keep it. It had the comforting feel that all rounded metal solidities possess. I put the little barrel to my forehead: it cooled and soothed. It had a long neckloop of durable twine. I hung it round my neck like a talisman. It seemed to send me to sleep.

I dreamt about my sister, who had become very young and tiny, more of a daughter. I carried her under my arm like a kitten through the streets of New York, but, as I had to make several purchases – vague things that were seen only as bulky parcels – she became a nuisance: there was no room for her under either arm. I threw her into the East River and she turned into a fish. It was a silly meaningless dream.

I awoke without pain to catch the swift sunset. Something small and hard tapped my chest as I got up. I started, then I remembered what it was. I was hungry. My shirt was dry. When I went downstairs I found the bar-lobby empty, except for the proprietress. She was smoking a Dji Sam Soe and cloves mingled with the cinnamon and camphorwood. She looked up from copying things from a small book into a big book and said:

– How long will you be staying?

– Oh, I said, I thought of leaving – oh, the day after the day after tomorrow.

She did not seem to catch the silly reference. She said something that sounded like *too late*.

– Why too late?

– *Tulat* is what I said. The day after the day after tomorrow the skilled workman will carry a burden over his shoulder on a stick with another stick over the other shoulder to support it.

– I beg your pardon?

– An example, she said, smiling now, I was once given at school to show how many words the English language requires to say very simple things. In my language, called Bahasa, we need three words only.

– Oh?

74

– *Tulat tukang tuil. Tulat*: too late the day after, etcetera. *Tuil*: too ill to carry, etcetera, etcetera. Perhaps you will remember the words that way.

– But I've no intention of ever having any need to –

– What has intention to do with it?

There was no reply to that. She gathered up her books and then, as if she'd just thought of this softener of what may have sounded like a rebuke to my brash youth, said:

– Dr Gonzi invites you to have dinner with him. Any time from six thirty on, he says. At the Pepeghelju.

– Who's Dr Gonzi, how does he know I'm here, why does he invite me, where's the –

– Such a lot of questions. The Pepeghelju is near, off Tholepin Street. Dr Gonzi met you, he says, earlier today. He was here for a drink. He was impressed, or some such thing. It is what is called here *uspijtelijtet*. He will be hurt if you do not go. It would be unkind to hurt Dr Gonzi.

She nodded and went to the little office behind her counter. She opened the door and acrid smoke, like asthma mixture, puffed out, and there was the talk and clink of quiet drinking. She went in and shut the door.

So. I went out on to Tholepin Street, smelling for garlic and hot oil. Shops, cinema, shops, shops. Which was Dr Gonzi, then? The jelyf scholar? It could hardly be that – But it might be anybody. Walking, I heard the squawk of what sounded like a parrot from a dark sidestreet: *Kraaaaaaarkh*, and then, in the sounds of New South Wales, *Ellow, Cocky*. Ah, wait: *Pepeghelju* ought to mean parrot, ought it not? So I went down the street and came to a discreet smell of frying fish, and there indeed was the restaurant. It was a small open yard with half a dozen tables, glassed candles on them, and bushes in tubs. There was a covered kitchen with a swing-door. A cage hung from a kind of gallows, with a droll-eyed red-and-blue parrot clinging to the wires. The sea whished just beyond. And there at a table alone sat the, as I should have expected, lionman. There was a well-punished bottle of Claidheamh whisky before him. Seeing me, he tossed off a glassful then unsteadily rose.

– Dr Gonzi?

– Surprise in your tone, as though the higher academic honours are to be considered incompatible with with – Never mind. Good of you to come. You did well today. You have funds of totally useless knowledge. I like that.

– You're not then a doctor of medicine, sir?

We sat, I very uneasy. His face looked ghastly in the candle-light. *Scratch Cocky, ahahahaha. Kraaaaaarkh.* There were no other customers.

– Of philosophy. *Real* philosophy. The consolations of, much overrated. Boethius. Metaphysics, an out-of-date and disregarded study. I have written on Bishop Berkeley. Call me an idealist. You may, knowing so many useless things, be acquainted with my edition of *Alciphron, or the Minute Philosopher.*

The voice still had that muted resonance of earlier in the day, though the whisky sharpened the consonants. I said:

– That kind of philosophy doesn't really appeal to me. I mean, I think the outside world exists.

– *Think*, you say *think*. A rather Berkeleyan position. Shall we now get down to *thinking* we are eating something?

He snapped his clawfingers. The parrot responded with monstrous hilarity, and then a little moustached Creole in a white coat came out. Dr Gonzi said:

– Leave it to me. Bisque, I *think*, followed by an illusion of grilled flying-fish with stuffed peppers. Will you think, that is drink, whisky?

– With pleasure.

– *Think.* You think that I took up this idealist stance prob-ably because I don't want, can't bear, an outside world which contains this sad mask and this ludicrous body. So much illusion, better that way. Yes? The reality is the soul. Sexual appetite an illusion like all the other appetites, the reflection of my face in others' eyes the work of a trick mirror. The children are not really frightened, their psyches are unagitated. I know what you're thinking. But tonight I don't care.

– No, no, really. I mean, I'm so wrapped up in the de-ficiencies of my own body. The fluxes, the pains, disease. I mean, no.

– Disease can be made romantic, sexually alluring. This you must know. Ugliness is defined in terms of beauty, is it not? But when, by a genetic freak, one is made to seem to pass out of one's own kingdom, when no normal aesthetic standard can be made to apply – Do I make myself clear? *Do I?* Have some whisky.

A claw grasped the bottle and the candlelit gold belched as it swam into my glass. He said:

– Only by entry into myth can reconciliation be effected. Do you understand? I have waited a long time for one such as you to come along. Does what I am saying at all make sense to you?

– Not really, not yet.

The waiter brought the bisque, upon which brandy floated. He ignited our plates with a taper he lit from our candle. Dr Gonzi looked across at me over the brief hellfire. I was very disturbed but didn't yet know what precisely about.

– A good illusion of goodness, yes?

There was no doubt that the bisque was good: hot, heartening, delicate. I said:

– He was always going on about tar water, wasn't he? About the supposed goodness of tar water.

– That was nonsense. There's nothing in tar water.

He seemed to brood on tar water, spooning in his soup. Then he said:

– Centaurs and that sort of thing. And, of course, Pan, the great god. *Panic.*

– What do you mean when you say you've waited a long time? For someone like me, I mean?

– A certain combination of mad talent and guilt. Yes, guilt. You answered all those questions *so sadly.* Ah, here come the flying-fish. Sad, sad, their play in the blown spume ended. Bedded down with peppers, stuffed. Could a stuffed pepper ever enter into the dream of a flying-fish? Man, man, the great sad unifier of disparates. Another bottle of this, yes?

He was drunk and growing drunker. But he ate his fish with great eagerness, fussily blowing out odd small bones from farting lips. He seemed to be trying to demonstrate

77

that, in spite of appearances, he was no carnivore. I too ate my fish, which was overdry. The peppers were stuffed with rice cooked in fishstock. The whisky was deliciously smooth, and I said so.

– Ah well, we must pamper ourselves tonight. No dyspeptic rotgut, gutrot. Tonight is a special night. As I said, I've been waiting a long time.

– You still haven't told me what you mean.

Aaaaaaargh. Cockycockycockycockycocky.

– You knew the answer to the riddle I asked, but you wouldn't give the answer.

– Well, no. It was so obvious, wasn't it?

– I have one riddle to which only I know the answer.

– You mean the riddle of life or something like that?

– Life is no riddle. Why are we here? To suffer, no more. But why do we suffer? Ah, that's more interesting. Hamlet's question, of course, and we all know Hamlet's answer. I too, like Hamlet, keep putting off the bodkin. The devil we know, and so on. But we must think of the prince as well set-up, though a little puffy. Mad, but alluring. Good my lord, dear my lord. Look at *me*, though, look.

– You said something about centaurs.

– Yes yes yes, Hyperion to a satyr. And yesterday I was offered money, do you know that, *money*, to be gaped at. The circus is in town. Money, by a man called Dunkel. So this has to be the end.

– I don't think I quite understand.

– The end, the end, *Ende, fin, konyets.* Damn it, boy, the end can only be the end, can't it, yes?

He had finished his fish and peppers and now began to hiccup violently. He drank off half a tumbler of whisky, while the parrot made crooning noises of what sounded like commiseration. The hiccups, fuelled by the whisky, became fiercer, and the lionface, as if in heraldry, turned green. The parrot listened with care, its head on one side, and then tried out *sotto voce* those noises which were probably new to him. Dr Gonzi got up and began to stagger out.

– I must. The indig.

I felt desperately sorry for him and he must, sick as he was, have known it. The indig, indeed. He lurched away into the darkness beyond the candles, off, I presumed, to be ill in the street. Should I follow him? Would he come back? There was the matter of the bill, a heavy one surely with its two bottles of whisky. I waited, sipping in apprehension still not clearly defined, while the parrot tried out a hiccup ineptly then abandoned the phonic project in a highpitched mating-call scream. I could have done with a cigarette.

After a few minutes I went out on to the street. It was very dark and totally empty except for Dr Gonzi. There was a sort of warehouse built of bubblestone, big and empty, and he was leaning against its wall. His being sick, if he had been sick, had not impaired his drunkenness. He was indeed drunker than before, to judge from what he had in his hand. He was pointing a small automatic at me. I pretended not to see it. I said:

– Feeling better? Good. Look, there's this question of paying the bill. I would have left money myself, but I haven't –

– Yes yes. There may be a hell, you see. The old Hamlet problem. If I kill you now and give myself up to the police, there's a fair chance that I may hang. This is a great country for hanging, you know. I'm quite prepared to plead guilty to murder.

It's astonishing how calmly one can take these things. I said:

– Motive, motive.

– Motive? The desire to commit evil, the best motive in the world. But I recognize the need for a certain demented fairness. Let me go out in a kind of mythic blaze.

All the time he spoke I was looking for dark angles of escape. There was an alleyway there, just beyond the warehouse, but it might be a cul de sac. The parrot broke into a florid cadenza of whistles. Whistle. I said:

– Fairness? You're talking of fair play?

– In my condemned cell there will be time for true penitence. Then the instant purgatory of the noose. There remains, however, room for reasonable Hamlet doubt. A play of uncertainty. I shall ask you my ultimate riddle. If you can't answer, then I shoot you. If you can, then I shoot

myself. I think I can promise both of us that you won't be
able to answer.

    – You're mad, of course.

    – Drunk, not mad. But have I not every right in the world
to be *furioso*? Mr Dark wanted me, Mr Dark can have me.
Dunkel. Are you ready?

    – This is just not possible.

    – *Think* that it is. Listen carefully.

And then, the gun pointing steadily at my sternum, he
came out with his stupid riddle:

> – Move and my own self enclose
> A land above the deeper snows.

    – That's more of a word-puzzle than a true riddle, I pro-
tested, bringing my right hand up to my chest.

    – But you can't solve it?

    – Of course I can. It's stupidly obvious. But I won't give
you the answer.

I was astonished at myself saying that. Why why why? It
was clear that he meant everything he'd said, and I could
save myself so easily, but I wouldn't or couldn't. My head
throbbed.

    – Then it is with the deepest regret –

At that moment the parrot, which was only about fifty
yards away, fulfilled William James's doctrine about
plateaux of learning and began to hiccup in earsplitting
triumph. I wrenched the whistle out of my shirt, breaking
two buttons, shoved it in my mouth like a kid's dummy and
blew. The double noise confused Dr Gonzi, who put his
gunless paw to his eyes as though blinded by sudden head-
lamps. I ran into the alley, still shrieking. Dr Gonzi recovered
and fired. The air winced in wow-wow waves at the crack.
Too much noise altogether: in a mad way I regretted con-
tributing to it. The parrot was laughing rather mechanically.
I whistled and whistled, keeping to the wall of the alley. He
again fired, following. In the alley's confines the noise was a
whole brief movement for percussion. There was no sense of
anybody in that street, or behind the backdoors of the alleys
which had, for I desperately tested three, no outer handles,

conceiving an interest in the noise: everybody seemed out, celebrating Senta Euphorbia. I ran on, all I could do. I paused an instant, pumping in a chestful of air which I then spent on a fortissimo blast. Dr Gonzi fired crack wow-wow-wow-wow and then stupidly called:

– Come back, damn you.

The alley was not deadended: it entered a cobbled street with empty market stalls. It was slippery underfoot and had a strong fish-smell. I blasted again and this time was answered: a police-whistle I took it to be. It and mine started a dialogue. Then I paused and panted. Dr Gonzi had stopped firing. Perhaps he had gone back to the Pepeghelju to pay the bill. I didn't need the police, then. The whistle that had answered mine was joined by another; a forlorn duet probed for the whereabouts of my signal. It came from the searoad, so I walked the other way. A siren started up: a patrol-car had been parked somewhere near, then, now activated. Running police-feet were approaching my rear, and the patrol-car, a spinning yellow light on its roof, turned a corner to meet me, and, meeting me, braked.

8

—Don't give us that, the inspector said. You picked a very bad one there, boy. Dr Gonzi, eh? That's a laugh. Why not make it the Holy Ghost or, while your hand's in, the President himself?

He clanged the base of his metal desk with his boot, a way he had of emphasizing strong points. He was a wellfed man with clever brown eyes which, alone of the police eyes there, were unshod with dark glasses. The constables who'd picked me up flanked him, standing easy, and they were quick to let their lower faces collapse in obsequious laughter. One of the two patrolmen, downing a quick coke, spluttered. The inspector looked steelily at both. They saluted, crestfallen, and the nonsplutterer said:

— *Muwvijemu.*

— That's right, move off. And deal with drunks on the spot. This isn't a toper's dosshouse.

— All I tell you is the truth, I said. Dr Gonzi shot at me. That's why I whistled. Three times. He shot, I mean.

— Oh, my God, Dr Gonzi as killer. How about telling us where you put the gun? How about showing us your weapon permit?

— Would I be such a bloody fool as to call the police if it was me who was doing the shooting?

— I've heard that sort of question before. We're not such *bloody fools* either.

The inspector inspected the referee's whistle, turning it over and over in his fingers as though rolling a cigarette. He said:

— It's got a name on it. Engraved. *W. Pozoblanco.* Are you W. Pozoblanco? Think carefully before you answer.

— I've already told you my name.

– So you admit to having stolen this whistle from W. Pozoblanco?

– I admit nothing except what I've already said.

– You're a foreigner, said the inspector ungrudgingly. There are things you may not understand going on here.

I eased my bottom on the cane chair. The office was clean and simple, as if to disavow the dirtiness that was evidently going on, in a complex montage of allomorphs, in the cells and interrogation rooms behind the plastic strip curtain. There was the noise of a man retching and someone shouting, as if to tell him under pain of new violence to get it all up. Others, more distant, sang what seemed to be a hymn, solemnly not drunkenly. A stick cracked rhythmically on a tabletop, an accompaniment to threatening monosyllables. Whiffs of faecal effluvia stole in shyly. I said:

– Do you think I could have a cigarette?

– Certainly, certainly. Any particular kind? Opium-tainted Turkish? Powdered peyotl? Asthma mixture?

That last was a shrewd shot. I was breathing with some difficulty: the lungful of air I kept seeking eluded my grasp by something less than an inch. I said:

– A Sinjantin for preference.

– Sorry, sir, out of stock, said the straightfaced inspector. The constable mouths grinned; the blank black eyes rebuked the mirth like law itself. The inspector said:

– We don't like guns here, you see, not in the hands of ordinary citizens, especially when they're strangers. Why don't you speak the truth?

I spoke the truth. Like all truth it sounded untruthful. The inspector said:

– As for this memory stuff in the market, visitors here aren't allowed to do paid work without a permit that has to be applied for in advance. So that's more trouble you're in.

– I didn't know. Nobody told me the law.

– Nobody tells anybody the law. The law assumes that everyone knows the law.

– I'm sorry.

The inspector looked again at the things that had been taken from my pockets. He said:

– Castitan dollars, illegally earned. We'll have to keep those. This cutting you have here seems to be about a dirty book. Why do you have it?

It was the *Seee* review of Yumyum Carlotta's novel. I said:

– I once met the author.

– You did, eh? Things are looking pretty black all round, aren't they?

– I don't see why.

The inspector at once became animated, though strangely impartially, as though I'd merely fed him a dramatic cueline. He uncoiled up, making the chairfeet on the linoleum briskly squeal, then, well upstage of the constables, who turned into caryatid proscenium columns, he loped up and down, his hands clasped behind him.

– You don't see why, eh, you don't see why? Oh, I could show you why well enough, why indeed, why why why, by the living heavens I could *icsplijeari*, if you know our native word, that why for you, my friend, and leave you without a single *why* left in your alphabet. What do you think of that, eh? Why why why, indeed.

He strode down centre, back to his desk and, handheels pressing it hard, nearbare arms very taut, he frowned from a great height down at the clipping from *Seee*. He said:

– Too much Chinese going on, for one thing. What have you got to do with the Chinese?

Strange he should say that. I answered:

– It's been proposed that I marry a certain Miss Ang. That, in a sense, is what I'm running away from.

– Ah, and she'd be tied up, would she, with Miss Tu Kang and those Chinese cigarettes you said you wanted?

– Sinjantin. Korean, not Chinese. And the lady at the Batavia Hotel (and how the hell am I going to pay my bill there, incidentally, since you took my bit of money away?) smokes a brand called Dji Sam Soe.

– Tu kang sin jan tin jee sam soo. Building up, isn't it?

There was no answer to that, but something newly disturbed me. Was it a sense of being dragged east, towards Miss Ang, despite all my efforts to go my own way? I didn't have time to pursue this, because a sergeant strode in, followed by two new constables. The sergeant did not wear dark glasses though, with such tired eyes, as though from an excess of recent deskwork, and so many elephantine folds around them, though the face was otherwise long and ascetic, he would have looked better with dark glasses. Were they a privilege of constables, a compensation for low pay, or a curtain on the callow humanity whose expunging went with higher rank? The sergeant spoke British English and was familiar with his inspector. Without saluting he said:

– Acted on the signal as ordered. Nothing going on up there, Jack. Fireworks, I should think.

– Premature petards, eh? No festive noises till Saturday says the regulation. Still, boys will be boys.

The inspector looked at me as if I were one of the boys covered by the indulgence. The sergeant looked too, looked away uninterested, then doubletook and said:

– So it's him, is it? You, is it? In trouble again, is that it? Having a go at a respected poor unfortunate citizen that can't hit back and anyway is calm asleep in his bed now, is that what it is this time?

I was astonished, but not so much as I might have been. There was this problem of getting enough air in, and there was the renewal of the throb in the head, and there was a general sense of the laws of probability being in a state of suspension on this ridiculous island. Still, I gasped:

– This is. Totally. I don't know. You and you don't. Know me. Is this. What they. Call a frameup?

– What name did he give? the sergeant asked. The inspector told him from his notepad. The sergeant said:

– *Llew* was the name he gave me last night. He was very particular about the spelling and how to say it. Something like Clew or Tlew, a lot of foreign nonsense. Got his full name written down at Marple Street. That's where he was brought in.

– Who was. Brought in? What is the name. Of.

– Brought in what for? the inspector asked.

– Calling up at a girl in an open window. Excuse was he

thought she was on the game. Calling up *how about it* and *what about a bit of the old*. And gestures.

The sergeant demonstrated a couple of these gestures. The inspector said:

– Where's he from, what's he on here?

– Up there with the Circus. And another thing is how did it manage to get in, what with the regulations? Animals and that. Subversive foreigners. Clowns and suchlike. Called himself the Cowardly King of the Beasts. Beasts is right. Thought he could rope in Dr Gonzi as a freak is my interpretation. My interpretation is Dr Gonzi gets rightly nasty and then this one gets wrongly nasty back. In my view of things it's no way to behave.

– That's not, I said, fair. It was another man. Dr Gonzi was depressed. Suicidal. In a killing mood.

– About this whistle, said the inspector, dangling it.

– A Mr Dark, I said. No, wait – a Mr Dunkel.

– There you are, the sergeant said, well-satisfied. It's this Dunkel who's the manager. My interpretation or recommendation is you shove him in for a bit and get Dunkel to take him home. Taking his time, that is. He knows Dunkel all right, you see. That proves who he is I would say, a matter of deduction or inference.

– Right, the inspector said and, to me, with professional cold quiet: Grow up, boy. Lying to the police won't do. This is a respectable community and we know how to deal with the disrespectful. Take him away.

He turned to an in-tray, with a show of disgust and preoccupation. The two constables flexed themselves, as if coming to life again after long enchantment, and began to flick and prod me towards the plastic strip curtain. The sergeant said, in a new mood:

– Old Ferguson was ratty tonight, Jack.

– Tantalic and yttria?

That's what it sounded like. I was flicked past dark cages where men groaned and one laughed bitterly. One of the constables barked a name like Fengoose. A bald man in only underpants came from his den chewing, keys adangle from his nowaist. He handed me a big tatty card which I thought,

86

for a mad instant, was a menu. But I saw, as I was slammed into solitary under a low wattage bulb, that it was a list of capital offences. The odour of the cell was a subtle attar of universal indignity, distilled from the relief-to-despair hidrotic spectrum with the additives of incontinent bladders and bowels, concentrated into a single drop that disinfectants had lavishly diluted. I lay on the bunk's hairy blanket and tried to breathe. Thank God, I was soon able to make that final inch, claw in the chestful without which I would die, and feel relief wipe out everything. I read the list with a smile. It was a long one, ranging from (but I may have misremembered) antipedobaptism to the illegal importation of zumbooruks. Incest was there in the middle – I remember that very clearly – but the copulation of first cousins was not to be regarded as incest: that was a different sort of crime and would be taken care of in a subcapital category.

I had shed apprehension and even surprise. I was rather curious to see what was going to happen next. Nothing happened for a long time, in which I read through the offence card twice. I had a memory from a great way back of a young man in levis carrying a wreath, and this for some reason triggered me into considering that a death-list might be considered a menu after all. A wide range of dishes to satisfy a culturally imposed desire for death, a kind of taught hunger, and each dish a full, nay an ultimate, meal. Nonsense, and a sign that my mind was wandering off into sleep. I thrust sleep back and concentrated on the pain in my skull: I had to be alert, I did not wish to miss anything. One moment of inattention, and that inspector out there would be performing a ceremony of marriage between myself and Miss Ang.

I st rted awake to the celldoor's being unlocked by, if that was his name, Fengoose. As though I'd chosen my meal, he took the bill of fare (farewell rather, oh very clever) away, and handed me over to a new constable who was, I took it, to escort me to a qualified freedom. He was much bandaged, as if he had been engaged in riot-quelling. He gave me the conventional push with a plaster-of-paris glove, and then I was blinking in the brightness of the outer office.

– Elaterite.

– Elastic bitumen.

The inspector and the man stopped talking. The man was grim, presumably Dunkel, and was smoking a cigar rank as a twitchfire. I was most curious to see how he would react: *That's not the bloody boy, what's going on here?* But he thought he knew me all right. I wasn't going to protest my real identity: I wanted to get out of there and have some natural curiosity satisfied. He was in a white tuxedo with black floppy tie, about fifty, his piebald hair brushed forward to disguise recession. He wore clear-paned glasses as thick as bottle-bases. He said:

– I'll leave what has to be said to your mother. Come on.

– Very well. Sorry if I've been a nuisance.

– Nuisance. I'll say you're a nuisance.

His accent was neutral, a kind of plastic. What was all this about a mother? The inspector made a weary gesture at my few pathetic pocket-contents, inviting me to sweep them back in again. I nodded, no more. He even let me keep the Castitan dollars. Then Dunkel nodded at the inspector and went out, I following meekly. I made a final headturn to see the inspector shaking his head in a sort of professional gesture of sadness. But yet what the hell was I really supposed to have done wrong?

Dunkel's car was a white Harrap Inca. With a syntax of cigar-puff and head-jerk he motioned me into the back. The upholstery was black-and-white ponyskin. A nice vehicle: the circus must be doing well. He drove down Strèta Rijal with skill, dodging revellers in the middle of the road who sang songs slow enough to be holy. The street looked pretty with its coloured lights and pennants. Public statuary – scrollholding administrators, an early Victorian brooder in tophat who looked like a poet, the odd bearded blessing archbishop – was lit from below, and strings of fairy bulbs made plum-orchards out of the balsamodendra and fustics. Dunkel drove on south, saying nothing but sighing occasionally. I tried:

– I know it's possibly asking too much, but would you be good enough to tell me the time?

– Don't use that special high-and-mighty way of talking to *me*, he said. It's nearly time for the second performance, as you know all too damned well. But you needn't trouble to be in this either.

He turned the radio on, flicking from pop and jazz that might seem to abet my nuisance-frivolity and at last finding a very grim violin concerto. We passed from the world of commercial buildings – Pancarib Savebank, Yellowbird Assurance, Collembola Electrics, Springtide Sanitary Engineering, Rhabdos Housesoc and so on – to the suburbs with their buses and box-houses, the sea to the left flashing odd messages. Supposed to be in the show, was I? Then we came to a large open green. Here was the circus – big top, cages, electric generators, restaurant tent, cars and trailers, a spectators' carpark filling up. Lights, the distant blare of a wind band. The grim concerto gave it all three fierce major chords in greeting. I was, behind all my confusion, excited. It was as if I were being taken to the circus.

Dunkel kept to the road which was a perimeter to the green. The trailers of these travelling people were parked on the edge of the trampled acre or so. He slowed down and stopped by a large cream trailer, cutting the music off in the middle of an obscure orchestral struggle in which the violin had no place. Then he did a curt headflick at me, meaning *this is it as you very well know and get in there and wait to be given hell to*. My heart crashed and crashed in readiness for a mad or bizarre or totally lifechanging encounter as I got out of the car, walked up to the trailer door, opened it, and went in.

He, the young man lying on a bunk and reading a paperback, was far more shocked than I. After all, I had more or less expected him, and he did not expect me. I recognize the difficulty my reader is now going to experience in accepting what I wish to be accepted as a phenomenon of real life and not as a mere property of fiction. The trouble is that he, you, is, are only too willing to accept it in that latter capacity, and this inevitably impairs ability to accept it in the former. A camera trick, a split frame! The deployment of coincidence to the end of entertainment. Excellent, a romance for bedtime or to splurch in with a peach in a summer hammock, its tradition being as old as Plautus and hallowed by Shakespeare, who had in his troupe the identical twins Walt and Pip Gosling, and yet light, lowbrow. Do please carry on. And it came to pass that I entered into that chamber and lo on his couch reading a profane book lay one that was as my twin self, though brother whether twin or younger or elder had I none as was well attested. And we did look on one another, and he was the more astonied since that I had a prior presentiment that such an one as he did in truth exist. It hath been said that each one in this world/Hath in an exact copy his true self/Though truly which th' original is and which/ The copy who can truly say? My Lord,/I have read of this in Bellafonte's work,/In Galen, Wace, Vitellius and him/That writ the Book of Sorrows. But that is not it at all, no. This was real, modern, now. My spitten image walking the garden of this world without excuse of true eggsplitting. A certain tiredness or inattention on the part of nature had contrived this, and it was meaningless.

His clothes were almost but not quite mine: they were wellworn and subfusc like my own, but the material was better. His shirt like mine was open at the neck, but a gay foulard pampered his throat. In the days before still and motion photography I would have been puzzled at first in the encounter to see that he was both like and unlike: unless my portrait had been done, he should to my eye be a mirror image, the only counterfeit of myself I would know. But cameras had made me familiar with how I appeared to the world. And this must be true of him too. We looked at each other for a long time, hearing faint circus music to help make more clownish the competition in jawdropping that was our first dialectic. His dropped farther, of course, than mine. There was no doubt about it: the whole thing was astonishing: one looked for mere resemblance and was given the whole works of identity. Only the captious could catch at points like his set of the mouth or flare of the nostrils in surprise, different from mine, stupidlooking. Now we had to get beyond this simple wonder. There is more to life than people discovering they have identical appearances. As it happened, it was he who made the first remark, and he preluded it with a silly laugh that confirmed at the start what I felt I ought to feel about him.

Only I, I think, listened to the other's voice with care, to hear if the identity subsisted on the auditory plane. Most people think voices don't matter; they regard a voice as a ghost or a garment or a cosmetic; it is a very detachable attribute of the visible or tangible body. When a voice is deliberately deformed, as in the toothless wartime oratory of Churchill or in glottal pop singing, it is not merely noticed but praised, praised because deformation has made it noticeable. But in reconstructing the personality of, say, Jesus Christ, glossohagiographs never come into the job. See him, yes, but never hear him in Aramaic that, for all we know, may have had a lisp in it. Not important. To most sound is mere décor. To this boy, Llew, my voice was a standard machine of communication, a jaloppy for getting around in and the hell with the make. To me his voice, which for some minutes I ate with nauseated hunger, was the hateful blessed key to a return to the total variousness of life against which he and I were blaspheming – no, he only, only he. His voice had much of my timbre, but the phonemes, learnable things after all, mere cosmetics, were American Welsh. Pennsylvania? Llew for Llewelyn, so he said.

This was his travelling room. A door led to the travelling elementals of gas and water, and then there was the door to his mother's room, not in use just now. Roomy, the whole contrivance. For travelling it was hitched to a Cyrano convertible which it was Llewelyn's job to drive. Llewelyn what? His second name that, for first name name he was usually called Llew. His mother had abandoned the dull name stuff of the registrar and notary. She was Aderyn the Bird Queen. How would I like to have a mother who was a Bird Queen? His father? Dead of smoker's cancer, a nervous eighty-a-day man who had had to retire from the tightrope. Neither of us even allowed the thought to materialize that we might have the same parents. Whatever he was, he was no twin of mine. The coarseness of his mind was glued to the fibreglass walls in vacant smirks and lolling bosoms, the odd sideburned guitartorturer, a quartet of haired and slobbering golden-disc musical philosophers. He had his spinner, his 45-r.p.m. plates scattered on the rushmatted deck like innutritious cakes of liquorice, vacant sleeves with brutal faces – *Shove Up, The Scumsliders, Om and the Im, A Prayer to Black Hell, Stick and the Snatches.* The paperback he had been reading was called *Giant Cock*, no fairy tale but obviously a loose story of crude leering conquests dripping with gissum, a representation of women's agony as pleasure.

The hate I felt had nothing of morality in it; it was what now, but not then, as I did not know the word, I see as ontological loathing. His very existence in the world was an affront to my innermost most tightly bound fibres of self. That this should look like me! I am sure he was too stupid to reciprocate. Rather he was vaguely complimented, as though a fullsize clockwork model of himself were going to be put on the market and I was a traveller's sample. All he could at first see in me was an alibi. And then I would be a means of his exaltation in a narrow world where, even in the least skilful of roles, he had failed through slackness. Bounding in in a lionskin to frighten the clowns, banging his chest in triumph, roaring and then coughing, he had to bumble off in a panic when the real lions came in, even though they were in cages. That was his sole contribution to the conspectus of mad empty talents that made up a circus. And then he had sold his lionskin when he was without money and Aderyn the Bird Queen would forward him none on his next month's allowance. Money of his own coming in, he told me, when he married, but he would not marry, oh no. His mother wanted him to marry, but oh no. He wanted his freedom. A tatty kind of freedom.

He had been brought in, wearing simple tights, to help gather up the dinner plates at the end of the act of The Great Giro, who span them in multiple accumulation on the tips of flexible upright poles. He had regarded this rightly as demotion and, after accidentally or otherwise tripping up The Great Giro at the end of his leaping and jumping bows to the applause and smart about turn for leaping and running off, there had been hard words and sulks. Now he was a chauffeur, no more, for Aderyn the Bird Queen. But, God, man, with my assistance – there were these chains, manacles and locks, masses of them, rusting away in one of the property baskets. They had belonged to The Great Bondaggio, or some such artist, who had died of a heart attack in his unretired sixties. There was also a cabinet with an inner revolving wall. It had been used for clownish mock disappearances, one auguste looking for another through endlessly circling blackness, an apparatus not now much in use. But think, man. If I, Selim (I called myself Selim to him; I would not dirty my true name by sticking it in his mouth), would be cruelly manacled and chained and locked by members of the audience who would hold the keys till the performance was over, then I would enter the cabinet, the curtain would be drawn, the inner wall would turn and he, Llew the Free, would appear almost at once unbound, though with duplicate chains and manacles in his hands like strangled snakes. It would knock everybody cold. It would exalt him, Llew. He would insist on a high salary and give me a percentage. But out of the ring there must be only one of us. Disguise was a simple matter. I have dark glasses here, also a hat. I will cut a lock of my hair and glue it on to you as a moustache.

I nodded and nodded, submitting to his presence as I submitted to the throbbing head he started up again, thinking that I had better get back to New York, wiring Loewe first for an air ticket. *Have seen light stop.* I got a wink or glimmer of it, certainly, with my growing sense of the need to have that face that moved inanely in front of me, as though I myself were acting an idiot, changed to not-me. A large sum of money for facial surgery needed. I must fulfil all that my father's will ordained. Or could I do worse and cheaper? Have, say, Dr Gonzi shoot him? But Gonzi would need ritual, not the benison of a chance encounter. Would he fall for my necessarily suicidal appearance in the pre-arranged lonely dark? Or I could get Llew drunk and throw him in the path of a couple of triggerhappy policemen. No, let me get away, having seen what I came to see, let me at least remove myself from the presence of this obscene abomination. But I delayed leaving, nodding, fascinated.

The first words he spoke, by the way, were:

— So that's why my mam thought it was me, see, watching the fucking procession while I was in bed all the fucking time, man. Witness I had, too, but I didn't want to bring her into it. Told my mam she ought to have her fucking eyes seen to, that's what I fucking said, man. And it's true, too, one of the fuckers anyway. Made her cry, that did.

9

And yet I did not leave right away. You can say that I was so
determined to go that I was able to put off going. Or that
the urge to leave was so strong that it seemed imposed from
outside and hence had to be resisted. He had a cupboard full
of tattered sex magazines published in, of all places, Adelaide,
South Australia, the cover of one of which showed a girl
screwing a complaisant kangaroo with a dildo. In the same
cupboard he kept a lime-cordial bottle containing a cocktail
of his own concoction – mainly vodka and stolen altar wine,
or so he said. It tasted of a debauch in an operating theatre.
Theatre, of course, came into my staying. I found it hard,
being the exhibitionist I was, to reject his proposal.

So Llew and a plump young man with dark glasses, a
moustache, and a kind of fedora went round to the back area
of the big top. I, as Llew, wore his clothes. I was not sorry for
what he was prepared to make a permanent exchange, since
they were better than mine. He had a cushion stuffed in my
pants and he kept spreading his left mouthcorner in a nervous
twitch – tiring, though, so he soon gave it up. This area was
rich with activity but not too brightly lit, and the performers
were too agitated with nerves, relief or malice to pay us much
attention. But the real Llew insisted on pushing me towards
The Great Giro, who was piling cold plates together like a
trattoria waiter. The Great Giro snarled at me and said:

– *Vaffa nculo.*

– Up yours, wop, I replied. Shit on one of those plates,
man, and give yourself a hot dinner.

It was the veritable Llew. It was horrible. It was also not
horrible. This was a grossly exciting place, warm with
animals. The string of lovely ponies was being led out, reeking
with nerves, still trotting in time to the tear-off of brass from

95

the band in the arena beyond. Applause was like the sea. As in some pornographic novel of the Edwardian age, the moustachioed ringmaster was cursing a nearnaked pony mistress and even cracking his whip. The baby elephant gave out a sort of Bach trumpet shrill, and its placid grey mother let her comforting trunk play over its back like a stethoscope. Elephant dung was being shovelled up smoking hot and filling many buckets. Llew said:

– That's her there, man.

I knew her, of course. I had seen her in the procession. She was erect, still, composed, with her back to us, waiting to go on. A red robe reached her ankles, her blueish hair her waist. A couple of ringhands were ready to push on two cages, both with perched birds in them. Meanwhile an interlude of clowns was lolloping on. I said:

– I want to see the act.

– Brought up on the fucking thing, man. But seeing as you're me you can take me round there.

We went round. The ticket girl looked at me with loathing, so I grinned. Llew was delighted by the whole simple deception, a boy easily pleased. We stood at the rear of the arena, our backs against the canvas. The tent was filled with Castitans whose joy in the show was expressed or sacramentalized in their fierce eating. Bread and circuses: that cynical summary was taken as a synchronic convention here: It was not only a matter of candyfloss, peanuts, chocbars, ices and fruitdrinks in cartons. Fat mothers had brought thick sandwiches and thermoi (?), and I am certain I saw one family with cold cuts on plates. Llew said:

– See that auguste there – the one on the bicycle?

– Yes?

– A fucking clergyman, man, believe it or do the other thing. Father Costello. Does the mass on Sundays and holy days of fucking obligation. Hears confessions. I can see you don't believe it. Right, then, you know what you can do, man.

– But –

A worker priest. I supposed being a clown was work. His trick cycle folded under him. He did a sort of soundless sobbing with his big painted mouth and then, without apparent motivation, the other clowns were on to him, buffeting and kicking, leaving the noise to synchronized rimshots on sidedrum and farts of tuba. Well, that violence had been done for real to his master, He Who Gets Slapped, again without apparent motivation. Llew said:

– Glamour of the big top he called it. Becoming as a little child. Kingdom of fucking heaven.

– Does he come under a bishop somewhere?

– He comes under nobody and on top of nobody. A dry-ballocked bugger. What you'd call very devout, never has a woman nor anything else. On the payroll but what he does with his money fucked if I know. Chaplain they call him, man.

Onomastically that was all right. Father Costello tumbled off carrying his cycle in two halves, howling loudly but silently. The other clowns waved in joy to the munching and clapping audience. Then the lights dimmed and a green spot picked out Aderyn the Bird Queen coming statelily on to music. It was *In a Monastery Garden*, complete with E-flat clarinet doing piercing birdsong obbligato, very banal. I wondered if Father Costello, still in clown's makeup, would go off now to read his office in the smell of lion dung. Then I became fascinated with Aderyn, though her son merely groaned and muttered *Oh Christ*.

The lights went up, and there was the austere brooding face with its curious patina as of henna. Two portable aviaries had been wheeled in, and scurrying hands were now skirring into position two headhigh metal perches, each about six feet long with two doublecastered feet. They faced each other across the arena. There was a third stand, at right angles to both, similarly castered, but this seemed to be a kind of bird buffet: a long narrow tray held bits of unidentifiable meat which, I swear, smoked as if recently torn from living animals.

One cage was full of hawks, the whole spectrum, as far as I could tell, from merloun down – gerfalcon, falcon gentle, falcon of the rock, falcon peregrine, bastard, sacre, lanner, merlin, hobby, goshawk, tiercel, sparrowhawk, kestrel. They perched unblinded, blinking, waiting, and, when their cagedoor was opened, they showed no impatience to be out. The other cage contained not hunters but talkers – the mynahs, starlings and parakeets of that morning's procession. When their door opened their tongues moved in no excitement. And now the sickly music stopped in the middle of a bar and there was an almost inaudible warbling from the throat of Aderyn. At once, easily, in senior order of rank – emperor's merloun first, knave's kestrel last – the hawks left their cage and soared to the height of the tent, there to flutter on the mount for five seconds. The mouths of the audience, chewing suspended, were up and open, as if to catch the droppings. Then, this time in junior order, so that the kestrel was first, they stooped gracefully on their meat, each taking one morsel, and ended on their long perch one at a time, an interval of a second between each landing. The band played fourteen chords, one for each bird, in three-four, crotchet at sixty M.M., the synchronization as though oiled. The final chord was an imperial fortissimo for the merloun. They sat still, unmoved by the performance, bored. A feather or two twitched like a nerve when the applause started. The applause was long and very loud. Gaunt and stony, Aderyn made a slight head movement of acknowledgement.

Now it was the turn of the talkers. They flew from their cage on a different signal – a sort of crooning sob, very quiet – and at once ranged themselves, in no particular pattern, on the opposed perch. Aderyn snapped thumb and finger. Without rush, the birds announced their names, one at a time. I forget the names; let us say they were: Iris, Angus, Charles, Pamela, John, Penelope, Brigid, Anthony, Muriel, Mary, Norman, Saul, Philip, Ivy. Then, all together, they began to make an astonishing noise which, in a moment, I was able to interpret as the noise of flying aircraft. For the hawks rose in group formation, the merloun as group-captain, split into two squadrons, then into four flights, and began to swoop down as if to pick the eyes of the children, who were nearly all in the front seats. There was delighted fear and then greater applause than before. The hawks took another reward of a meat morsel, then settled again, indifferent, on their long perch. The talkers, so far, had been fed nothing. To Llew I said, clapping my hands raw:

– She's astonishing.

– She's a fucking old bitch.

– But she's wonderful.

– Ought to be, man. Birds birds birds all her fucking life. Me, I've no gift, see.

I saw, I had seen already.

– Try living with her is what I fucking say.

The talking birds now gave a more extended demonstration of their skill. In turn they perched on the right wrist of their mistress, each to form an item in a sort of ornianthology of familiar quotations. A starling, in Hamlet black appropriately, started off:

– *To be or not to be that is that is the kwaaaark question.*

– That one, Llew said, will get its little fucking botbot smacked later on.

– *Here and now*, a mynah went over and over again without rebuke. A parakeet contradicted with:

– *Tomorrow and tomorrow and tomorrow.*

Another mynah, uninformed about Auden's later self-excisions, cried, to applause:

– *We must love one another or die.*

– *A robin redbreast in a cage*
Puts all heaven in a hahahahahahahahaha rage.

– She'll be in a fucking temper when it's all over, man. I'm going off to get bleeding pissed.

– How does it end?

– One lot keeps on changing places with the other lot to music. Like a dance, man. And then the mynahs and the rest sing *Abide with me* and the others, bloody bad tempers they have too as you'd know if you got near them, fly around in like a cross formation.

– You're kidding.

– Make them do anything. You've no fucking idea.

A falsetto mynah cried:

– *Oh mummy dear what is that stuff that looks like strawberry jam?* A gruff starling responded:

– *Hush hush my child it's only dad run over by a tram.*

– Not very enlightening, I said.

– You've got to remember they're only birds, man.

We got outside while a parakeet was doing something it was charitable to think of as coming from *Finnegans Wake*. I said:

– Not on form perhaps tonight?

– They're not getting the response, man. Need a more educated audience than this fucking lot. Why, in the States once – Norman, Oklahoma, I think it was – she had one man up from the audience answering questions the birds fucking asked him, and if he got the answer wrong they'd all fly on to him like to peck his fucking jellies out.

– Incredible.

We stood outside the tent under the moon looking at each other. I didn't like him any better, even though some of his mother's glamour had now rubbed on to him. The disguise just made him look like a parody of myself in disguise. But he had to have some virtue; nobody could really be as horrible as that. I said:

– You admire her really, don't you?

– Who? Her? She comes to kiss me goodnight, me at my age, man, and she stinks of all those birds. Look, you're my pal now. We're buddies, aren't we? We have to be buddies because we're the same. That stands to reason, man.

– No, it does not. We look alike, that's all. It's a *lusus naturae*. A freak.

– Are you calling me a fucking freak?

– No, but both together we are. I'm going now. I've things to do tomorrow, and then I've got to get away.

– That's right, go off and leave me when you could be my pal. We could go into town now and get drunk, like buddies. I don't give a shit what she says or does. We can go into town in the car. I've got money. The one I was in bed with screwing this morning when the old bitch thought it was me watching the procession and it was really you, a laugh that is but nobody to share it with except you and that's one reason why you've got to be my buddy, I took the odd buckeroo or three out of her bag when she went into the toilet to put the thing in, you know, the gissum stopper, forget its proper fucking name, man.

From the big top came applause and better music than *In a Monastery Garden* – the finale of Respighi's *Gli Uccelli*, I think – so I took it Aderyn's act was over.

– You're a bit of a rat, aren't you?

– Who? Me? A rat? If I'm a rat you're a fucking rat too. That stands to reason if we're like the same.

– We're not the same.

– All right, we argue that out over a fucking drink. The old bitch will be coming out now looking for her darling sonny bunny and stopping him getting his what they call lawful pleasure. So we'll get in the car and off now, man, yes?

He jingled his keys. Attached to their ring was a miniature plastic representation of a male sexual apparatus. I said, starting to walk towards the main road:

– I've got to go to bed. Tomorrow's going to be a busy day.

There were three doubledecker buses waiting, evidently to accommodate the circus audience. From the festal bray of the band, which suggested the heraldic posing of animals and insincere teeth and cordial armwaves of mahouts and whipmen, it was clear that that audience would soon be flooding out. I walked rapidly. Llew walked rapidly with me, panting:

– What do you mean, busy? You and me have got to sort out this worldshaking act, man. Llew the Free. No Chain Can Fucking Bind Him.

– I'm getting a boat to –

I stopped just in time. But the mere act of beginning the statement clarified my decision for me. There were plenty of boats in the harbour. There must be somebody who would start me on the searoad back to America and a little money and Hidalgo or Manzanillo and the writing of my play. First, though, tomorrow morning, Sib Legeru. That jelyf scholar had told me where he was. Llew said:

– A boat to where, man? I'll come with you, we'll go to fucking gether, we'll do this act independent like of this fucking shambles of elephant shit and birds. One of them nipped me, do you know that, only the other day. See, I'll

show you the mark. Eyases, they are, see, always more fucking badtempered than the caught ones.

– Go home, I said. Get back to your mother. Keep out of
trouble. If it hadn't been for you the police wouldn't have
grilled me as they did.

– What do you mean by that? If it hadn't been for you the
old bitch wouldn't have been on to me about going into town
without permission to get pissed or fucked. All you are is an
imitation of me, man, so keep off that pigshit about things
being my fault.

We were not yet quite at the bus-stop. I halted and looked
at him. I said:

– Get this straight. You're an affront and an insult. You're
a filthy joke played on me, me, me by stupid nature. You're a
nothing that happens to have my face. If you crumbled to
dust now and got blown away by the wind, nothing would be
lost. Do you get that, you wretched filthytongued parody of
a human being? I'm leaving tomorrow, and one of my
reasons is to get as far away as I can from you. I'll convince
myself, if I can, that this has all been a nasty dream.

Llew trembled with rage and selfpity. His moustache, cut
from his own backhair and fixed with the gloy his mother
used for her presscutting book, was a little askew. I had to get
away before it was dislodged completely. He said, dithering:

– Right right, bastard, it all depends on who was born first,
doesn't it, that's what it fucking depends on, right right? So
you say when you were born and then we'll soon know who's
imitating fucking who, right, man?

I experienced a small internal dithering of my own at this.
I feared irrationally that he might pull his passpoort out and
triumphantly wave a proof, backed by the might of the
State, that our identity was total. *Miles Faber, also known as
Something Llewelyn. Date of birth: December 24th, 19—* I said:

– Saying's no good. We need documentary proof. And I
can't give you that and I'm not going to take you where it is.
Anyway, this is a lot of nonsense. I'm getting on that bus
now.

The audience was streaming over the green. Cars were
starting up. I moved quickly and Llew, wheezing like an old

man, moved quickly with me. He cried, as I climbed on:

– I'll find out where you are, you bastard. I'll bring my fucking proof. I'll not have any swine telling me I'm only a fucking imitation.

– You won't. Find me, that is. I'm going tomorrow.

– Swine, swine, bastard, why won't you be my pal? Why can't we be buddies, like I want?

I had my windowseat. Passengers were crowding on now, pleased with their evening. There was high praise of the Bird Queen. Her son stood at the stop, abandoned, his hands stuck deep in my jacket pockets. I checked that I had transferred all my belongings. The whistle was cold. Had I whistled this wraith into being? A wraith was a simulacrum that portended death, was it not? Nonsense. As he stood there, seeming to whine to himself, his moustache became completely detached and began to drift in the seawind circularly towards the ground. Some passengers began to laugh. Or was I *his* wraith? Nonsense. The bus moved. He still stood there, whining something. Then he took his right hand out of my pocket and waved it shyly. He still wanted us to be pals, buddies, man. We sped towards the town and lost him. I willed my loss of him to be total, even in retrospect. He never existed. Then, as we passed the Magus Emporium, an uneasy recollection of one of Professor Keteki's lectures came up like the taste of an old meal. Shelley. Was it *Prometheus Unbound*? Llew the Fucking Free, nonsense. The lines were:

> The Magus Zoroaster, my dead child,
> Met his own image walking in the garden.
> That apparition, sole of men, he saw.
> For know there are two worlds of life and death –

What came after? And why did he meet his own image? I couldn't remember. Not that it mattered much. I was desperately tired and my head ached. Moreover, the wound had started bleeding again: there was a trickle by my left ear. The woman next to me saw it and tut-tutted, as though the blood were an obscenity. Like that non-existent Llew. But it was with Llew's handkerchief – gissum-stiff – that I wiped the blood away.

10

And the following morning, when I awoke – late, as I could tell from the quality of the light – after a totally unhaunted sleep as heavy as syrup, his clothes waited for me on the chair like Llew himself. The trousers were (*was*, Llew would probably say: *trousers* was a dual word in his dialect, like *ballocks* as a parson or term of abuse) of the creaseless kind that one does not lay down folded: I had seated them on the chair on their bottom with the legs dangling to the floor. The chairback wore the jacket like a film actress of the 'thirties. What a fool I had been to bring anything of his into a life that determined to vapourize his memory, unperson him. And I could not afford to buy other clothes, not yet: everything pointed to my capitulation to the lawyers. The shirt was my own, and I had handkerchiefs. That defiled one, defiling, of Llew's I had left on the bus deck. I didn't have to admit Llew's more intimate contact.

Tiredly I gave myself a dry shave sitting on the bed with my eyes closed, closed eyes being better than a shaving mirror: you learn at once the razor skill of the blind. I peered out on to the corridor, found it empty, so ran naked into the washroom for a shower. Dressed and welshcombed, I pocketed my luggage and went downstairs. The lobby was empty except for the proprietress, who was exhaling the smoke of Surabaya cloves behind her counter. I said:

– I'll be checking out.

I put all my paper money down in a single fistful drawn from my trouser pocket. Yumyum Carlotta was among it and, before I extricated her and stowed her in my breast pocket, the proprietress saw her and said:

– Strange. That is one of the words I mentioned to you yesterday. You will need no tricks for remembering it.

I did not understand. She gave me my passport. She said:

– You will be going to the Dwumu for the miracle?

– Miracle?

– *Mijregulu* in their language. In mine, *mu'jizat*. It is their superstition to expect a miracle at this season. One small boy this morning was shouting round the streets that the *mijregulu* had happened and happened to him only. He had been to the dawn *mijsa* with his mother and taken the bread which, in their superstitious way – but perhaps you are yourself of that faith. The boy swore that in his mouth he had felt a small hairless animal, very small he said, crawling around and heard it through his head bones cry in a little baby's voice. And then he had swallowed it. This is, to me, cannibal work. But perhaps you are yourself of that faith.

– Well, in a vestigial sort of –

– As this was not a *mijregulu puwblijgu* or public miracle it was ignored. For a *mijregulu puwblijgu* they have to have blood flowing from impossible sources. Well, but an hour ago, while you were still I suppose sleeping, the blood began to flow. Not from the statue of their Senta Euphorbia, as most expected, but from the *pipit* or little *zab* of an infant Isa, Jesus would be your name I think, held in his mother's arms. This is distasteful. The blood is, they say, still trickling. It is being collected in teacups. They have called no chemical analyst to take a sample. It is all distasteful, I fear.

– From his –?

– Exactly. I hope you enjoyed your stay here.

To get to where I had been told to go, which was Indovinella Street, I had to pass through Fortescue Square. There stood the great mosquy Dwumu under the hot Catholic repressive blue of the forenoon. It had a skin of gold which peeled in places and thus looked like the foil on a mousegnawed wrapped biscuit, especially as the stone beneath was the colour of rich baking. The square was crammed, chiefly with blackclad women singing a hymn. The police band accompanied, augmented by the mufti ensemble of yesterday's procession. The hymn went something like:

Up and down the wide stone steps of many treads people
went and came, into and out of the ornate arched doorway,
carrying tiny vessels lightly as they mounted and entered –
eggcups, pill-bottles, one hopeful woman with a jug – and
bearing them with foot-watching care as they left. One small
boy had a Coco-Coho bottle with a drop or two of the
precious blood in it, which he kept squinting at through the
bottlemouth like a rare captured insect.

Sengwi ridimturi,
Suwcu d'sentitet,
Leve mij –

There was a sudden unholy effect of discordant parody as the
police band started on a new tune while the mufti one kept on
with the old. The new tune was secular and martial,† like a
national anthem, which was what it turned out to be. For
sailing into the square, preceded, flanked and followed by a
goggled uniformed motorcycle escort, came an open car
with the state flag on its bonnet. The President himself, come
to see the *mijregulu* and, giving it a presidential blessing, draw
into himself and his office some of its numinosity. Fat, beam-
ing, cleverlooking, capped, braided, medalled, in spotless
navaltype white, he stood up to accept the subdued homage
of his people, who did not immediately (and he seemed, in
his cleverness, to nod a kind of appreciation of this) forget
God because Caesar had arrived. He got out of the car with
his aides and bowed his head humbly at the ringed blessing
of the baroque cleric who came down the Dwumu steps to
greet him. I pushed through the crowd towards Indovinella

Street. To hell with order, ecclesiastical and civil. To hell with miracles. Miracles? But miracles subverted order, did they not? Nonsense, no: they confirmed it: they kept the people on their knees. But you're for the irrational, which is what miracles are. No no no, the irrational confirms the rational as night proclaims day. Let me get between the day and night into the world of, oh, eclipses.

On the periphery of the crowd I saw Dr Gonzi. He nodded at me as pleasantly as that grim leprous mask would allow. He wore a dirty black cloak and a matching sombrero. I would have moved on, willing to forget his drunken madness of the night before, but he clawed my sleeve and said:

– You have nothing more to fear. I've found another instrument. I did little in the philosophy of politics though I have always accepted the notion of the *contract*.

– Look, I have to get to –

– Yes, I too must be in a hurry. A matter of unphilosophical practicalities.

I could smell whisky on his breath and it was not a stale smell. He was then perhaps habitually a drunkard. He said:

– Hobbes is good on the contract, read Hobbes. I shall play the same game with the appropriate authorities. They may in concert be able to work out the answer, though I doubt it. Singly not one of them has your peculiar gift. It may still be your responsibility to encompass my end. Do you take my meaning? I sent the silly thing to headquarters, but they will have filed it among the other missives of madmen. I didn't, of course, sign it. Not signing it, as you will recognize, is the whole point of the enterprise.

– You'll forgive me now if I –

– Look after yourself, boy. The pleasures of the world are not less acute for being phenomenal. I look forward to different ones. Meeting the bishop, for instance.

– The bish—?

But he went off through the crowd, his torso forward, claws forward as to engage the ground, a failed lion. The crowd courteously let him through. He apparently carried no vessel, but he was going to see the *mijregulu*. I was going to see something very different.

I found Indovinella Street after inquiries of sceptics who preferred their shops to the bloody *zab* of the infant Isa. It was a cobbled street, steepish, with one or two old-fashioned taverns and dwellinghouses with walled gardens. These houses were thin but, in compensation, high – four or five storeys. In one of them were the disregarded works I had come so far, and with so much effort and, yes, pain, to see. The jelyf man had not been able to give me the name or number of the house. There had, he thought, been a wooden sign outside it, but it had been long wrenched away, by idle boys or a poor family in need of fuel. He had paid one visit, many years before, but had not liked what he had seen. The key to the house had hung on a nail in a tobacconist's shop and was probably still hanging, oxidizing. He had recommended that I not pay the place a visit: I would surely see not refined art but sickening madness.

I climbed up and down Indovinella Street but found no tobacconist. I went into a tavern called the Yo Ho Me Lads to ask for information, and, while I stood waiting at the deserted counter, I heard a voice call *Hey* out of the darkness. I turned and probed the empty gloom for its source.

– Hey.

I radared on to a dim shape and went up to it: the drunken host perhaps. But it was one of those two faggots, Aspinwall, bald, fleshy, ill-coordinated and trembling with drink. As I grew used to the dark, I saw the label of a bottle on his table clear and give off its name: Azzopardi's White Cane Rum. Aspinwall, as he spoke, breathed out a powerful sweetness:

– Didn't take him long, did it, the bastard?

– Who? Gone off, has he? Your boyfriend in the holy shirt?

– Interior. Into the interior, as the bastard called it. A great poet there, he says. Pilgrimage to great poet. Have drink.

– Not on an empty stomach. What great poet?

– Have breakfast, then. Lunch, brunch. Any goddam thing. Hey, you in there, he called to a curtain. More corned beef sandwiches and a raw onion and plenty of mustard.

– I don't suppose they have Dijon here, I said, sitting down.

– That's not the name. Some goddam British poet with one of these pantiwaist names, like Vere de Vere or Marjorie Banks or Sir Marmaduke Upyourass.

– He's missed the miracle, then. He could have dipped his precious Godshirt into the precious blood.

– That goddam Godshirt as you call it near did for us on that run. Bad medicine, religion on board.

– I though it was me who was supposed to be the Jonah.

– There you are – *Jonah*. Religious. And there was that other one I never thought to hear mentioned again. Specially in bitch of bad weather like that. Though not your fault altogether, I guess. Bad medicine that man.

He drank down a large tot, good medicine, an act of exorcism.

– Oh, I said, remembering. You mean Meister Eckhart?

– Meister Shyster. Jack Eckhart was the biggest two-timing bastard that ever picked teeth in comfort watching orphans starve. He drove me out, defiled dry land, the fink and rat. Stole two big money ideas, both mine, pocketed kill money for them, the doubledealing rattler.

– What's kill money?

– Money a firm pays for an idea it wants dead. Like everlasting match, would have killed Kruger, Kruger bought it buried it. What you call that animal that goes backward and forward, head at each end?

– Amphisbaena. A kind of lizard. It doesn't exist.

– Got a name, eh? And doesn't exist. This thing *did* exist. Refrigerator with two doors. I made it.

He waited for me to show some emotion. I showed none but said:

– I thought you did dress-designing.

He moved his hands in impatience, saying:

– Dresses only machines, for Christ sakes. You dumb like the rest, but that shyster Eckhart not dumb, oh no. You not know why two doors? Because things get left at the back of a regular icebox. You put beer in, right? Take beer out, empty space, put more beer in. Keep taking from the front. You never done that?

– I've never had a refrigerator.

– You kids, you kids, all same these days. Pot and heroin, too much hair.

To my surprise, a man in shirtsleeves brought sandwiches with a raw onion and a daub of mustard made with vinegar. He was a small wellformed octoroon, perhaps quadroon, with a lot of hair that caused him to look reproachfully at Aspinwall. I said to him:

– I'm looking for this museum. Sib Legeru. Near here. A key in a tobacconist's shop.

He shook his hair in regret and went off still shaking it. The quest was proving difficult. I took a sandwich while Aspinwall said:

– So with doors front and rear that doesn't happen, right? No frozen crap left at the back. A good idea or else the bastards wouldn't have paid to kill it. Conservative bastards. Know what the other idea was?

– No.

– Go on. Guess. *Guess.*

– Look, surely you mean that the doors would be at the *sides.* At the back you have to have the works – that grill thing and the leads and so on.

– You kids. Got no icebox but know all about it. Go on, *guess.*

– A nondrip oilcan. A frame to take the weight of a very heavy copulator.

– He could always get underneath.

– It might be his partner that was the very heavy one.

– I don't go much for that, not now. You come with me and you won't be in any danger. Funny you should say that about a nondrip can, though.

– What do you mean, come with you? When are you leaving?

– Tomorrow at sunrise, I guess. One or two things being done to the craft. Get a real overhaul on one of the keys. That storm was a bitch. No, about that drip.

– You're sailing for Florida? You're not waiting for God-shirt, then?

– Screw that phoney with his phoney poetry. Confucius or some other guy said that the last drop always goes into a guy's pants. Rots the material, as you'll know. This is where the dress-designing comes in. Detachable sponge insert, shaped to crotch of pants, catches drips. Anything preserve ervative like that they just don't want to know about. Dedic dedic dedicated to to what do you call it.

– Destruction? Consumption? Obsolescence?

– I guess that's what it is.

– I can sleep on board tonight?

– I guess that's what it is.

He had finished the bottle of rum with no assistance from me, who had merely eaten an onion and sandwiches. I dipped the last corner of crust in the mustard, swallowed it, then coughed. My body shook: I was never well.

– What it is, I guess.

He was dazedly, I could see, wondering what to drink next. It was not yet noon and a long day's solitary boozing lay ahead of him. Well, anyway, my getting away from here, soon too, seemed taken care of. I didn't like Aspinwall, but he was a good sailor. He seemed more tolerable without the holyshirted poetaster. Anyway, any port in a storm. That, I realized, was not really an apt proverb. Various riddles buzzed in my head, but I could ignore them now. I was moderately content. It was cool and dark here. In a short while I would continue my search for Sib Legeru. The golden mean oblong of the doorway let in golden sun that, like a swimming bath, one was not urgently concerned with replunging into for the next minute or so. Then that doorway let in something else: a very familiar shape, severely corseted. Miss Emmett fisted the bar with vigour and called:

– Manuel! Manuel!

She looked into the gloom but saw nobody she knew, nothing she wanted. The only thing she wanted, as I saw when Manuel, the haired man, appeared, was a packet of ten Honeydew cigarettes. She hadn't changed. Scissors dangled at her waist. She would go back, wherever she lived or stayed, to overboiling eggs and crunching sugarlumps. I, slow as ever, began to realize what she was doing here on this remote island of Castita.

II

The embarrassment of my sister and myself, meeting each other for the first time with no particular desire to meet each other, was eased by the news of a failed attempt on the life of the President.

Her name was Catherine, a very ordinary name suggesting stone saints. Miss Emmett called her Kitty and sometimes, horrible, Kitty Kee. I said:

– Well.

The television newsreader, a bald young man with a blow-up of shocked Castitan faces behind him, gabbled:

– . . . while His Excellency was paying homage. The bullet lodged in the statue itself, shattering the plaster and disclosing the simple mechanism by which the hoax was being perpetrated. An inquiry is being initiated into what His Grace the Archbishop has described as the most flagrant act of blasphemy ever to desecrate the sacred edifice. His Excellency the President expressed himself to be more shocked by this evidence of a sinister and cynical plot to throw doubt on a fundamental feature of the religious life of a devout Christian community than by the mercifully and, he might say, miraculously frustrated attempt on the life of the democratically elected . . .

Miss Emmett switched the set off. She said:

– We don't want to hear all that. Not now. Not at a moment like this.

– There must be some very complicated emotions going around, I said.

– Yes, said Catherine, complicated.

Kitty Kee, indeed. She was a fat girl of seventeen, perhaps fed by Miss Emmett only on hardboiled eggs and sugar. Constipated, perhaps; her complexion was blotchy. I searched her face for signs of myself. The eyes, certainly. Not the nose, far too bulbous. Miss Emmett said:

– And to think we shouldn't be here. We would have been on our way to France –

– Kingston, London, Paris, Nice, Catherine said with the pride of the young traveller. I'm to go to a school in Nice.

– Don't interrupt, Kitty Kee. We got this cable from the lawyers telling us to get off earlier than we intended. It's as though they knew there was going to be trouble here.

– Why the delay then? I asked.

– Oh, we had such a terrible storm, real tropical, and the aeroplanes weren't leaving. And now we're all packed and ready to go just when you get here. Providence, or somebody.

– Well, I said. I looked round the sittingroom of their rented house, which gave out no sign of anybody's character. Marmetone floor with a couple of dirty goatskin rugs. One easy chair, on which Miss Emmett sat, the colour of over-cooked saffron cake. Two Windsor chairs, I on one, Catherine on the other. Her skirt was short in the fashion of the time, showing her fat mottled legs almost up to the crotch. This is a young girl, I told myself. What of physical do you feel for her? I felt nothing except indifference tinged with the salt of revulsion. I was glad of that, but also I had expected it.

– Tomorrow? I asked.

– By the midday flight, Catherine said. We spent the night in Kingston. I've never been in Kingston.

– Not a nice town, Miss Emmett said. The natives sing rude songs and bang on old oildrums.

– You've been around, I said to her. It's been a long time since we –

– And you never wrote. You never wrote one little letter to say what you were doing and how you were getting on.

– I've never been much of a one for writing. For that matter, I didn't know where to write to.

– It's all been very mysterious, Catherine said. The fierce light smote her unkindly from two windows – the street one, directly looking on to the Yo Ho Me Lads, and the one facing, which showed a dead orange tree. Comedones, a small boil-scar on her fat chin, a dusting of scurf on the shoulders of a dress which was unwisely mauve and had a greasemark or two at bib level. My sister. Miss Emmett, despite her age, looked far more wholesome. Perhaps there had always been massive doses of protein in her diet, ingested in what the doctor had told her were pills for the faints or flushes. Her lined face seemed set in a pose of firm content, as if she had won the battle of life. She was not unsmart in her seablue cotton dress patterned with flights of guillemots, her cord belt from which shining scissors dangled. I had always taken the scissors for granted, a badge of office which became by sheer chance an instrument for cutting cupboard paper or snipping parcels open. Why did she wear them?

– Wear them?

– A scissors is *this*, not *them*, you ignorant boy.

Why did that disturb me? Ah yes: a trousers, a ballocks. Had she always used that dual singular? A death of plurality for some reason this morning.

– A scissors is always hard to find even in a wellrun house. It gets lost. You forget what drawer it's in. And a good scissors will always frighten somebody who comes to the door. It is not, as you should know in your newfound cleverness, what they call an offensive weapon. In America they tried to say it was because it was threatened to be used as such. But any woman is entitled to her scissors.

– In America?

– In Seattle, Catherine said. Miss Emmett didn't like the look of a man who kept coming every day trying to sell something.

– It was hair-straighteners, Kitty Kee. I asked him if we looked like the sort of people who needed hair-straighteners.

– She said she'd stick the scissors in his face if he kept on pestering. So he complained to the police.

– You were in America when I was in America? What were you doing in Seattle?

– My father, *our* father I should say –

– Let's not talk about your father, Miss Emmett said in a kind of liturgical tone I divined she must have used many times before. The dead are dead, and there's nothing to be gained by resurrecting them. Like poor old Rufa the Fifth you dug up in the garden when we were in Rotorua.

– You certainly *have* been around. Where's Rotorua?

– N.Z., said Catherine. Rather a nice place, full of trees and sort of heaving all the time. And lots of geyzers pronounced *gyzers*.

– Above the southern snows. Why so much travel? Didn't you want to settle down anywhere?

– My, our – It's all right, Miss Emmett, I've gotten over it.

– Got, not gotten. Try to speak *English* English, Kitty.

– I mean, why here of all places?

– You're here of all places, Catherine said. The reason you give is a pretty odd sort of reason. We came here because I was ill – it's all right, Miss Emmett, I've gotten *got* over it – and the climate's supposed to be good and there's a man here who – I suppose I ought to say there *was* a man here. He was no longer in practice but he took me as a favour. Now he's given it up and just writes poetry. There's a book of his – see –

There was one of these folding extensible Indian bookstands by the window, unextended, one carved zoomorph sideflap fallen in – in dejection one might fancifully say – at the fewness of the books. She seemed to gesture at something thin and white.

– That must be where the Godboy went, the scribbler in the holy shirt.

– You do say mad things.

– You knew all about me, I said. And I knew nothing of you.

– But, of course, Miss Emmett –

– Miss Emmett must have known about you when she was with me. Didn't you know, Miss Emmett?

– Nothing, Miss Emmett said. It was a great surprise when your father turned up with her in Christchurch.

– N.Z.?

– That's right. I was with my niece and her husband. He works, worked I should say, with the Butler Collection, whatever that was. I saw a picture of this Butler – a sneering looking old man with a beard.

– And yet, I said with a bitterness that I recognized was

totally insincere, a posture expected, he never wanted to see me at all after my mother, our mother –

– It was all a very sad business, Miss Emmett said, and I think we ought not to talk about it. I think I'll go and make a cup of tea. I want a cigarette, and I feel *unclean* if I smoke without a cup of tea. It's like eating a boiled egg without bread and butter.

She went out, very upright. At once Catherine reactivated the television set, as if shy with me without a chaperone. She said:

– I can talk about it now. Miss Emmett doesn't believe in psychotherapy. A bit too modern for her, I guess, suppose. Our father – oh, that sounds so mocking but what else can you call him? – he may have turned against you but he was all over me. Very loving, then one day he became too loving. He'd been away on business a long time and he said he'd missed his little girl. I was frightened. When she found out Miss Emmett went for him with the scissors.

– Oh no.

I saw the bald newsreader distractedly. It was the same bulletin as before:

– . . . than by the merciful and, he might say, miraculously frustrated attempt on the life of the democratically elected leader of a free . . .

– I got over being frightened, and then I started doing puzzles all the time. Crossword puzzles, quite hard ones, and always getting them right. And then they knew I was ill. This doctor in San Francisco said the best man was – That seems to have shaken you, you look really shaken. I'm sorry, I forget that it shakes people. It doesn't shake me any more, you see.

The newsreader was saying:

– suspect more than one person is involved. The police are engaged on the rounding up of suspects. Roadblocks have been set up outside the capital. During the period of the emergency no exit permits will be issued. Grencijta International Airport is being closed to outgoing traffic until further notice . . .

– But they can't do that, Catherine cried. Oh, how stupid they all are with their stupid politics.

– Stupid? Who? How?

I hadn't been listening to the news. I was, as she had said, shaken. How then am I able to set down verbatim the words spoken on the news? The same words, or something like them, were spoken later on the news. I listened attentively to that news. There is an explanation for everything.

– Miss Emmett! Do you hear what they've done, Miss Emmett?

– Look, I said urgently. Were you given any information by anybody about the precise nature of the relationship between our father and mother?

– Oh, they were happy. That's why he became so deranged when she –

– What's all the shouting about?

Miss Emmett had come in, chewing on a sugarlump: *votf orver fyouting avouk?*

– They won't let anybody leave. It's because of this stupid shooting at the stupid President.

– Ah, Miss Emmett said. So they knew, you see, when they sent us that cable. They knew there'd be trouble. The Americans are not stupid. They have their spy organizations. The C.U.A. and F.B.I. and U.S.I.S.

– But we're packed and ready. Oh, how *silly* they all are.

– Fetch in the tray, Kitty Kee. In a way, of course, it's Providence. Dear dear Miles has been sent to us by Providence and it's only right we should have some time together. Fetch the tea in, girl. I made a few sandwiches.

She looked at me lovingly. Her reaction on first seeing me had been surprise, and this had led straight on to a resumption of her governess approach. In the kitchen alone, slicing hardboiled eggs for sandwiches, chewing sugar, she had been hit by a realization that I, Miles, her dear boy, was back with her again after all those long years.

– You're so thin, poppet. You need feeding up. Who do you stay with now during your vacations? Poor boy, with no home of his own. Let me turn that horrid telly off.

– My generation doesn't believe in home any more. In the vacations I just get around, seeing America, picking up the odd job. Or used to. No more vacations after this.

– Poor poor lad. Well, we shall have a little time together here. They have lovely meringues at the supermarket on Craig Road.

– No. Sorry. Tomorrow morning I start working my passage back to Florida.

– Tomorrow morning you what?

That was Catherine, just come in with the tray. I saw what I'd expected: the gleam of set albumen between thickish slices of bread and butter; sugary cakes. Catherine said:

– If we can't leave, neither can you. If they won't let planes out they won't let boats out either.

– Oh.

– Weren't listening, were you?

She had become bossy already, really sisterly. I looked at her in distaste, a fat girl who had already poured herself a cup of tea and was slurping it in with unnecessary noise. She put a whole small chocolate pastry in her mouth at once and showed me her teeth, which were yellowish and glinted with fillings, grinding it into sludge. A chocolate crumb fell on to her big sloppy bosom and she rubbed it into her dress with her fingers. Then she scratched her bosom since her fingers were already there.

– That's awkward, very awkward, I said.

– You must stay, my dear boy, Miss Emmett said, until this business is over. The Americans are clever people. They gave us very good warning, but then this storm came, you know. And this airline they have here –

– *Arija Castita*, Catherine said through the blown crumbs of a salmoncoloured macaroon, showing off her bit of knowledge.

– They only have two trips a week to Kingston.

– Flights, they're called.

– I know that, girl. Pour me a cup of tea. I'm dying for a cigarette.

– Cleverer at spying than at Caribbean meteorology, I

said. The Americans, that is. I think, really, I'd better go back to that hotel. If you could possibly lend me –

– What's the matter? Catherine said. Do I smell or something?

It was not really a fair question. Miss Emmett said:

– There's a nice little bed up in the attic. You'll be comfy there. And I can feed you up and we can talk. Oh dear, she added. There's hardly anything to eat in the house. Emptied the larder, you see, because we're going. I used the last of the eggs just now. Have an egg sandwich, dear boy.

– No, thanks, I've already eaten.

– Don't seem able to give you anything, do we? Catherine said, before working into a cream horn.

– Well, then, if you're sure it's no trouble.

– I'll go round to the supermarket, smoking Miss Emmett said, when I've finished this.

– No, no, I'll go, I said too eagerly. I didn't want to be alone with Catherine. I didn't want her to go on, in her cured cold way, about my father. I wanted to chew all that over alone.

– Perhaps I could find out about this museum at the same time. It's on this street somewhere.

– No museums here, Miss Emmett said, nor art galleries nor anything of that sort. Just residential except for those two drinking places. Horribly noisy late at night that one opposite. But Manuel is nice. They order these cigarettes for me specially.

– I like to see them coming out drunk, Catherine said. It's quite a little entertainment. Stupid drunks shouting stupid things at each other.

– Funny about that, I said. This is the street I was told. The man seemed in no doubt about it.

– Which man, my dear boy?

– This man I met in the – the jelyf man. Sorry, of course that wouldn't mean anything to you. This man I –

– Oh, yes, Catherine said. We're not all that cut off from civilization, you know. We have Jellif here. Jellif's nice. Specially with canned peaches and whipped cream on top. If you're going shopping get some Jellif.

– And some of those lovely meringues, dear. They come in packets of six. Get two packets, we must build you up. There's some money under that little china owl by the door.

– Meat. Meat is what I'm going to get. Meat.

They both looked at me as if meat were something obscene or explosive. Miss Emmett recovered and said:

– A little kiss, dear boy, before you go out.

That went right back to my childhood. She'd forgotten my self-conscious teens when I wouldn't kiss anybody. I indulged the old darling and put my lips to her grey well-washed hair. She laughed and said:

– And one for Kitty Kee. Do you realize you haven't kissed your little sister yet?

I swallowed the bolus of distaste that at once arose. Catherine looked at me with no warmth. I said:

– Do you particularly want to be –?

– Of course not.

– Right, then.

I took the dollars from under the china owl and, going out, heard Miss Emmett complain:

– A very unaffectionate generation you all are, I'd say.

Wittig Street, Buckley Avenue. I kept repeating to myself, as I looked for Sib Legeru: *Had to be his own flesh, his own flesh.* A kind of cannibalism. I'd said I was going to buy meat, and the phrase put me off meat. And I had a sort of image of a sort of postman dressed in white going down some long avenue or other, shuffling his letters and parrotcocking his crest to read the addresses. At length he would deliver to me an official envelope and I would open it trembling, knowing all the time what was inside, what was inside being an official notification of my insanity in a single brief sentence, very large typeface, upper case only. Insanity as the crown of the other inheritances. She, Catherine, had had a brief spasm of it only with, so to speak, a historical cause. Now she was sane; did I want to be sane like that? If I were insane, being sane would probably be like having to be like Llew. I needed Sib Legeru. Desperately. I asked people I passed if they knew where Sib Legeru's works were, but they did not know, nor did they wish to know. They looked at me as if they knew I was mad. Why was I not full, as they were, of the bogus miracle and the hunt for the murderers of the true miracle? They were all alert, in holiday mood. *Had to be his own flesh*. The double horror had sparked in them a desire to live and be cheerful, since life was so full of blessed surprises.

Own flesh. I shuddered at the conformist order of Craig Road, where a supermarket was the sole provisioner of an endless double row of overcleanlooking semidetacheds, a long flat treeless ribbon where the sun was dismally naked. Also earth in the form of grit, unheld down by vegetation, swirled in the wind and got into my eyes. Full of tears, they were ready to accept the mechanical irritant as a priming of wretched abandon, the release of all my tensions. But there were too many gay shoppers around. Meat. I would not buy meat here. I turned into Pocock Street and then left on to Ross Crescent. Nin Street, Ventura Street, Redvers Lane. Nobody knew of Sib Legeru. I came to a little huddle of shops – stationer's, knitting materials, butcher's. In the butcher's window there was a frozen sirloin, Argentinian doubtless, about six pounds weight. I would buy that. *His own flesh*. I had a yearning for a big burnt roast.

– Sib Legeru?

– Who? What?

The butcher shook his head sadly as he weighed the joint. He was thin, like so many butchers, and probably ulcerated: a packet of Stums lay among the knives and cleavers. And then, an accession of memory suddenly acidly stabbing him:

– Key in a tobacconist's? That what you said? Five dollars thirty.

– Yes. Yes yes.

– Lee's. Try Lee's. Shadwell Park Road. Off Indovinella Street. Know where that is?

– Yes. Yes yes yes.

I walked out with the joint wrapped in three newspapers. At last I was getting somewhere. I found Indovinella Street, again with some difficulty. First to deposit this glacial beef and let it bleed out its water. And then. I carried it with speed and gingerly like a timebomb whose hour was soon due. And then the musical retching hooter of a car sounded behind me. I turned: it was police patrolmen. They too, sensitized by today's urgent duty, seemed to think in terms of an explosive ticker. I stopped and so did the patrol-car. It was a handsome scarlet vehicle, very well polished. The driver, in mandatory dark glasses, did not get out, but that sergeant of the previous night did, followed by a skeletal dark glassed constable. Oh God, I thought. The holsters of both gleamed fatly in the sun. The sergeant, who seemed to have grown more elephantine folds under his eyes, said:

– So. Still not learning your lesson yet, eh?

– What do you mean? What lesson? Is there some law against walking the streets?

– Yes, said the sergeant. For immoral purposes as the whole world knows. But we'll keep off insolence and stupid little jokes, won't we? Your mother was very upset and rang up to apologize. And she asked us special to make sure you're where you should be, which is where she can keep an eye on you.

Llew, then, as was to be expected, had told her nothing about what he thought stupidly was his image, though he was really parodic mine. Llew had not given up. I would be seeing Llew again if I wasn't careful. I said:

– Look. I'm not the one you think. I'm just like him, that's all. I've got my passport here. Just wait a –

I transferred the insule of iced meat to my right arm so I could dip my left hand into my inner pocket. Both the sergeant and the constable jumped. Ineptly, the constable put his hand to his holster. The sergeant said:

– Never mind about passports. Hand that thing over.

– It's a joint of beef, I said. I bought it for my sister and my er former governess. They live along here.

– Governess, eh? the constable said, making a governess sound like a wardress.

The sergeant grabbed the parcel and unfolded the three copies of the *Timpu d'Grencijta*. He could not deny that he was looking at meat. He prodded it with a long forefinger but a wall of wine-coloured ice pressed back. He took a gloomy look at one of the front pages but there was nothing subversive there.

– There's too much insolence going on. What's your sister doing here if your mother's up there?

– It's not my mother.

– We could run you in on suspicion, especially after what happened in the Dwumu. But we're on to bigger game than what you are. Rod, he said to the constable, get on the carphone to Mr Whoeveritis, the manager at the circus –

– Dunkel, I said stupidly.

– Yes yes, let on not to know but you know all right. Tell Mr Dunkel, Rod, that we don't want this Lou boy running round the streets. We've enough on our plates without him. Go on boy, do what you've got to do and then get back where you belong.

I didn't want Dunkel knocking on the door, though Miss Emmett would certainly have the scissors ready. I didn't want the police to have too exact a knowledge of where I was. I walked towards the Yo Ho Me Lads.

– There, is she – your sister and the other one?

– I want to buy a bottle of wine.

– What does a lad of your age want with wine? Going to get drunk again and make dirty gestures?

– I'm going to cook *bœuf à la bourguignonne*.

– Foreign muck.

The constable, I noticed, had not done what he'd been ordered. Probably there was no carphone, only the usual radio link with headquarters. Headquarters would not be happy, this day of the failed assassins, with a request to put through a message to a circus. In any case, surely a circus, being a travelling entity, could not have a telephone? But perhaps Mr Dunkel had his office in a rented permanent fixture. Still, it was clear that the sergeant was only trying to scare me. Nobody could possibly really believe, despite the superficial evidence, that I was that foulspeaking leerer. I had got the sergeant worried, and worry was, with men like him, the father of bluff.

There was only one customer still in the Yo Ho Me Lads –

Aspinwall, snoring through the dark. Manuel came at length and sold me a bottle of something local that looked black with iron. It cost only twenty-five cents: one could not go far wrong at that price.

12

I could have cried with frustration, but there was no priming grit. The roast spat away in the oven; Catherine chewed her nails at an old movie on television; Miss Emmett sat upright in her chair (some distance from where I was sitting) smiling gently to herself while her inner private projectionist ran some clumsily edited film about her own past, probably with me in it (Miles Faber played by an unknown prodigy). I smoked one Sinjantin after another, drinking it in to the very diaphragm, grudgingly thanking God for one small mercy. The Lee who ran the tobacconist's shop was an undefined Oriental and stocked some of the brands of the East (Dji Sam Soe, for instance), very dear blame import duty sir. He handed over the key, which he said he had not been asked for for years. He recognized it, bunched up as it was with others, because of the three knife nicks on the handle. He believed the place was on Indovinella Street, but which number he did not know. He had never been there; he had a shop to look after.

I had knocked all along Indovinella Street, my heart knocking almost to knock me over, but people thought I was selling something or was mad. In nearly every instance it was a man who came to the door chewing crossly, sometimes with a napkin in his fist. A good class residential district, with napkins. No place for Sib Legeru.

– My dear boy, Miss Emmett said after I had exclaimed on my frustration for the third time, a young boy with his life in front of him shouldn't want to go round looking at old museums. My brother-in-law in Christchurch was a museum kind of man, and it did him no good. You forgot to bring the meringues, you see, thinking of your old museums.

– And the Jellif, Catherine poutsneered.

– Bugger the Jellif.

– Miles, that's not a very nice thing to say to your sister, nor in front of me either. I don't know where you pick up such language.

And then we had the television news, with a plentifully haired young man reading it against the same blowup of shocked Castitan faces. Four youths known for previous attempts at acts of disaffection were being interrogated and the police were hot on the trail of the ringleader. A private twoseater Troll had been prevented from taking off at Grencijta International Airport and its pilot and passenger arrested for contravention of the emergency regulation, about which they alleged total ignorance. The guards posted at the dockgates and all along the yacht marina had been augmented following certain warnings whose nature could not at present be divulged. The meteorological report that followed the news promised fine weather. This was a sort of compensation for everybody having to stay in Castita whether they liked it or not. Then the M.G.M. lion snarled welcome to an old movie.

– Quiet now for this, Catherine said.

– Is this all you do in the evenings? I mean, don't you read or drink or play the guitar or have boyfriends or anything?

– Poor Kitty Kee never got much education.

– What's education got to do with drinking or boyfriends?

– Reading, I meant. She's much too young for those other things. She had to go about with her father, you see, and she couldn't have regular schooling.

– Quiet, can't you see I'm watching?

The movie began with longbreasted women with metal hair in bathing costumes of the thirties, drinking Chichis on the beach at Waikiki, Diamond Head in the background.

– Honolulu, Catherine said.

– Yes, Kitty Kee dear. And you flew straight to Auckland from there and then to Christchurch and that's where we met. Such a coincidence.

– What is, was? I asked.

– Oh, do be quiet.

Soon the film settled to New York smartness and wit, with

the eggfaced women in paddedshouldered suits, wisecracking at sleek moustached men in doublebreasteds who had cocktail cabinets in huge society lawyers' offices with a vista of Manhattan. The accompanying music was quick on the ball to underline comic discomfiture with waw-waw trumpets, and if anybody went comically to bed the strings did two dissonant bars of *Rockabye Baby*. You could, I supposed, call it a sort of social history lesson for unschooled Kitty Kee. There were references to Tammany Hall and Roosevelt's New Deal and the Forgotten Men. I said:

— Look, dinner's nearly ready. Are you going to watch that horrible thing through to the end?

— It's not horrible, it's sophisticated. I'll eat my dinner here on my knee.

— Aaaargh.

This thin house had four storeys but no diningroom. I set the formica kitchen table, not forgetting the wine, and got the beef out of the bottled-gas oven. I dumped the sizzling carnage with its smoking blood and fat on to a willow pattern dish, sharpened the blunt carver with its matching steel and called that food was on the table. Miss Emmett came in. She insisted on cutting some slices for Catherine and making a couple of doorstep sandwiches. She said:

— A bit tough, isn't it? Poor Kitty Kee had to have some teeth out, poor girl. She has what's called a bridge. She can only really eat soft things really.

She delivered the telesnack and came back to sit to her plate and complain about toughness on her own behalf.

— Thank your stars you have your own teeth, dear boy, if you have, that is. I had the last of mine out in Christchurch. Not a good fit these dentures. Sometimes the top ones drop. There's a kind of glue you can get at the chemist's called Dentisiment, but I keep on swallowing it all the time. *Very* tough, isn't it?

It wasn't all that tough. I tore into it with ferocity, spooning bottled mustard-and-horseradish on at intervals. I was trying to eat everybody and thus get them out of the way: my father, Llew, Kitty Kee, myself.

– I don't think I'll have any more, dear, nicely as you've cooked it. I'll just make myself a cup of tea, I think.

– This wine's not tough, you know.

– Strong, isn't it? Nice though, very nice. It'll make me sleep perhaps. I haven't been sleeping too well lately.

– Don't you *ever* have proper meals?

– Well, you know how it is, dear boy. It's always an encouragement just to have little snacks, you know, when there's nowhere proper to do your eating. I didn't like the idea of turning one of the bedrooms into a diningroom. A bedroom's a bedroom, all said and done.

– Why didn't you get a bigger house?

– Well, this one's sort of in the family in a way. My cousin bought it for letting.

I opened my mouth at her.

– It's very illmannered to show what you're eating. It turns my stomach, dear.

– Cousin?

– He was in the Colonial Service, not very high up but he got a knighthood when he retired. He thought rents might help his pension a little. Jim Pismire. His liver got very bad.

– Sir James –

– That's right. How ever did you know?

– But, good God, it was he who – What's in this house? What's upstairs?

– Only bedrooms.

– But, damn it, this is the place, this *must* be the –

– Finish your dinner, dear.

I was on my feet, the still-hot oven burning my calves. I had the key in my hand.

– That's not the key to this house, Miss Emmett said. It's a Yale lock. Really, Miles, I wonder sometimes if you're all there. But I shouldn't say that, knowing your poor father. What I mean to say is that this is no museum, is it? I have some little ornaments, as you know, but nothing for anybody to come and see. Now sit down and finish your dinner.

I groaned, sitting down. I poured more wine for us both. I had not dared previously entertain the fear that Sib Legeru's work had mouldered back to its basic physical elements through neglect and then gone to the incinerators or the sea like the rest of the detritus of the world. The wine steadied my throat as I said:

– When you took this house over was there anything in it?

– Nothing, dear, except spiders, these big tropical ones. One, I remember, carried eggs on her back. There's an outhouse in the garden, of course, and that's where they seem to have put the old rubbish that was here before.

The wine had flushed her. She began to waver a bar or so of *You will be my summer queen.*

– What sort of old rubbish?

– It's locked up, but you can just about see through the window, all cobwebby. Rubbish, the usual sort of thing. It's not nice to have dirty things even in the garden, the garden properly speaking being part of what you pay rent for, but the bushes have grown all round the shed so you can't really see it. American red-currant and laurel. And lots of weeds. Out of sight out of mind. Goodness, this wine *is* strong. And now where do you think you're going?

– To have a look at this shed.

She laughed vinously.

– You will have your own way, always did, would. It's dark now. You won't see much. And you can't get in, can you?

I held up the key fiercely.

– This'll fit. It's got to fit. Is there a torch or lamp or candle anywhere?

– Well, have it your own way. There are candles in that cupboard there, but don't start setting anything on fire.

I opened the cupboard and found a bag of raisins, two empty sauce bottles, a packet of icing sugar, a tube of *dragées* and a paper packet of candles. I said:

– Don't wait up for me. This may take some time.

– Silly boy.

The way to the garden was, I had seen, a narrow passage by the side of the house, separated from the next house and its mirror-image passage by a rickety creosoted fence. There was only the front door to get out by, and, passing the livingroom open door, I saw Catherine with her dental bridge in her hand, licking with delicacy an adherence of chewed bread. The television movie said: *He's the worm in the big apple*, and a clarinet arabesque followed by a soft drumthud illustrated this. Catherine heard me and said:

– You leaving us?
– I'll be back.
– We go to bed early here.

I fixed the catch on the front door Yale lock so that I would not shut myself out, then I felt my way towards the shed, trembling. The garden had been totally neglected. My feet crunched on broken glass and squelched on a small dead animal body as I fought between bushes and branches. There was not much moon. I took out my local matches and struck several before I could light one of the candles. The foliage kept the wind off. I could hardly get the key into the lock of the warped door, I was dithering so much. But it fitted. This shed, then, all its paint eaten away by the salt wind, housed the immortal remains of Sib Legeru. It was for me a moment so solemn that I wanted to retch. The door groaned an arabesque, opening, and there I was, inside.

How, to use a fictional cliché, can I describe what I saw? I lighted all my candles and planted them in their own wax on every utilitarian surface I could find – the narrow window-sill, a mineral-water crate, a couple of dried-out paintcans I upturned. Then I looked around voluptuously, though somewhat disturbed by a stink of decay whose provenance I could not place. There were canvases leaning against the walls, gnawed and dusty. There were a couple of teachests full of large filthy manila envelopes, springback manuscript folders, loose and unprotected sheets of scrawled foolscap. I stretched, like one waking to a long summer day of arranged pleasures, and then began to look at the canvases. I raged with anger and cried aloud *Bastards* as I saw the defilement of soil and mildew, but then I ignored the accidents and became absorbed in the essences. Tomorrow I would bring daylight to the works and a closely examining eye; tonight was for a generalized awe and a gloat over multiplicity.

The pictures, which were all oils, were not notable for good draughtsmanship – a prerequisite for surrealism, and surrealistic was what a crude taxonomy would term them. But instead of the juxtaposition of disparates or *cauchemar* attributions (a trombone on fire; a water closet in a lunar desert), there was a consistent attempt at the representation of metamorphoses unbound by the restrictions of the sciences. Thus, a wrapped loaf reproduced itself like a living thing by the process of extending itself in space, trying to hold its offspring of miniature wrapped loaves with wax paper wings, while their solidity deliquesced into blood that glistened in the candlelight as though newly shed. It was freedom, it was imagination untrammelled even by unconscious laws of dissociation. What I took to be a companion picture showed blood turning itself into a subtle attenuation of golden filaments that became white pudding. Then the raw canvas showed through before a naked thigh strove to become a glass jar in a coruscation of noisy firework colour that settled into the delicate pink, green and white of the segment of a human arm. These were large paintings, about three feet by two. Smaller ones showed similar acts of daring that soothed my soul by their disdain of what the world calls meaning. An open first folio (recognizable from a crude reproduction of the Droeshout portrait) walked a sea that was all buttons, sleeves and tabbysilk lining, but the whole composition was shining black framed in strings of crimson. I saw clearly how that old surrealism really truckled to the world of cause and effect: a trombone proclaimed, by being burnt, that it could not be. Here was the ultimate liberation of the spirit.

I dipped into a large typewritten work of fiction, its folios damp and mottled and smelling of old apples. Soon I did more than dip: I read in complete absorption, standing. The story was of a man due to give a radio talk. Sitting in the studio, waiting for the red light, he feels a need to go to the toilet. In the toilet a great fly emerges from the flushing water and addresses him in a language he recognizes as Canaanite. It glows in a kind of numinous gold and leads him through the ceiling to a room in which there is a robed congregation of Shiites. Mirza Mohammed Ali strives to make himself heard over loudspeakered music from *The Pirates of Penzance* which modules to the mindless clatter of an adding machine. The man sees that the fly has changed to a middleaged American named George, who leads him to an arena where a popcorn-eating audience roots for two youths fighting a huge engulfing python. Leaves fall from the air, the snake becomes a dead tree trunk, the boys shrink into sleeping infants and then expand into blonde Viking women over whom a man in green silently laments: he is their brother and he has killed them before learning their identity. The sky and the forest that has replaced the arena erupt into laughter and a procession of Roman revellers with cups, wineskins and garlands dances through to baroque music. George has turned into a bronze statue. The man follows the revellers through a doorway. He finds himself in a booklined study, alone with a bearded scholar who speaks Latin at him at length, at the same time slicing shive after shive of pink talking meat. Each piece of meat is transformed into a place or a person – an Iberian landscape full of redcoats and artillery smoke, a gamecourt, King Arthur III, the Sultan of China's daughter, the outer wall of a feudal castle with a blind lady balancing on it, the Crimean coast, Cabourg in Normandy, Hödur with the mistletoe sword.

This was all in the first chapter. I would have read on to the end of the candles (the book must have been about as long as *War and Peace*) if a spider had not startled me by unwinding from the roofbeam on to the back of my neck. It was a reminder: now was only for dipping, sampling. I sought shorter things, poems. Like this:

> London Figaro infra pound
> Threejoint dackdiddy Solomon
> Delay delay thou Gabriel hound
> Mucklewrath IHS brilliging on
> Ants alley jackalent Meckerbound
> Skysent stone threw sinkiss black
> And caged Cardinal Mabinogion
> Though M is NN copied slack
> A freehand onestroke perfect round
> Took that bony face aback!

Almost a nursery rhyme, kid's stuff. But I read freer things while the candles gently obeyed the laws of geometric and chemical dissolution but moved towards their own wax abstractions.

I was reading the fourth canto of an epic poem rather in the style of Blake's prophetic books, full of gauzy giants quick to change to and from moods and coffeepots. It was, I thought, very exciting. The candles were nearly wicks in wet wax. I should, to be sensible, have taken the work, or some other work, up to the attic to read in bed and comfort. But this, I reminded myself, was the night of the preliminary survey, and I could hardly transfer the entire *œuvre* up from here. Really it was physical inertia complementing intellectual excitement and making me tolerate the stench which the fumes of Sinjantin did little to mitigate, as well as the pain my thin haunches took from the empty mineral-water crate I sat on. I paid little attention to the noise of drunken men leaving the tavern, though I wondered for a second if Aspinwall, frustrated and paralytic, was the lump I heard hit the pavement before the banging of a door. This noise was more real, the denunciation by Laman of Rosh:

> Forecap, neigh, sprue, drench of scallions
> In asaph and kentigern, your abaces fall, your log
> Stalk in a clone of bartlets –

I seemed actually to hear the whimper of Rosh and the breathy timbre of Laman's voice. Amazing. The sound rose from the page as from some miracle of electronic contrivance, but it continued when the canto came to an end, with Laman cantering off on a mortise into an empyrean that was a clause and opoponax. I raised my head. The noise was coming from the house.

Noise in the house. Trouble. Burglars. Police. Miss Emmett fighting back but her weapon wrenched away and clattering, while she whimpered, to the floor. I fell stiffly out of the shed, angry at this intrusion of the boring violent world. I saw light shining raw from the uncurtained back windows of three storeys. The noise came from above ground level. I stumbled over glass and brambles towards the front of the house, noting an empty street, no police-car. The door would not yield: the catch had been released. The sittingroom window was a sash one and the lower light was down to the limit. But the frame was old and swollen, and the two elements of the metal fastening had grown apart, never more to engage properly. I pressed my palms on the sash and forced it up an inch, then I got my claws under and sent the whole light whistling up. I climbed into the dark sittingroom, which smelt of sweat and vanilla. The television set, after its long heat, was crackling in its contracting wooden casing. Light from out there. I went on to the corridor and saw Miss Emmett asleep, still fully dressed, on her chair at the kitchen table. That would be the wine. She, then, was safe. It was Catherine who was in trouble. I could hear her from upstairs, being in trouble, and the voice of the male she was in trouble with. If it was really trouble. That specialist in the interior of the island might, for all I knew, have prescribed nightly fights with men, followed by yieldings. It seemed improbable, though.

I ran up to the first landing – bathroom, empty bedroom, Miss Emmett's presumably, their doors open, landing light blazing. I ran up again and came to the source of the noise. The door was closed but not locked. I opened, and new emotions enriched, then replaced, those already proceeding in Catherine's room. The room, if I may be permitted to describe it briefly, expressed Catherine well enough. Its décor followed trends at third or fourth hand, since she was out of touch with the direct influences that animated her volatile agegroup. On one wall was Che Guevara and a poster advertising a corrida in Algeciras, September 1968. On another was W. C. Fields, a dead, child-hating, drink-loving, bulb-nosed American comedian of the thirties, who became briefly a youth fad perhaps because of his cussedness (he would never learn the lines of his scripts, for instance) and the weary corniness of his wisecracks. There was also

Humphrey Bogart, an ugly but, I always had to concede, curiously attractive tough-part film actor with a slight lisp. There was a big pop-art poster whose crude yellows and blues were an obscenity and whose design was as flaccid as a two-year-old's penis – concentric circles, lower-case Gothic letters exhibited as asemiological artefacts in a kind of illiterate glee. There was the inevitable recordplayer with discs and sleeves scattered – *Punishings from the Rods*, *The Dea Dea Tease*, *Nekro and the Philiacs* and so on. Dirty underlinen was everywhere on the floor. There was a powerful reek of shoes and stockings, also of ancient snacks which had been overzested with tomato ketchup. The chest of drawers had something like a dozen and a half empty soft-drink bottles arranged perversely neatly on its surface; most of the drawers were halfopen, with bunches of creased apparel thrusting out and the two cups of a brassière dangling down (the fastener probably caught in the wool of a nearly fully endrawered sweater) like miniature windsocks. The rear or garden window was, in fact, open an inch or two at the bottom, admitting sufficient breeze to justify the fancy.

The bed was a single divan, with the heavy shaped embroidered cover (of bright and fussy design – red leaves, green pagodas, orange parrots), that made it a piece of day furniture, thrust to the floor unfolded. On the bed was Catherine in a not over-clean nightdress that had been concertinaed into a sort of cummerbund by, I saw now, that male who was her assailant rather than her lover. Her big dancing bubs were exposed, and the male was kissing the one after the other in a brisk rhythm that made him look as if he were doing a head ballet to, say, the slow movement of Haydn's Clock Symphony. She let him do this because her hands were wholly occupied in fighting off the lower attempt at engagement. She was weak, though, for some reason. Perhaps the fight had been going on longer than I thought. The male was fully dressed, but his fly was open, as if he were in a urinal and not a boudoir. One hand attempted to guide the penetration, which had not been achieved, the other – cynically, in view of the Haydn ballet – tried to keep Catherine subdued with odd fisted belts on the face or body. It was, of course, Llew.

Catherine was the first to see me, and the sight of the exact duplicate of her ravisher, standing there at the door in a brief posture of undoubted satisfaction, gave her energy for new screams. Satisfaction was perhaps inevitable, because she was being punished for daring to be my unpleasant and unsavoury sister, though this was not the mode of punishment I would myself have considered apt for insolence of that sort. When I saw that it was Llew, my first attempts to explain to myself how he had managed to get here and do what he was doing were held back, like the beginning of a queue, by a portly commissionaire who gave precedence to an awed acceptance of the appropriateness of Llew as minister of either pain or pleasure to my sister. They were, and The Severed Head or some other group could make a song out of that for them, complete with sneering intonation and tortured vowels, in a way meant for each other. The queue was still not allowed to start moving in, for the first awe was followed by another, of a very high mystical or metaphysical order. My father had been undoubtedly mad. He had been granted a mad vision. He had envisioned his daughter set upon sexually by someone of my appearance, and he had mistaken that person for myself. Madness, like great art, marched through the scrub of space and time and lopped it all down as it went with a mental *parang*. Like, I nearly thought, Sib Legeru, but I stopped the thought in time, space.

It was up to one of these two to say something to me, but it was up to Llew first to feel ashamed and stow his weapon and creep away hangdog from the bed, tail indeed between his legs. Things never happen as propriety or even probability dictates. Llew recognized me without surprise, with a nod of satisfaction rather at my being here and providing the true explanation (which was true) of how he himself was able to be here, and at the timely entrance of one who really had to want to be a buddy, despite previous disavowals, and give a buddy's help. He said:

– Fucking strong bitch she is, man. You hold her down so I can get him in. And then like I do the fucking same for you, man. Ah, but no, you wouldn't, because you're a –

– This, I said, is my sister.

Catherine heaved him off with strength I should have thought impossible in so flabby a sweeteater. She had to be unencumbered in order to stagger over to Che Guevara's wall and look from one to the other of us openmouthed, in the same rhythm and roughly the same tempo as Llew had used for the tenderer aspect of his assault. Her nightdress had, because of gravity, readjusted itself from the waist down, but she had, in her consternation, neglected to resist gravity above the waist, and her big nipples looked at some point between Llew and myself. What sort of a cruelly tasteless and heavyhanded joke was this? The same man appearing twice in her room synchronically: it was too much. She tried to say that she thought she thought something.

– You thought he was me?

– Thought thought –

– I'm sorry, I said. I suppose I could have mentioned that this thing here exists, existed. And in the same town at the same time. But I had other things on my mind.

– What do you mean? Llew asked, buttoning up. I don't like the sound of that *thing*, man. If you're trying your fucking insults again –

He was drunk but, as he had demonstrated, not incapable. He sat on the edge of the bed with his risor muscles out of control, however, and even that involuntary smirk was not easily excusable.

– Thing, I repeated. Mindless animal. Coming up here to rape my sister.

– She told me to come up, man. I was just coming out of that fucking place opposite, pissed but as good as fucking gold, and there she is leaning out of the window saying to come in and go to bed. So I come in and go to fucking bed but she lets on not to fucking like it, man. There's a word for her and you know what it is, man.

– What were you doing round here anyway?

– Thought thought –

– Yes, all right, you thought it was me out there with a skinful. You're out of this. This is between him and me.

– Well, Llew said, it's your fault, isn't it, for being like an imitation? I'd come into town to go to the fucking movies, this dirty sex film called *The Day After*, and then I go into this hotel where the woman running it thinks I'm you, which is a laugh, just to have a drink, see, before it starts, man, and then there's this fag with dirty words on his shirt comes in and he thinks I'm you too. A laugh it was, I'll say it was.

    – Chandeleur?

    – All like printed dirt all over his shirt. Anyway, he says –

Possibly Chandeleur had changed to something secular, but it would be typical of Llew to see even the words of holy mystics as dirty.

    – He says let's go off together in this other fucker's boat, see, because he can't look at him any more without wanting to spew. Well, it was a laugh and I said yes yes, thinking all the time about me not knowing you were a fag, man, because you didn't look like one last night.

    – What do you mean, me a fag?

    – Thought, thought it was –

    – She'll get it fucking out in a minute. Well, he was going on about my lovely body, meaning yours, and he knew I, meaning you that is, liked him though you let on not to and all that crap. But then we go off and have some drinks and all the time I'm speaking like you, man, big words and all and a fucking plum in the meathole. And then he starts crying and says he loves this other one really and he loves me too and let's all three of us go off and leave this crappy kip, but somebody in one of these like beercaffs says nobody can leave, man, because of this law they bring in on account of somebody trying to blow this fucker's brains out.

    – I want to be, Catherine said clearly, sick.

    – You go and do that, I said. Catherine tottered towards her door, hoisting her straps at last, though sick, to hide her bosom from the view of nobody.

    – So we go to this place here where his pal said he'd be and there he is, fucking stoned, man. And the one waiting on says to me, Wine all right? but we weren't drinking wine, we were on this white rum, and then it was a laugh again, so I got it you must be round here somewhere. But this one here

I just took to be on the old job, no connection with you, and certainly not your sister, no, no, not a fucking idea of that. Anyway, that like explains everything, right right, so I'll go. We ought to get thinking sometime of when we can get off and do this great act together.

He rose from the bed, smiling voluntarily. Really, I supposed, he had by his standards nothing to reproach himself with. A girl in a nightdress at a window, telling him to come in. I said:

– And the other two?

– Those? Fags, man, but then you're a fag, right? No offence though with you, man. You've got to be different seeing we're alike.

– I'm not a fag.

– Have it such ways as you want. They ended up all over each other as though each one was a fucking big chunk of ice cream to the other, and they won't go.

– Won't go?

– Won't go. They're there. The one that runs it says he's going to get the fuzzpigs to them.

Catherine was on the floor below, evidently trying to be sick though without success. She called, in the voice of one spectacularly dying:

– Emmy, Emmy, Miss Emmett.

I had forgotten that Miss Emmett, if awoken and told, with Catherine assuming a great act of shivering and hysteria, would be less reasonable than I about this business. I said:

– If the police are coming round here you'd better get home or whatever you call it. I don't want any more trouble.

– That's all right. My mam knows there's been a bit of the old mistaken identity. I didn't tell her the whole lot with fucking stupid Dunkel bringing you instead of me in the car, because this is too like precious, if you see what I mean, I mean me and you being really the same, not just like *like*, I mean, and going to do this big miracle fucking thing together. A pity this one knows, big fat ugly bitch as she is –

– My sister. Look, you'd better get –

I could hear Catherine down at ground level now,

thwarted of being sick and so groaning louder than before.

— That's all right. You can get her to keep quiet about it, threaten her with a sock on the puss and that, and anyway we'll be right away from here soon, two buddies making the big zooma zooma. What I was saying was the pigs call Dunkel's office in this hotel he's in and say to keep me out of town because there's enough trouble without me adding to it and they reckon they see me on Indiarubber Street with a high explosive in the old famble wamble, and all the time I was laying on the bed in the old —

— Indovinella Street. That's this street. It was beef, not high explosive. Look, you'd better get out of —

There was a kind of ill-coordinated quadruped on the stairs.

— Just going. This street? That explains it, then. And they said I was supposed to say it was beef and it looked like beef but they weren't taking any fucking chances, man. Anyway, my mam said I could go to the movies, in the car too, and it's not all that late. I parked it by the hotel where I met the dirtshirt one, so I'll get round to it. Sorry about tonight, but you can see how it was. I mean, her being your sister and you my pal. But I didn't get him in, so that's all right, man.

Him, indeed: a dwarf accomplice. It was not all right, far from it. Miss Emmett came in first, her blear eyes fast clearing, and Catherine was behind her. Miss Emmett registered expected shock, though prepared. The likeness was so good that it was me she went for first, but Catherine put her right. What I didn't like was the snipping noise of those scissors. She had them in her hand though anchored to her waist, and their opening and shutting jaws went *ee ah ee ah*. Llew said:

— Who's this one? Look, lady, I meant no fucking harm, see. Asked me in she did. So what did I do? You'd have done the same if you were me.

— This, I said, in cool introduction, is Miss Emmett. You could call her my sister's lady companion. She's devoted to my sister, as you can tell.

Then I stood back to watch. I had done all I reasonably could for Llew, asking him to leave before the advent of avenging Miss Emmett, not having even hinted to him that I was not disposed to show a brother's blind rage and hence he was lucky. And so on. Catherine stood back too, though with a vindictive sneer that looked wholly sexual and was as good as a participation in what now proceeded. Miss Emmett was vocally incoherent, but her scissors were, was, incisively articulate.

– Filf. Toag. Gretchit gillon.

Bogart seemed interested in her technique, but Che's violent mouth and eyes were above nonpolitical acts of violence. Llew cried:

– Keep her off. You're supposed to be my pal. Tell the fucking bitch to stop it. You're my buddy, aren't you?

– No.

He backed to the rear or garden window, thrusting both hands out to the weapon that jawed *ee ah ee ah*. Miss Emmett snipped at a finger and drew blood. Llew howled and took in the tiny flow with the wide scared eyes of a haemophiliac. Miss Emmett clackclacked at his crotch, thus bringing into the same area of action the three dual forms: *scissors, trousers, ballocks*. Llew yelled:

– She's fucking mad, man.

He mounted the narrow windowledge with his bottom, his intention being to kick out at her with both feet. She did a swift tailor's job on his left trouser leg. He howled for the injury to the material, madly identifying it with the flesh underneath. Miss Emmett now turned the weapon into a genuine singular. The jaws snapped to silence, she grasped the pointed unified duo by the waist or pivot, the surprised eyes of the thumb and finger holes peering from her tight fist. She stabbed and stabbed at anything of Llew that offered. Llew was going to go out by the window, the only way: treetop there, jump for it. He pulled up the sash, howling and clumsy. Miss Emmett started minimally at the influx of cool air, and the cups of the brassière filled with the breeze and danced. Miss Emmett daggered his back, not too deeply. He turned towards her, cursing and pushing, bringing me too into his curse:

– Fucking ow ow swine bastard get her ow ow ow fucking off my fucking ow ow.

She went for his eyes, and instinct, so often wrong, told him these were more vital than his balance. His hands weaving at head level, he seemed to sink into a chairback that wasn't there. He went out, howling loudly now, head first, backwards, into the upper air of the garden. I had the curious momentary conviction that that would really be the end of him, the artist who maintains his own creation just erasing him from the pattern between window and ground. No Llew after this, dead or alive. Miss Emmett stepped back, panting, saying:

– It was. Like. Seeing. His father. Again.

If she wanted to be Mrs Alving, then the departed actor would do well enough for Oswald. What she meant was not my father in the incestuous attempt but in fear of the scissors. But no time now to think of that. I remembered life was not a cartoon, and that there was something solid down there, dead or alive. I pushed Catherine aside and ran downstairs. As I clattered breathily, hoping to God that asthma would not return, I had a sudden realization, which I should have had before, of what Gonzi had meant that morning. But that would have to wait.

14

– Before this happened, I said or think I said, certainly no more than a quarter of an hour later, it was just a matter of the delay being a bit of a nuisance. Now, of course, it's very urgent that you get out of Castita.

Catherine had a dressing-gown on now, an unseductive dark brown cerement associable with up-patients in state hospitals, constellated with the souvenirs of old meals.

– I can't take it in I can't take it in I can't –

– Never mind about that now. Think of *what to do*. Insist that the police take this business with the utmost seriousness.

– But they mustn't be told must they mustn't be –

– That. That. That in your hands.

She was not disposed, despite my gravity, to take the business seriously herself. She was still bobbing up and down in the wake of the other matter. She looked at the shaking piece of paper again, already grubby although it had been in her hands less than two minutes, and said:

– They'll laugh they'll laugh they'll. Oh, and I'm so ill. It's not possible, none of it's possible, I can't believe –

– You're the only one who can bloody well go. Got that? I can't go, can I, and she certainly can't go.

Miss Emmett was chewing sugarlump after sugarlump from a red square box of sugarlumps. She was upright in her armchair here in the sittingroom, eyes smiling on inner cinema images of an old person proud of violence, triumphant in prescience, jammed together by a mad director. When not taking a new lump from the box on the table beside her, her fingers stroked the scissors in her lap like a cold thin cat. I called her name but she didn't respond. I flicked my thumb and finger before her eyes and she jumped to posthypnotic attention.

– Yes yes yes.

– Listen, Miss Emmett, listen.

– Yes yes yes.

– Get this absolutely clear. You did the right thing. Have you got that? The right thing. Assault may legally and morally be met by counterassault. But we daren't tell the police. The police just won't understand. And if they do understand it won't be for a hell of a long time. The police here are not very intelligent, and today, tonight, they're very very jumpy. Have you got that, Miss Emmett?

– She hasn't got it, Catherine said. Not got it. I haven't got it. Nobody's got it. Oh God God God. She's not very well. I'm not very. Nobody's very.

– She was well enough up there doing what she did.

– This is the this is the. Reaction. Oh God God, I think I'll have to be sick again.

– Yes yes yes.

– What do you mean, *again*?

– Try again, I mean. If at first you. Oh God God God God, you have messed things up for us, haven't you? Everything was all right before you came along.

– Ah, shut up.

– He shouldn't have done it, Miss Emmett said clearly. It's in the blood, though. Driven to it by something in the blood.

– Oh God God, I wish I could be sick.

– That's right, I said to Miss Emmett. You go on thinking that. It was Miles and you went for Miles with your scissors and Miles fell out of the window. And then Miles ran away and you won't see Miles again.

– Ran for miles. Yes yes yes.

– You did the right thing. But now it's all over and there's no need to mention it again. Miles has gone back where he came from. You've scissored Miles out of the film. No more Miles.

– I can't go while she's like this, Catherine said. You can see that. You can see that I can't. Go while she's.

– The bad Miles, Miss Emmett said. But I didn't get the good Miles.

– There was only one, I said loudly. I'm not Miles, if that's what you're thinking. I'm somebody quite different.

– While she's like this.

– Go in the morning then. First thing in the morning. Then the planes will be able to start flying again.

– There but for the grace of God go I, recited Catherine, closing her eyes. To New Zealand. Oh, it's mad it's mad it's. They'll laugh, I tell you. Laugh ha ha ha ha.

– Stop it. *Stop it.* Give Miss Emmett a couple of sleeping pills and get her to bed. Give yourself a couple of sleeping pills and – Is that clear? Am I making myself clear? Am I succeeding in making myself –

I took a few calmative deep breaths: the asthma, thank God, was not obstructing the process. Then I said:

– I'll be round here tomorrow as soon as I can.

And then I left. There was little I had been able to find in the house in the way of disguise materials, so I went along the back streets as a limping young man with dark glasses (from Llew's breast pocket) and a bad faceache (handkerchief held to it). There seemed to be no police around and very few night walkers. A woman peeped out of a doorway and said to me:

– *Fac fijki fijki?*

I ignored her and went on to the Batavia Hotel, where some upper lights were still on. There were two or three cars parked outside it, and several more on Tholepin Street. The cinema was dark and shut, the show long over. I was late then, very late, but I could always say, if need be, that I went for a cup of coffee somewhere. I took out Llew's keys and their obscene attachment and then I forgot the make of the car. Fuck it, man. Llew's voice came back with clarity: *A Cyrano fucking convertible. Me, I'm her fucking chauffeur.* And there it was: creamy, fender-dented, longnosed, SKX 224. I got in and shed toothache and dark glasses. I started her up and schooled my right hand in the feel and position of the controls. Then I drove off carefully. I had a lot to think about. But I couldn't for the life of me see any other way out of the problem than this.

I had not been surprised to find Llew dead. Other men

falling backwards from a third-storey window would probably have limped off with bruises or, at most, have lain with a broken limb or head till the ambulance came. But Llew had with total efficiency cracked the back of his skull on the ruins of a birdbath – irony there – and, as a garnish, gashed a brachial artery on what looked like a smashed wine carboy. There was no accident but also no murder, unless you could regard the great sustentive creator as a murderer. He had made a mistake, he had repeated himself, and he had at last found time and opportunity to erase the error. Indeed, the fact of that error had only been brought to his notice by the chance collocation of myself and my ghastly likeness. But what the shamed artist could not now do was to pulverize the various extensions of that liquidated identity; he had to leave that to others, another, me. There was the body itself and the image on other retinas of its path through the world. There was the mother.

My fear of the coming of the police to the Yo Ho Me Lads, a possible report to them from somebody of the noise in the house opposite, the interest of the police in the presence of a disruptive force in that region of the street – these had prevented me from doing what is so often done in murder stories of the more lurid kind. I was sensible enough to know that to bury a body is not easy and it takes much time. Even to drag it to the middle of that dark overgrown garden and cover it, as in a token Greek burial, with earth and leaves and branches could have been dangerous in its aftermath, my entering the house with earthy arms and sweat on me. *Well well, doing a bit of midnight gardening, eh? I'm a bit of a gardener myself, let's examine your handiwork.* And to tell the police the innocent truth – No, the truth would never do here. I had already tried the truth with the Castitan police, and they had put me in a cell with a menu of capital crimes.

But the police had not, so far, come to Indovinella Street. They might come later; meanwhile those two landed faggots could snore in each other's arms. And the police would certainly have no occasion to look for the body of Llew. The body of Llew was in Llew's mother's Cyrano, driving carefully to a sleeping circus.

I had lugged that corpse to the outhouse to desecrate the works of Sib Legeru. All the candles had burnt out except one that had been doused earlier, before its half life was done, by an incoming draught. Relighted, it was able to melo-dramatize the settling of Llew behind teachests and can-vases, throwing gross Bram Stoker shadows. There, locked among masterpieces, he could await the opportunity of a permanent disposal. Meanwhile I must be he. Fucking him, man. I had a general scenario worked out, but there were so many things – the things that are of no moment to God but matter in domestic life – I must feel towards, guess at.

I tried to make the journey last as long as possible. I was helped in this by a minor or preliminary roadblock just be-fore that green that had flowered, transitorily, with the cir-cus. It was as if the way to the circus was a way out of Castita, which in a sense it was. Failed assassins and miracle exploders as clown recruits, temporary ringhands hiding in the straw of departing elephants. No wonder a state like this was uneasy about even peripheral circus men – Llew, for instance. Llew had tried rape and cracked his occiput. He had not actually harmed the state, but there had been good potential nuisance value there. A circus was international bolshevism or Jewry or the Vatican. This one must have had great influence to get in at all. And think of the cost of transportation. Ele-phants trumpeting in holds, tiger cages sliding down stormy decks, the thunder of terrified hooves in the tossing night, birds crying over the gale. For what profit?

– Papers? Passport? the young constable asked. His dark glasses reproduced in duplicate the spinning crimson stop-light in the middle of the road. His companion had parked his black lenses on his brow, like a presbyopic granny, while he looked at the cartoons in the evening paper.

– If you want fucking identification, man, I tried, you come to the fucking circus. There's plenty'll say who I am, see.

– Oh, circus. Any free tickets?

– You come any fucking time. Mention me, Mr Llewelyn. No fucking trouble at all, man. Caught your murderers yet?

– Won't be long.

They waved me on, and now I was face to face with the weary old paradox of a journey, however prolonged, slowed, made circuitous, still being in its very essence a yearning towards a destination, and here was the staff carpark. I parked with care. There were the trailers. I walked on legs of jelly. Jellif. The stupid bitch my sister had not really taken anything in. She had not even taken in properly the fact of a corpse nestling in the outhouse. I feared that perhaps in the night it would all dawn on her with the first cock and she would panic and bring people in. But Miss Emmett, temporarily deranged, might be a calming sugary presence as well as a sufficient responsibility. Me, I had my own fucking problems, man. In one of the trailers there was singing and glass-clinking. Probably not clowns, who were said to be sad and abstemious people. But the cream trailer of the Bird Queen was in darkness. Where did her birds roost, by the way? Probably over there in that animal park, a bloodwarm compound of gamy and atavistic dreams.

The trailer door was not locked. I seemed, as I entered, enclosed like a foetus by a loud pounding of exterior heart. I felt for the switch; subdued light came on and showed the mess of Llew's room or cabin no longer as sordid but pathetic. That cheap stilled music and its timid little makers to whom learning and skill and the whole of history were a dead scene, trying to shock with hair and rebel moustachios and tight pants embossed with the shape of genitals. I had in my pocket a notebook, one of Sib Legeru's, totally out of Llew's character but a hold on sanity that I needed. I would read it through the night; I had to keep awake and alert; I could not risk surfacing from sleep as Miles Faber, perhaps with the Bird Queen looking down from her great height to catch deception, like a gannet a fish. I had to think of all possible dangers.

On Llew's bed was a pair of puce pyjamas newly laundered. This was a lucky chance: I could not have borne the wearing of anything soiled, even microscopically, by his body. I undressed, folded the clothes that were his, and prepared for bed. As I was turning the sheet down, peering for any small sign of his night incontinence, I heard the voice of his mother calling his name. There were two doors between us, but the deep sharp tone carried. Now to act, not without an excitement that was partly pleasurable.

– Yes, mam?

I went past the kitchen and bathroom to her door and opened it gently. She lay yawning. Some light overflowed from Llew's cabin: I could see her long shape under a coverlet, the doors of the wall wardrobes, a couple of fixed mirrors. Her long dark hair was proved removable: I observed grey short curls on the pillow topping the strong face in deep shadow. She spoke kindly enough. The accent was, like Llew's, Welsh tinged by American. But how deep the voice was. She said:

– What was the movie about, then?

– Oh, sex, mam. Like all movies these days.

How far should I garnish with obscenity? Llew had seemed to make no distinction between men and women interlocutors. His mother said:

– Nothing about the sea? Giorgio said the sea came into it.

How pure that vowel in *sea* was. I said:

– Something about the sea, yes. It wasn't all that good, mam.

And then she said something that made me freeze:

– Taking meat to your sister.

– T – tay –?

– Keep away from people, *bachgen*. The police don't like strangers in places like this. Clever strangers like us especially. And you had what they call a perfect alibi. They made it sound as though taking meat to your sister is a kind of –

– Euphemism?

– *Duw mawr*, big words is it now? But it's all big words nowadays in whatever you read. Like this big word in my eye. What is it again?

– I've forgotten, mam.

– Well, I hope he can put it right. Don't let me oversleep now. The appointment's at ten.

Me and my big mouth and big words.

– Conjunctivitis?

– No, not as big as that. But something itis. Well, we'll see.

How different your voice sounds tonight, *bach*. You've not been drinking again?

– Only coffee, mam.

– Coffee? Coffee? Big words and coffee. Well, you're growing up, of course. I have to face that my boy is growing up. Nothing stands still. I'll try and sleep now. *Nos da*.

I didn't know whether Llew kissed her *nos da* or not. But to be on the safe side I leaned over. I could see the sharp strong face clearly. One of the eyes was red and sore. A bird bite? The good eye betrayed no doubt that this was Llew leaning over. I caught a slight odour of a poulterer's shop as I kissed her forehead.

– *Nos da*, mam.

Back in Llew's room I had a brief syncope. I fell on to the bed and was out for a heartbeat. The strain. I could not put up with this strain for long. Perhaps tomorrow the airport would be open again. Miss Emmett had money from the lawyers. I would fly with them as far as Kingston, Jamaica, and breathe there before the next phase could be assembled. But I would leave as Llew. Or be Llew at least till the sanctuary of the international departure lounge. Big boy now, mam. Go my own way, see. Settle down. Marry, perhaps. Change my name, even.

> Muskseed on white poplar
> Caraway biscuits for
> The roughhaired siskin
> Aberdevine

But, lying in bed with that notebook, I found Sib Legeru no longer a total release from the world's shaped and bony madness. Llew had to be removed from among those works, yet, perhaps because of the Poe guignolizing of that solitary candle, I would find it difficult to extricate crass corpsedom from all this free cleanliness. Sleep would enable me to think of tomorrow as a separate time, with my problems resigned to it, but where there is no sleep there is no tomorrow. The problems were here and now. What had I done to deserve these problems?

15

– Healing nice though it is. Funny you never said. Nasty gash like that.

– Didn't want to bother you, mam. Had enough on your plate, like. That eye and all.

– Still. Funny you never said, *bachgen*. Changing you are. For the better in some ways. Still. Fighting, was it?

My boldness had the panache of desperation, which is, after all, the usual state of mind of the artist.

– It was on the ship, mam. That time it kept lurching.

– Yes. The ship. Nasty rough old crossing that was. I wonder sometimes whether it's worth it, this kind of life. Never settled, always on the move.

– Yes, mam. I've been thinking a bit lately. It's time I thought of –

– It was a quieter life with Professor Burong in the aviary. Science, that was. But a lot of science gets turned into showbiz as they call it. You remember the Parkingtons that place in Missouri?

– Yes yes, the Parkingtons.

– They'd been doing real research as they called it. At that place that sounds royal. North Carolina I think they said it was.

– Duke?

– Something like that. You remember better than me. E.S.P., whatever that stands for.

– Extra-sensory perception.

– Learning you are, *bachgen*. Changing for the better with your big words. But they'd been lured, as they put it. I never forget what he said. You remember what he said?

– Is that fucker going to cross the road or isn't he? Sorry, mam, I shouldn't have let that word slip out. Exasperated they make you and that brings out the short words.

I was tired enough to be exasperated. And I was probably giving away more through my unconfident mode of driving than through my speech or even the back of my head. She had a good view of my head, sitting in the back, a lady being driven to a medical appointment by her chauffeur. She looked like, say, last night's M.G.M. film's idea of a lady . . . long, slim, in severe slategrey suit and stockings of black mist, the short grey hair blued, drop earrings. Earrings, she had said, and had undoubtedly said often before, were supposed to be good for the eyesight. There was no henna glow on her cheeks: that was just part of her professional makeup.

– Real Tiger Bay language. Well, you've tried to curb it lately, I'll say that. What Eric Parkington said was that behind every art there's a science. That's true, *bach*.

– That's what I wanted to mention, mam. I've no art and no science. Time I got down to something. Time I got away and did something proper. I lay thinking all last night. Tired I am this morning, see.

– Thinking, is it? Well, there's a change for the better, too. I know how it is, boy *bach*. I'll never stand in your way. As soon as you want to settle I'll give all this up. I've said it often enough before but you only laughed. *Chwerthaist ti*. A job and a house and birds in the garden and your mam taking it easy for a change. What are all those people doing?

– They want blood.

We were passing the Dwumu where the devout refused to be cheated of their miracle. There were old women with vessels angry outside the locked doors.

– Want blood, is it?

Her voice thickened, as though blood had been stirred into it and I wondered if the gooseflesh were visible on the back of my neck.

– But I want to get away *soon*, mam. I've wasted too much of my life.

– Looking after your widowed mother was waste, was it? Ah, here it is, then. Marrow Street, a queer name for a street, especially where doctors are.

She laughed, *chwerthodd hi*, and I had to laugh in duty without comprehension. How much Welsh was I supposed to know? I found out much later that *marw* was the Welsh for *dead*.

– Park over there, she ordered, where it's clear. Wait for me. I may not be long.

– A book I want to buy.

– A sexy one, is it? No, you've changed, isn't it, *siwgr*? A sexless book, one full of knowledge. Right then, don't be too long away.

I watched her mount the steps outside the big oak door of Dr Matta, whose name was engrossed in copperplate cursive on a brass plate. She rapped the brass dolphin knocker and then turned for a last look at me before being admitted. Her look was hard and puzzled but, as the door was opened by a girl in white, she turned it into a swift smiling one of somehow hurt affection. I didn't like the way things were going: the strain was already inducing in me pains in the rectum, difficulty in breathing, a loosening of the top incisors, as well as a recurrence of the throb in my head. She went in and the door was closed on her. That morning I had said I would have coffee, and this was the first time Llew had ever wanted coffee for breakfast. But it was hard for her to be more than merely puzzled by evidence of change of habit and manner. The great undeniable was the face, Llew's face, and the so to speak pendent body. And the voice was right, I knew it was right. Vocabulary was a different matter, but she seemed to like the first shoots of a new, maturer, Llew. If he had lived, even Llew would have had to start growing up. The main point was that the three-dimensional essence was there; the rest was a matter of accidents. But I had to get away as Llew regretfully leaving his loved mother for his own good. A human right to be free, a thing talked of much those days.

I thought these things marching on my, his, thin and urgent legs towards Indovinella Street. I itched to be in the outhouse with Sib Legeru, but that would mean also having dealings with a corpse already set upon by Caribbean heat. Tonight that shed would be cleansed of the presence; I felt sure that, with a few nips of hard spirit inside me, I could do the interment in something like thirty minutes. Very light sandy soil, none of your lead loam to crack back and lungs. A spade, there must be a spade about. Perhaps, most inappropriately, in Sib Legeru's own shed. Spades were for Wordsworth, not that earthfree radiance.

I wiped my wet forehead, ringing the bell. Catherine came, looked cautiously through a crack, then opened the crack into a silent way in. She didn't look too bad all things fucking considered, man. Her dress was clean simple blue and she'd knotted her hair behind with, I saw after, an elastic band. We went into the sittingroom. I noticed on the way that the kitchen table had not been cleared: there were flies dancing around the cold joint. Miss Emmett was not to be seen.

– In bed still, Catherine said. I gave her a pretty big dose.

– What of?

– I mean another dose this morning before I went out. We've only got aspirin. She was willing to take any amount of them. Feeding herself in rhythm, like sugar. Not a lethal dose, though. Just enough.

– So you went?

– Only to the telephone in the post office. I couldn't go and tell them face to face, I just couldn't. It was a very long job finding somebody who'd listen. But it was there all right, still in somebody's tray on a desk. The same. Just the same as you gave me. How did you remember?

– Ah.

– And they saw that the move and myself and New Zealand did give a kind of answer, but they wouldn't commit themselves about doing anything about it.

– God God. *Duw*. Were they inquisitive about who you were?

– Yes. Name and address and all. I said I was Dr Fonanta's secretary.

– Dr who, Dr what, whose secr—

– Dr Fonanta. The man I went to to be cured. He's a poet now, though. That poet there.

She shrugged towards the thin white book in the Indian bookstand by the window. This was something else to be – Later, however. I threestepped over to the book and handled it, however.

— We're innocent, Catherine said. Remember that. We did nothing wrong. And they couldn't do anything to Miss Emmett, could they?

The title: *Structures*. The name: Swart Smythe. I said, flicking the pages:

— Innocent is the word. Innocence is no good to anybody these days. Who lies best wins.

Fonanta. *Shmegegge, chaver*. Gaston de Foix. It would all fit together when there was time. Here was a sonnet:

> Two aircraft trails make barlines on the sky,
> The weak sun lies between, a semibreve.
> The dog's fur smells of cowpats. Trees unleave,
> Leaves lie like fillets of fried fish. Untie,
> Autumn, summer's corsage. Apples lie
> In rotting fallowships, making believe
> My twitching nose that round it soon will weave
> Companion odours of roast pork —

— Oh my, I said, God. This is terrible. I'll take it, I'll read it later. I said I'd gone to buy a book. I must get back to her.

— Yes, her. Is it going badly?

— She's puzzled. But it may be a kind of epistemological puzzle.

— I've had no education, remember.

— A question of her own perception. It may not be me who's transmitting the wrong messages, it may be her own perceptive apparatus that's garbling the right ones. That's what I hope she's thinking.

— I've been thinking, too. Is it possible we have, had, a brother? Your twin? Is it possible? There's been so much mystery and secrecy and —

— It can't be possible. You can see that it can't be possible. How in God's name could it possibly be possible that —

The doorbell rang. In the best tradition of sensational fiction she and I looked at each other, wide-eyed. Clichés of action have to wear old gloves. I mouthed: *Who?* She gestured: *Only one way to find out*. I mouthed, with a violent headshake: *Ignore it*. Her eyes told me to look at the front window, to which my back was turned. Someone peering in through the lace curtains. I saw who it was. I began to conceive a sort of wry admiration for destructive providence. I said:

– I'll go.

– Is it –?

– It is. She must have cancelled her appointment.

Aderyn the Bird Queen strode right in on my opening. I got in first with:

– Fucking quick he was then, mam. Everything all right then, is it?

The reddened eye had turned into a dangerous weapon. She saw the fly's banquet in the kitchen, then Catherine at the sittingroom door.

– *Chwaer*, she said bitterly. Where is my son? What have you done with him?

– You going fucking mad, mam? I cried. Here's your son. Is something wrong with both your fucking eyes, then?

I could not think that Llew, in such an emergency, would have quenched the obscene word. My danger, after all, was much as his had been in the bedroom upstairs.

His mother seemed to push Catherine into the livingroom. I kept talking.

– Told you I was going to get a book, didn't I? Well, here it is, man, mam. They hadn't got it in the shop but she was in the shop and she said I could borrow –

She turned on me with deep incisiveness.

– Followed you. Followed you as far as this street. The man in the drinking place opposite knew you from your photograph.

I noticed that she had in her hand an open passport, her thumb keeping it open. I was clearheaded enough to want to try to read it, but with a kind of sob she snapped it shut and stowed it violently in her handbag. I said:

– That's right, my photo. My fucking photo. Me. Why do you keep saying I'm not me, then?

– Where is he? What have you –

– I want that passport, mam. I'm leaving, I'm getting out, I'm a big boy now.

– You and your sister and a piece of rotten meat for the

journey? No more tricks, whoever you are. If Llew's in on this trick I'll kill him. But I'll kill you first, whoever you are.

In a mad way I was enjoying this. Despite the danger of innocence in a naughty world there is something comforting about the knowledge of one's innocence. It is the comfort of knowing that there must after all be a protective God (different from the cunning providence that was playing this destructive game); otherwise there would be no point in anybody being innocent. It is exhilarating to have an irrefutable proof, however discardable it may be later, that a good God exists. Vitally integral, pure of scelerities, no exigency of Moorish jacules –

– Sit down, mam, I said, sitting down. I see I have to tell you the truth. But if I've been lying remember it's your fucking fault. Scared I've been of you, see.

Catherine sat, but the Bird Queen remained standing. She was, I saw for the first time, not unlike a stork. She clutched her bag between index and pollex, her keelless sternum heaving, a nictitating membrane coming down over her sick eye. I said:

– Birds, birds. Sick of living with birds. Well, she and me are going off together, mam. A new life away from birds. I'll get a job, I'll work for her. You've always stood in my way as far as that goes, mam. A man can't live all his life as a fucking servant to birds.

Aderyn the Bird Queen sat down; her pygostyle engaged a hard wooden bottom. She said, quieter than before:

– Not true. You know I always wanted –

– Some nice little thing of your own choosing you could like boss and lady over. Another unpaid servant. To stop your darling sonny bonny whoring and to bring you breakfast in bed.

Catherine was impressed but frightened: Llew was alive again. That *sonny bunny* surely must convince the mother, on whose face a kind of agitated oil or sweat was spreading thinly, an uropygial secretion. I followed up with:

– Selfish you are, mam. Live for your art you do. Your son wants something like of his own to live for.

Aderyn's response was to make moaning noises in her

syrinx and then to add to the noise with a kind of dry weeping. Catherine and I looked at each other and I, fool that I was being young, gave her a sort of parodic Neapolitan tenor amorous leer. She winced in quiet horror. She was perhaps after all not a bad girl, though ugly. She had perhaps after all, though now cured, known suffering. Aderyn said to me:

– I don't know her. I don't know anything about her.

To Catherine:

– I don't know you, see. I know nothing about you, see. Terrible shock this is. So quick everything happens.

– Oh, I improvised, we've known each other a long time, without you knowing, mam. Afford to travel she can. An heiress. She came here because we're here, I'm here. Rented this house.

– Don't know her parents, don't know anything.

It was time for Catherine to speak. She said:

– I have no parents. I'm with with a sort of governess. Miss Emmett.

– *Governess*, yes, that was the word, *governess*. But *sister* too, *sister*.

– And quite right too, I said, to say *sister*. These people here on this island respect only mothers and sisters and wives. I couldn't say *wife*, could I? A man best protects his his his girl by calling her his sister. That's in the fucking Bible in the Song of Solomon, man, mam.

I put in that final flourish to mitigate what had been too Mileslike. Aderyn ignored it as, as I could tell now, she would ignore my other obscenities, or my other uses of the same obscenity, or my same obscenity put always to the same use and employed, almost literally for me, *ad nauseam*. English was evidently not her first language; its foulnesses were hypothetical ones. But for me it was monstrous that such speech should be a device of safety. She siad to Catherine:

– What's your name, *geneth*? Want to be his wife do you, is that it then?

– Catherine Faber, I said. And she does, yes she does, she does, mam. Going off together we are, as soon as we're let out of this crappy kip, see.

– Let her speak for herself, *bachgen*.

– I must go and see how Miss Emmett is, Catherine said, getting up. She was less than halfway to the door when Aderyn said:
– Stay, girl.
She stayed.
– What is the matter with this Miss Hammered, then? Ill, is she?
– She had a bit of a heart attack, I said. She's resting.
– Know all about it, is it, boy *bach*? Not much good as a governess any more, I'd say. Sit, girl.
Catherine hesitated.
– *Eistedd, geneth!*
Catherine responded as to a powerful cantrip. Aderyn got up professionally as to address an audience. She said:
– The world's changing, I see that, see it every day. And as you get old you don't change with it except in your body perhaps and then always for the worst. What the young want the young must have, that we're told in the newspapers and on the *teledu*. Life being perhaps short in the future for us all but most specially for the young. I've had my life and it was not always a good one. My marriage was not happy except for my son here, you, *bachgen*, and perhaps I was too selfish in my work and my talent. I was given the great *anrheg* of power over living things, meaning birds. Birds, girl. The fowls of the air, as in the Bible. Girl I was myself, no more, when I first showed the power, teaching my auntie's budgie so well that they made a gramophone record of it – *Georgie Porgie* and *Little Tommy Tucker* and such rhymes, as if a bird was no better than a snotnosed *plentyn* whining for loshins. Well, what my birds say now is better, university lecturer he was that gave me on paper what he said was right for an Adult Repertoire as he called it, and Professor Burong and his connections came in nicely there. And now, *geneth*, heiress as you are if what he says is true, you will no doubt be despising me for being part of a circus show, and if you are educated, which you will be if you are what he says, you will despise me also for bringing down what could have served Great Learning to the level of spit and pennies and brass bands and taffysucking gawpers. If you will say the word *prostitute* I will

not say no. For Professor Burong said, when I was but a girl feeder in the Aviary, that the gift I had was better than all learning and should be put to the service of The Science of Living Things as he called it. But I had my son, who is sitting by you now and says he loves you, and I was sick of watching each *punt* and *swllt* and never able to afford a good present for my dear *mab* on his birthday at *Nadolig*. And so when I met this circus man I was filled with the glory of lights and crowds. So I went with him into that world, taking you, *bachgen*, for, you may know it now on this day of change, the man you called father till he died was not your father.

– I sometimes, I improvised, thought it was like that, mam.

– Yes yes. It is not important. It is your own life that is important. And sometimes I think of my proud birds, both the hunters and the talkers, which is the division of men as well as birds, I think of them as brought low and degraded. But if I opened their cages and said *Go, fly away*, it would be only to me they would fly, for they know no different. But my own *mab* is not a bird and he can be free, and now the cage is open. So then there shall be a marriage, and with my blessing too.

I got up at once on that, mainly to eclipse Catherine's visible sick palpitations, and tried to embrace Llew's mother with:

– *Diolch*, mam, wonderful, I knew you'd like see it was best for all of us, and now we'll get off this crappy island soon as they'll let us and go to the States and get married and get a home ready for you and –

But she hadn't finished. She resisted my grateful arms and said:

– But it has to be now. No more putting off since they tell us time is so short for us all and specially the young. Today is Saturday and tomorrow there's no performance, so we shall have the ceremony tonight so all can drink to you and rest tomorrow.

– To to –

– Tonight, yes. After the second show. I was brought up Calvinistic Methodist and you, *bach*, were brought up nothing. Your religion, *geneth*, I don't know. But now they tell us all is one and the Pope himself will go to *capel*, so Pongo, that is Father Costello, will do it tonight and gladly. We must prepare. A white dress you have, girl, surely, and Llew has a good suit. We must tell the refreshments people.

Catherine was on her feet now, looking manically (but it could be taken for delight) for an egress not just from the room or the house but from this whole spacetime capsule that throbbed in the continuum of sense. Aderyn said:

– Love and gratitude and joy you should both be showing now. In each other's arms you should be in bliss. But the shock of joy can sometimes look like the shock of disaster.

I grabbed Catherine and hid her collapsed face in my shoulder. She shook and shook. I nodded at the tricky Arranger of Things, disguised in a ceiling corner as a spider.

– There, Aderyn said tragically, is happy I am.

16

– I mean, regard this as theatre, as a mere extension of circus. Brothers and sisters have acted lovers before. There were Beth and Bob Greenhaulgh who did Romeo and Juliet at the Princes Theatre in Manchester, England, in, oh, about 1933. Connie Chatterley and the gamekeeper Mellors, in the stage version of Lawrence's dying sermon, were acted by Gilbert Zimmerman and his sister Florence. And they actually went through the motions, naked too, flowers wreathing genitals and all. That, of course, was much later than 1933.

– Oh God God, what a mess you've landed us in.

– Soon – maybe tomorrow, perhaps even tonight – we'll be able to make our separate getaways, if you can lend me some money that is. The police can't afford not to lose face by not producing – after a decent interval which is supposed to cover hidden skill and diligence – a ringleader of some sort. They're probably deciding, perhaps with the President himself, who it ought to be. The Minister of Education maybe, breaking down and confessing, a big trial, a general purge, the President glowing in new glory. And the Minister of Education, being a freethinker or freemason, will be proved to have rigged the exploded miracle, having put the true one to silence.

– You've made a hell of a hell of a –

– That's unjust, and you know it.

I had taken some money from under the owl and then crossed the road to the Yo Ho Me Lads for a bottle of Feileadhbeag (pronounced Filibeg), a Scotch whisky distilled in Port of Spain, and I was drinking this. It made me elated and talkative.

– But what does it mean, what does it prove?

– Or it may, of course, be the only possible candidate – *our* candidate. Mean? Prove? Oh, tonight's affair. It's naïve, really. Nobody would dream of marrying his own sister. If I marry you, you're not my sister. Ergo I'm her son Llew. And as Llew I'll leave her, with my bride. And then everything will be saved, including honour. They can't *force* consummation, though they'll probably get near it.

— Consumm consumm —

— I can act it out, but can you? You'd better drink more of this. It's better to be giggly than the way you are now.

The way she was was haggard and tremulous, the fat body shaking like, I presumed though I hadn't of course bought any, her favourite Jellif, the fat face wearing haggardness as a fat foot wears a thin shoe. I went on talking:

— The situation, as far as I'm concerned, is what you might term an interesting one. In two days in a strange country I've acquired a mother in the form of a Welsh-speaking Bird Queen who scared me —

— She scares me too.

— Maybe, but you haven't seen those damned swooping hawks of hers. One false move and down they'll come. They go for the eyes.

— Oh God God God.

— Act. Drink more whisky. To continue, I've spent some hours in prison, I've discovered the works of an unknown superlative artist in a garden shed, and I've been shot at by a riddling lionfaced expert on Bishop Berkeley.

— Oh God, it tastes awful.

— Think of the awfulness of the taste, then, and not of any other awfulness. Most interesting of all, I'm due tonight to be married by a circus clown to my own sister — whom I first heard of last Sunday and met in the flesh for the first time yesterday — and I have the problem of burying in this garden the corpse of a young man who is, was rather, my double. The only time for doing it is what the world would call my wedding night. Work that fucking out, see, man.

— You're horrible.

— Maybe, but I'll save you from those bloody beaks.

— And then there's her. There's the problem of her. She just won't wake up.

She meant, of course, Miss Emmett. Catherine and I sat in Miss Emmett's room, on either side of her bed. It was a beautifully clean little room but curiously decorated with framed reproductions of neither commemorative nor aesthetic value. There was a photograph of very ordinary beechleaves with what looked like mould growing on them. There was what looked like a Soviet poster of the Second World War, showing workers and soldiers marching arm in arm under a great star, and for some reason the soldiers had bigger heads than the workers. There was a crude drawing in water colour of goldfish in a bowl, but this seemed an original not a reproduction – by Catherine, by long-dead me? There was what seemed to be an architect's drawing of a projected box-like factory. There was an advertisement for plastic furniture, lovingly framed as if it were precious art. Seeing none of these, Miss Emmett slept deeply and, I thought, healthily. Would she wake cured of the shock that made her say yes yes yes? It was safer for her to be asleep, of course. But what if she awoke while Catherine and I were out and ran off healthily but dementedly to the police about something she had become convinced she had done last night? I had to get that damned corpse buried, but not now while the sun raged and people sat, this being Saturday afternoon, in adjacent gardens.

– What shall we do with her? Catherine asked.

– I'm being altogether serious when I say that we ought to wake her up in order to give her something to make her sleep again.

– Oh, you're horrible and impossible.

How clever, or how foolish, was the Bird Queen? If she was convinced I was an impostor, then her leaving me alone with Catherine till the evening was a fair stroke of nastiness. She knew, and I knew, and I'd patiently laboured at making Catherine know, that any attempt of ours at hiding in the town or getting locked up by the police for some contrived misdemeanour, would be proof of my imposture, meaning my or our or some accomplice's at best kidnapping, at worst liquidation, of her son. We were supposed to be in hell in the livingroom, Catherine and I, looking at each other in horror when not at the wallclock (a cuckoo one, incidentally, whose bird had been put to silence and entombed behind his little double door), while the flies blew the cold beef on the kitchen table. If, on the other hand, she thought I was really Llew and this (but how improbable that had to be) was the girl I loved, then she was merely kindly leaving an engaged couple to kiss and cuddle and moon about sunnier delights to come while – having skipped the doctor and, little as she liked to drive, driven herself back – she told the good news to Mr Dunkel and the circus company, including her birds.

Catherine said she was hungry and went down to the kitchen while I drank more Feileadhbeag and neared the end of my small supply of Sinjantin. She came up again with the red box of sugar lumps, and I thought for a moment she intended to bring Miss Emmett round by forcing some into her mouth – a way reserved, surely, for bringing diabetics back to the world's doubtful sweetness from the coma of disturbed chemistry. This still looked like healthy sleep induced by aspirin. But Catherine meant the sugar for herself. She crunched and crunched and said:

– And that meat down there is horrible. Full of sort of heaving white things. Ugh.

– Why didn't you throw it out?

– Nothing to do with me. You bought it, you cooked it, you ate it.

– You ate some of it.

– Only a little sandwich. It was Jellif I wanted and meringues, and you were too selfish to get me any. Or Miss Emmett any.

– If you were less bloody selfish yourself you'd do something about cooking a meal or something instead of golloping sugar like some great glossybottomed mare.

– I don't like to be spoken to like that.

– I'll speak any way I want to.

– Not to me you won't.

We stared at each other in the realization that this was a fair simulacrum of the start of a married quarrel. Fate, or the procession of events, or the manic economy of nature (a bizarre idea, I suppose) took over our big eyes and opening mouths and made them the response to a new ringing of the doorbell. A schoolfriend I used to stay with – Gabriel Bellini – had a collie dog which, in a quite friendly spirit, used to take the head of the Siamese cat in his mouth. One day when I was there he yawned and, seeing the cat near and knowing his mouth to be still open, he thought he might as well take advantage of this to have the cat's head in. A rare kind of economy, really. Anyway, the bell rang and the only thing to do, after the cliché responses, was to go and answer it. I went downstairs, heart hammering, etc., and she followed me.

The person at the door was familiar to us both. Catherine cried:

– Dr Fonanta, oh, Dr Fonanta!

To me he was the jelyf man, but he was also, I now realized, someone I had seen before coming to Castita. That name *Fonanta* phonated a memory: the New York eatery, the crippled man dictating notes on French history and French peasant soup to a tape-recorder. He was hatless and on crutches, he was gloveless and showed a ceramic hand. Parked by the kerb behind him was a long polished Origen 70 with a thuggish driver at the wheel. He said, in the French voice that, I heard now, was the same as had dictated in New York and riddled here in Grencijta towards the end of my little openair show, with soft courtesy:

– I considered I had better come round.

– Oh yes, oh yes, Dr Fonanta, come in Dr Fonanta.

He hobbled in and Catherine got him to the armchair in the livingroom, fussing as if she thought he ought to have rugs around him and his feet in a footcosy. She evidently thought highly of Dr Fonanta. For me, there were a lot of new puzzles here to be worked out. I said:

– First you were in New York and then you're here and now you're here, in this house I mean –

– Yes yes, I remember very well. I had to lecture at Columbia that evening. You, by the way, must be Catherine's brother.

His baldness shone at the ceiling and his eyes at me. It was a clever goodtempered face set above the wreck of the body.

But I remembered that he was a rotten poet: not so clever, then. Catherine said to me, him, both:

– How did you, where –

– I had a visit from Inspector Preparatis, Dr Fontana said. He was flanked by motorcyclists, very impressive. Something about a message emanating from my secretary. I have no secretary now, of course. Only Umberto out there in the car. The inspector wanted to know what they, the police, ought to do about the message. He talked of improbabilities and being made a laughing-stock and so on. I told him he could act on the information received, insane though it appeared, but he seemed doubtful. It's a matter of waiting till the serious big men at headquarters realize how wide the bounds of seriousness are.

– So the airport remains closed, I said. Ah, God.

– What I meant, Catherine said, holding her chair down firmly in this world where so many reasonable laws were being suspended, was how you two know each other.

– Many things, smiled Dr Fonanta. Questions and answers, a dead artist called Sib Legeru, poor leonine unleonine Dr Gonzi.

– Sib Legeru, I said. You knew precisely where his works are. Why did you let me waste time searching?

– Ah, a waste of time, was it? Interesting.

– Oh, we're in such trouble, Catherine cried out, oh, we're in such terrible trouble.

– And while I'm here, Dr Fonanta said, ignoring her and reading my face as though it were really a printed book, lines and all, I'd like to have another look at those *works*.

The nuance of contempt came ill from so poor a poet. Then an orchestral crash of despair made my body shake. I said:

– It's. Not. Really. Poss.

– Not really possible. Again, interesting. You've burnt them? Sold them? Packed them off already to some great academic conservatory of nonsense in the United States?

– I've. Lost. The.

– Key. No problem there. Umberto has an iron shoulder.

– How much, I asked warily, gulping and regulping at a lump of ghastly bread that would not go down, flattening myself as if at bay against the wall where the cuckooless clock tocked, letting down its chain entrails, do you know?

– Know? *Know?* About what?

– About about – You've no right to say what you said, nonsense you said. Apples and roast pork, you –

– Not the best of my poems, true, but it does at least make sense. We'll come to aesthetics later. You, Faber, put on a creditable performance the other day, though you were fascinatingly reluctant to answer riddles. I had Umberto follow you. Did you not perceive his shadowing bulk? At the Batavia Hotel he obtained confirmation of your identity. But I knew already, well enough. All the rest follows. Girl's voice to police, riddle answer, the name Fonanta. You've succumbed, Faber, I surmise. It was *your* answer, not hers.

– I don't see what –

– Time enough. Let us skip dull intermediacies for the moment. How and where is dear Miss Emmett, by the way?

– She comes into it, I said, as you damn well probably know. She's under sedation now. A matter of shock.

– Things are going well, Dr Fonanta beamed. A pity there's no eclipse tonight. I gather there'll be fireworks, though. There's probably some rotting meat about somewhere.

Catherine and I shared a look of guilt at that. I went out to the kitchen without a word. The beef was as alive as a telephone exchange. I picked up the dish, averting my eyes, and walked as steadily as a waiter to the front door, out, up the narrow path, the meat computerizing like mad, and then safaried through the overgrown garden to a point from which I hurled the gesturing meat into bramble, ranunculus and monstrous cocoacoloured leaves. Newly environmented, the decaying horror became part of the life cycle. For good measure I threw also the china dish, but that would be only a fracted artefact, unabsorbable into any ultimate meaning, a mere mean signpost of transient frivolous culture. Then I went back to the house. Dr Fonanta shone at me:

– Catherine has told me curious news.

– Cur curi –

– Things are proceeding very nicely to their consummation. As I said before you went out, there's probably some rotting meat about somewhere.

– I threw it away.

– I think not, Faber. Never mind. All will end well. You are good at wordgames. You should also be good at palinlogues.

I did not understand for a moment what he meant. I was thinking that his glee was the inhuman one of some fictional intellectual higher policeman who sees suffering as the expulsable pipesmoke that fills a room devoted to the pleasures of jigsaws or battleplans. The whole of history has been taken up with pretence after pretence that the void between the two voids can be filled up with something other than play. Yet if nature does all the serious work, what is there left for man?

– I approach something like elation, Dr Fonanta said over his crippled body and ceramic left hand.

17

Here is an account, which my drunkenness at the time and later impairment of memory have probably rendered inaccurate, of my marriage to my sister.

The elephants had buns and the performing seals fish and the growling carnivores meat. The birds, caged hawks on the bridegroom's side of the ring, talkers on the bride's, had nothing. Most of the congregation was still in ring gear, including makeup, but Father Costello, or Pongo, had dismantled his face and was disclosed as an eager and ascetic cleric in bags and checks and rags that were perhaps no more bizarre than any of the traditional sacerdotal outfits. His voice was refined Anglo-Irish and he preached at some length.

– Not altogether fanciful to descry something of our lost prelapsarian innocence revived here in this perfect round, symbol, like the marriage ring itself, of God's eternal unity.

We stood there, I swaying slightly, Catherine in a kind of creased white sack dug from the bottom of a packed bag, Mr Dunkel by my side with the ring ready. Dr Fonanta, in his elation, had sent his ironshouldered thug out to buy something cheap and simple from a chain general store called Bwunmirketu. He was undoubtedly mad but so, of course, was everybody else. He would be along later, he'd said. He would revive Miss Emmett and give her certain discreet instructions. He had talked no more of Sib Legeru but I had, of course, like you, read his palinlogue.

– Adam and Eve and the tamed and feeding beasts on the terrestrial level. On the celestial level the entire creation glorifying its maker through the divinely bestowed gift of diversion. We are all God's *jongleurs*; we play and tumble before His throne for His weary delectation.

– Get on with it and get it over, tuxedoed Mr Dunkel muttered. Then he gave me another of the so-termed baleful looks that, I perceived, were all that he had ever given poor Llew. Llew had not been liked at all by anybody, except a couple of girl bareback riders with pert hard faces but really superb bodies who, standing now near naked with the rest of the congregation, could hardly take their eyes off Catherine. They obviously believed that I had put Catherine in the family way somewhere along the endless circuit, and that, lugging her luggage and pregnancy, she had caught up with me here.

– It is no accident surely that those pioneers the martyrs under the Caesars attained their first glimpse of the ultimate in a circus ring.

As for Aderyn the Bird Queen, she stood behind me, stony and hennaed, in a turquoise robe and a cataract of false hair. It was totally impossible to tell what was going on in her mind.

– And so I return to our present joyful purpose.

Was that irony intentional? I tried to stiffen as the moment of untruth approached, and Catherine succeeded in stiffening. She had been well premedicated by Dr Fonanta, who had had his thug bring in a black bag which contained, along with a sphygmometer and an enema machine, a ranged spectrum of pills. One of the barebacked riders, oval bitchy face and madonna hair, smirked at me, and what with this, the sight of her breasts and thighs, and the whole generalized randy atmosphere of any wedding (but here there were also hugemembered beasts, though caged, and uncaged docile elephants whose long copulations, since they had been exulted in by Cardinal Newman, were able to form a legitimate subject for a brief cadenza in Father Costello's sermon), I found myself segmentally stiffening, and perhaps visibly to some, since Llew's best blue suit had skintight pants.

Father Costello's marriage service was either something new and ecumenical, or else a work of his own composition. I was asked:

– Do you, Llewelyn, take this woman Catherine willingly into the temple of matrimony, to feed and fructify her, clothe and adorn her, make her sleep sound and her waking pleasant, as time shall run to the loosening of the bond, the garland become a chain and amity turn to acrimony?

What could I answer but that I did?

— Do you, Catherine, take this man Llewelyn as your pillar, helpmeet, support and stay, as a source of joy and fury, of bread and brood, so long as lust shall last and love live?

I may not have remembered that quite right. Catherine, like any regular bride, fought dry tears and would not answer. Father Costello said kindly:

— Courage, child.

Catherine seemed to nod, and this was taken as sufficient assent. Dunkel handed me, at Father Costello's gesture, the ring that Dr Fonanta had had bought, and Father Costello guided my ring-carrying hand from Catherine's thumb to ringfinger, each phrase of his formula passing a finger over till the right one was reached:

— The Father be your house, the Son be your table, the Comforter be the sweet air blowing through. And this holy act be you-and-you made You.

At that he thrust Catherine's finger into the ring, which was a little loose. The band, which had brought its instruments down into the other ring, immediately brayed and thumped into a wedding march I had never heard before:

Aderyn gave us both a cold kiss and, while the released congregation made for the buffet tables, Dunkel dragged me to one side to give me a sort of blessing:

— Now, you young bastard, let this be the end of your stinking games and filthy irresponsibility. She doesn't look much and I'm screwed if I understand how you got tied up with her, but I'll bet it was something nasty and typical. Anyway, it's only because your mother asked me nicely that you're having it for tonight, so keep it clean, get it, pig?

— Fuck you, belly, I said amiably. What tonight, what's *it*, man?

– My trailer, Dunkel said, raying out hate from behind his pebble glasses and looking, perhaps because of the glasses, a little like Pine Chandeleur, thought older. I yearned towards that holyshirted bastard as to the unincestuous dolphined seas of freedom, thinking at the same time that there was too much duplication going on, as though the Llew-me duo had infected the nearer world, thinking at the same time that Dunkel had no right to a trailer if he did his work and sleeping in hotel rooms.

– Clean, he repeated, you filth. Then he went over to join the glass and bottle clinkers.

– Clean, yes, I answered, meaning it. There would be no spilling of anything tonight. There would be a vigil with the transistor radio I would borrow from that young elephant dung sweeper over there, who was playing pop all to himself, oblivious of the blasts of the band. The news must come through soon, and with it the reopening of the ways out of Castita.

Meanwhile there were the jollifications to be got through. Aderyn had done everybody well. On trestletables there were gin, whisky, wine, cauldrons of ice, Coco-Coho, sandwiches and even a sort of improvised wedding cake – a cherry affair smeared with icing and crowned with two celluloid dolls that, appropriately, had no sex. The Great Giro, in tight braided pants and a claret messjacket of the sort called an arsefreezer, was stuffing himself with bread. I said, smiling:

– Your plates have come in useful, yes?

Figlio d'una vacca puttana troia, stoppati il culo.

– Not fair to my mother, that, man. Stuff you too, garlicky pisspot.

There were, I found, plenty of simple circusfolk ready to sneer or snarl at me, and in a variety of languages. One blond muscular trapeze artist called Carlo drew spits and umlauts out of a black Finnish night, and a lady like a schoolmistress who was in charge of the seals (these had now been put to bed in a tank and could be heard roaring plaintively, left out of the fun) spoke bitterly at me what sounded like debased Sophocles. Well, perhaps poor Llew had deserved all this, but he had paid the price. It was my duty really to give the assembly, on this final or postfinal appearance, the full rich randy rank nasty quiddity of that dead useless boy, but somehow I hadn't the heart, man. Almost meekly I told the baffoed liontamer (and lions too, it was all lions, from Loewe on) to get pedicated by that lousy scratching old mog with an unwashed mane and be newly infected with jungle syphilis. One of the bareback girls, I saw, had taken Catherine aside, presumably to instruct her in techniques of eluding my filthier demands. Aderyn, whose bad eye looked worse, was statelily sipping raw gin and ice with the ringmaster, who had removed his corset and was scratching his released paunch. I went over to join the clowns, who, still in tomato noses, were arguing metaphysics with Pongo or Father Costello. Perhaps this was really an underground seminary. The band began to play a lumpish waltz, hoofed and heavy, with trombone farts and clarinet squitters. The liontamer danced with the sealwoman. A nearly toothless mahout made Jumbo, or Alice, prance on hind legs, weaving the fore ones, wreathing its lithe proboscis. But this was like talking shop in the mess and was soon put a stop to. The drink softened some of the enmity towards me and converted it into mere sneering pity. One of the clowns, breaking off his critique of the Kantian *Ding an sich*, said:

– You're landed, *Kerl*. There's justice in the world and I say no more.

– As a man rose, Father Costello twinkled, so shall he seep.

I saw the bitchy madonna bareback girl turning alone from a table with a sandwich in her hand. Rose, yes. I would dance with her to hide what the sight of her made rise, what her pressure would make rise further. Filthy, coarse. But I was Llew. I was also Miles. Would Llew have leaped with such relish on a piece of yummy protest? For some reason I caught a sudden memory of the proprietress of the Batavia Hotel talking of the day after the day after tomorrow. What was the word now? And, whatever it was, why? I went up to the girl and said:

– A dance, eh? Like for the last time and old time's sake, eh? May I like have the pleasure of?

– Dance? But you don't dance.

Her accent was of the kind I liked least: provincial British entering the big world via America. But how can a man doubt there is some great beneficent or evil ultimate when his hands tremble towards such bowls of junket and firm yet delicate erections of curves and silver? I said breathily:

– It's not the dancing. In my arms, I want you like in my arms, man, for the last time before the darkness of wholly mattress money.

And I had them already clawing her. She filled her mouth with her sandwich, trapping a squirt of ketchup with her tongue, then made big droll eyes, wriggled her pelvic basin, and swam with a parody of abandon into my embrace. So we danced under the working lights to the tier upon tier upon tier they towered of yawning seats, while the band thumped and farted its waltz, my cock crowed through the darkness, and Catherine, whose face showed nothing but drugged eager tranquillity, was still being instructed in matters of total irrelevance. Then the ringmaster, dancing near, the pony mistress he had but recently cursed in his arms, cracked the whip of his voice with:

– Manners and propriety, lout. This dance is for you and your bride.

Christ, yes, so it was, and me with that, man. Cheers and jeers, and I had to hurl myself and my burden on to a Catherine pulled out by supple circus arms into the ring. Hiding it in her, I clumsily whirled her about, but that warm fat flesh was like iced water to it, and it receded in shock and rage like an exorcized devil, shaking its fist with a promise of return. And then.

– The boss! cried Dunkel.

The boss? I was past all surprises as you, the reader, must be. What, incidentally, are you like? Yawning and idle, looking for a *good read*, have you picked this idly from a public library shelf or remainder table or barrowload of dogeared joblot hasbeens and followed distractedly, with an apple or a cigarette or/and casual puttings down and takings up, certainly with detachment, this dripping of the heart's blood of an innocent sick boy set upon by the madness in the very core of life? Be sympathetic; more: *believe*. I might be your own son or father. The boss was Dr Fonanta (but had I not heard that name, or something like it, when the circus first brassed, whirred, roared into my life at the tail of Senta Euphorbia's procession?), and he was being pushed in an altropropel wheelchair down the raked aisle of the big top by his thug. The thug did this with one hand; with the other he steadied on his shoulder a lightly sweating Frigoportatile which, as we all soon saw, contained a dozen of champagne. Only Dunkel seemed to know that this was *the boss*; the rest of the circus company watched his descent to the ring in wonder and curiosity.

A sort of wedge in the ring's plastic circumference was removed to allow Dr Fonanta to enter. He sat cheerfully, nodding at all impartially while the bottles were taken from their box and exploded by the thug Umberto. Umberto, who kept his peaked cap on, had an exaggerated and brutalized version of the face of a longdead Canadian tycoon called Lord Beaverbrook. Dunkel said to the company:

– Very rarely we have the pleasure.

– Very rarely indeed, Dr Fonanta interrupted with a face of pleasure, and the pleasure is all mine. This is your first appearance on the island where I have made my primary home, and it will probably be your last. The expense of transportation, as you will have guessed, far outweighs any possible profit. But a remarkable and happy event has emerged from your visit, one that contents me a great deal. I apologize for being too late to attend the actual ceremony, but I have had various things to do. I have also witnessed a sad and strange thing. The failed assassin of His Excellency has publicly regretted the failure of what must be termed not merely murderous but also blasphemous. The police, acting on information received, arrived at this man's house, which is in Nattermann Square, a populous place, to find him waiting armed at his front door, warned of their approach by their sirens. He made his loud declaration of dissatisfaction with life in general and, in particular, the organization of life in this republic, and then he fired at nothing, though the police thought it was at them. Rightly nervous, they counter-fired, and the man dropped on his own doorstep, full of bullets. He was a man who had been much respected for his gentility and learning, and also pitied for the cruel deformity he carried from the womb, being truly misbegotten. Many were shocked to find he could conceive an assassin's purpose, if not achieve an assassin's success. His name was Dr Gonzi. Mr Dunkel had, I believe, made professional overtures to him, but he was not, I think, known to any of the rest of you here.

Dr Fonanta smiled around but gave no special gesture to indicate the part that Catherine and I had played, I alone really, in the accomplishment of Dr Gonzi's messy quietus. I bowed the head inside my head in grave acknowledgement of his happy release, and then I allowed my heart to leap, since my own release could now not be delayed much longer. Somewhere on one of the imagined corners of the ring, behind his elders, the elephant boy was still playing his little radio. I fancied that the news was coming through in Castitan. Catherine said:

– Miss Emmett, how is Miss –

– Better, my dear, as you will soon, I hope, see.

I said:

– My bride and me, like. We ought to be on our way to the old nuptial like couch, man.

That phrase, despite the tmesis, sounded too literary for poor Llew, so I qualified it with two or three iconic loin thrusts and an openmouthed leer, adding a couple of Zulu clicks for good measure. Dr Fonanta, with merry regret, said:

– Ah, my dear boy and girl – I know them already, ladies and gentlemen, and they have many fine qualities – there are certain secular hymeneal ceremonies to be performed – a tradition with circus weddings. First, an epithalamium has to be recited. I have such a composition here, as it happens, newly written, its writing one of the reasons for my lateness. Clink glasses freely, since, frail as I am, my voice can rise well enough to this occasion.

It could too, by God. Dr Fonanta took a sheet of typescript from an inner pocket and then must, from the volume he poured out, have activated a hidden amplifier. While the company drank in embarrassment, he declaimed an English poem in a French voice:

Let the marriage demons shed
Grace and blessings on this bed
That these two shall occupy,
Where with laced limbs there will lie
Youthful bone with youthful flesh,
Fresh as blossom, blossom fresh,
One already, now more one
In predestined unison –

I couldn't help it. In my own voice I cried out:

– Oh God, to think you have the nerve to disparage a genius like Sib Legeru –

The response to this was various. Most seemed to think I was putting on a bad and badmannered act, some saw me with new and narrowing eyes, others knew too little English to perceive any difference between this and the regular Llew. The Bird Queen betrayed nothing. Dr Fonanta spoke goodhumouredly:

– Very well, my boy, let us have no bedding poem. Let us, or rather you, have the bedding itself.

He nodded to the bandleader, a beery man who had removed his frogged tunic. The bandleader shrugged and made his players blow and thud that unfamiliar wedding march again. Dr Fonanta called above it:

– Carry them to their wedded bliss.

I was at once picked up with ease by a little man of superb development who doubtless did that sort of thing professionally. But this, like the elephant dance, was too much like shop. A varied gang soon had me roughly aloft, and Catherine was chaired more gently, with compassion even, by a team which contained all the ladies of the troupe, Aderyn excepted. She was not to be seen, she had disappeared with birdlike suddenness. As we moved out by way of the backring area, The Great Giro came up with one of the celluloid dolls from the weddingcake, grinning in plenidental malice. He drew a lighter from his pocket, struck it aflame, and consumed the doll in less than a second. I said:

– Might be the wrong one, you shitbrained salamiarsed mortadellastuffer.

There were fireworks out tonight, thudding and searing the samite air. Dr Fonanta, down there alongside pushed by Umberto, remarked on them, the happy coincidence of the festal sparks and skytrails and violet bursts, but the happier coincidence of the noise. He said:

– Charivari one might see it as, hear it rather. And now, ladies and gentlemen, *trot them.*

And so we were jolted at the double, Catherine going faintly *oh oh oh*, towards the trailer park, and we stopped before the door of one fine blue chunk of mobile living luxe, eight feet high and twenty long. Dunkel, who had been following in the rear, somewhat subdued (probably because of that massive *faux pas* with the late Dr Gonzi, its indiscretion at last revealed to him), now came with a key, opened up, and switched on a light. Dr Fonanta said:

– Now perhaps the ladies would be good enough to prepare the bride for the consummation of her joy.

With Catherine still feebly going *oh oh oh*, and then, in sharper stabs, *No* and again *no*, the ladies giggled her in, on her feet now, to a vague prospect of softness and shadow. Then the door was closed and I was left with the men, who dropped me pretty much as I once saw a treed monkey drop a puppydog she had stolen from its dam – the supporting arms losing interest, the burden consigned to the air, a bump which caused yelps. I picked myself up and dusted off Llew's suit and found Umberto offering me a drink from a silver flask.

– Stick it, man, I said. I've had enough for one night.
– *U trink.*

And, by God, I had to. It was all right: cherry brandy with a metal brace of something, but I was really drunk already. I had to be drunk. Dr Fonanta said:

– Dutch courage as they call it. Now I don't think you'll begrudge me my reading of the part of my poem which is addressed to the bridegroom only.

He had the paper in his hands. He could almost read by the whizzing exhalations, and the noise, which was distant enough, meant nothing to him. The strong men who had upheld and then dropped me stood around with folded arms, grinning. He recited:

> Donor of the honeyed pang,
> You, whose kingdom is the *yang*,
> Generalize the yielding *yin*
> Much before you stand within,
> Hanging Phryne's likeness on
> Undifferentiated noumenon.
> Do not yearn for Helen – ask!
> All identity's a mask,
> Even swords of sib and kith
> Wait for melting by the smith,
> *Orang tukang, homo faber*,
> And, by dint of his tough labour,
> But by godlike *vis* enpassioned,
> Gladly seek to be refashioned –

– What's that? I asked feebly. What was that word, name – I may not have got, gotten, all the lines right, but I was certain that among them – I was very drunk, there was no doubt. The circusmen laughed. Dr Fonanta smiled kindly. And then the door opened and the ladies, also laughing, came out, indicating that I might now enter, and I heard the rich voice of Father Costello somewhere in the background intoning:

– God flow in your seed.

But then I was inside the trailer, the door shut on me violently but silently, and I faced poor scared Catherine – naked, as I could tell from the neat pile of her clothes on a wallseat – with the bedclothes up to her chin, timehonoured useless shield against entering man.

– I've got to, I said, flopping on to that very seat where her over and under clothes lay, think.

– Oh what a mess you've you've –

– Think, I snarled, I've got to *think*.

Outside the trailer was the crunching of rockets and petards, also the noise of retreating simple circusfolk who were going off to finish the champagne. Inside there was as much luxury as it seemed possible to get into a mobile home –

white sheepskin rugs on the marbly composition deck, a fine double bed with black silk pillowcases and a crimson, gold and white silk coverlet, a complicated wallpanel to control a radiogram, lights, toaster, teamaker and the sliding door of a small bar. There were embroidered hangings – a Flemish hunting scene, a naked mythological rout with grapeclusters and winecups – and also some good reproduction of modern painters like Rostral, Ombro and Indigène. But there were no windows or lights or whatever they're called on a trailer. There was a desk fixed firmly in a corner, also a glass-doored inset cupboard full of files. Reduced in size and made static, this cabin or stateroom would be called a bedsitter. A heavy brocade curtain led to what I supposed were a kitchen and bathroom. The first would have, I was sure, Fortnum and Mason delicacies in it, including a fussy brand of Assam or Cameron Highlands tea; the second would gleam with lovely bottles – Penult, Divan, Incog, Pro and Con, Rondeau.

– Think, I said.

And I was struck by what I should have been struck by in the Batavia Hotel – the meaning of *Tukang*, Yumyum Carlotta's name. It meant what *Faber* meant – a skilled workman. I was struck by what I had done before making that al fresco protest – answering what should properly have been the unanswerable, for I doubted whether Professor Keteki had known the answer. A man with a clubfoot had once answered the unanswerable and moved on to sleep with his mother. Riddles are there for a good purpose – not to be answered. They are like those do-not-touch wallpanels set in the great buildings of the modern world, which you can take as a rationalized translation of the natural order, panels decorated with Black Hand Gang warning signs – skulls and crossed bones, stylized lightning streaks. Fifty thousand million volts, mortal danger. As for Swellfoot the Tyrant, how much was he to blame? If he hadn't answered he wouldn't have banged his mother. If he hadn't answered he would have been eaten alive. Take your choice, man. I'd had to answer Dr Gonzi's riddle at the last; the first time, though, I'd risked being eaten alive. I'd done better than Pusfoot, but it made no difference. I had no excuse. I'd answered the unanswerable, and the bloody unanswerable was often as easy to answer as the four-two-three nonsense that brought plague and famine and blindness and death to a Greek kingdom. What goes up when the rain comes down? An umbrella. You could build a whole tragic cycle on that. It isn't the difficulty that makes the riddle unanswerable; it's the unanswerability.

I hardly started at all when a voice came out of the ceiling. Catherine looked up, petrified as a saint, and I noticed that the poor girl had a quite nicely made throat. The voice was not human. It said:

– You can be seen, you know.

It said that three times. It was a bird's voice, of course. It had, like a telephone time signal, been prerecorded: the repetitions were exact. It came from what I had taken to be a ventilator but was evidently one of a cunningly disposed set of hi-fi speakers. Presumably the recording was coming from a tape machine somewhere in the wall: it wasn't worth my while to investigate. After a pause it said it three times again. Easily done: transferred in endless repetition from one tape to another. She was mad. But cleverly mad: witness this use of impersonality. *You can be seen, you know.* By anybody, everybody, nobody. Spoken by the voice of all three.

And then another point came to me: why did it always have to be a bird or a half beast? Birds spoke; demianimals spoke. The riddle couldn't have been asked by a portly shiningfaced man in a robe, offering Oedipus a couple of ripe figs, or a hetaera offering more, showing glowing shoulders. Like, now, Catherine's in her fear. The riddler has to be itself a riddle. But no: the ultimate organic creation's emissary, rather, granted a voice. With this voice it says: *Dare to try to disturb the mystery of order.* For order has both to be and not to be challenged, this being the anomalous condition of the sustention of the cosmos. Rebel becomes hero; witch becomes saint. Exogamy means disruption and also stability; incest means stability and also disruption. You've got to have it both ways, man. I needed Dr Gonzi to clarify all this for me, but Dr Gonzi had to be dead. The other doctor had moved me on from Berkeley to Kant. That flesh on the bed was the nameless intuited; on her I had to impose, along with my person, some legitimate, meaning sensuously acceptable, phenomenon. I was drunk, remember.

– You can be seen, you know.

– I don't doubt it, I answered, beginning to take off my, Llew's, clothes. And I didn't, either: behind those tapestry hangings there were probably, after all, miniature portholes coinciding with the blank eyes of the hunters and revellers.

– Heard too, probably, I answered. Under the mattress a microphone would be eager to drink up the whole drama of sonorities. I was totally trapped, but I had initiated the process that night on the campus. 1 plus 1 equals 1 when you're dealing with capital crimes or mortal sins. It was a mere formality now to see if the door was locked. It was. I already had my shirt off when I tried it. Catherine was, of course, aghast, appalled, incredulous, speechless, to see me standing at last naked, drunk, grim.

– You can be heard, you know.

He changeth his tune.

– We've got to push on, I told her, to very nearly the limit. Trust me. I won't cross the border. We're on the stage, that's all. The acting ends when they unlock that door and let us out.

I brushed my hand along the control panel and the lights went off. And, in mid-moneme, the bird went silent. Then I was in the roomy bed struggling briefly with Catherine, who was too weary and tranquillized to hold me off. That viaticum I had been made to drink had undoubtedly been spiked with cantharides or something, but the bitchy madonna barebacked girl had been the true stimulant. What she had started could now be finished. She was in my arms now, grown plump. Catherine did a very tired row of breathless protests, but I whispered *An act an act* in her ear. I remembered a couplet of the Earl of Rochester's, once quoted by Professor Keteki, whose name, I realized for the first time, was pronounced not unlike Kitty Kee: *Swift orders that I should prepare to throw/ The all dissolving thunderbolt below.* I must withdraw stay withdraw stay withdraw stay.

A hellish hammering on the door and the shrilling of female

voices imposed a counterspasm. I was out of that bed at once, pumping seed on to Dunkel's sheepskin rugs. I groped, still pumping, to the control panel and had light on again, also the birdvoice saying we could be heard, you know. To Catherine I cried:

– Get your clothes on. It's all over.

18

— Only reasonable, I think, Dr Fonanta repeated, to let them spend the remnant of their wedding night – whose happiness so far has been grossly impaired by the trauma of that sudden interruption – back in the town; back, shall I say, in the bride's own premarital lodging. A circus does not perhaps after all provide the proper ambience for the start of a honeymoon. This young pair needs and deserves tranquillity.

The fireworks had ceased and a quarter moon had risen. Dunkel was in his trailer looking for marks of my defilement. His eyesight was such that he could not easily see the floor without getting on his hands and knees, and this he did not do. Catherine stood beside me, unnaturally jaunty. Her ring-finger lacked its ring. Dunkel would find it later in his bed perhaps. I was back in Llew's suit, my own few possessions in its pockets. Umberto still held Miss Emmett back. Her scissors were at her waist, bright in moonshine. She had said:

— Filthy woman, filthy filthy woman. Listening, trying to look. Luring my Kitty Kee into that thing with this horrible boy, and then looking and listening. If poor poor Miles was here he'd rend mother and son alike. Filthy family.

Aderyn the Bird Queen seemed to have had her good eye clawed at, though the blood that trickled from near the tear duct was minimal. She said:

— He's not to go. Not yet if ever. Mothers have their rights. We have things to say to each other.

— Your son is a married man now, Dr Fonanta smiled from his wheelchair. He must go where he wishes to go, and that is where his bride goes.

— Married indeed, cried Miss Emmett as she had cried before. I won't have them married. A filthy trick behind my back, that's what it was and is. I'll have the police in.

I felt very strange – weak though not ill, sinner and martyr, in and out of danger. Dr Fonanta said very gently:

– We won't talk about the police, Miss Emmett. Not the police. Let's leave the police out of things.

She was quiet then. I said:

– I'm getting out of here, mam. With Catherine. I've played your fucking game, see, and I've like had enough. We're going a long way away. There's the money, see, we're all right for money, she's got plenty, see. You agreed to it all, mam. By letting us get married in the first place you agreed. Like to us living our own life, see.

– Yes, Aderyn said very tiredly. But there's something still to be settled, *bachgen*. I'm not satisfied yet.

– What is it you want, mam? Haven't you had enough out of me?

– You and me together, boy *bach*. Just for a little while.

Dr Fonanta shrugged himself brokenly, saying:

– Only reasonable. Umberto will drive Catherine and Miss Emmett into town. Your stay here has been short, Miss Emmett, but not uneventful.

– Marriage, indeed. While I lie there out like a light with my horrible dreams.

– You, my boy, will, I take it, find your own transportation later. Go with your mother, then. It must be the last time for some time, I think.

– And if I say no, mam?

– It's not possible for you to say no, *bach*.

No, it wasn't. She led me back towards the big top, while Miss Emmett called:

– Keep away from her, do you hear? Marriage, indeed.

I think, looking back, I knew pretty well what was going to happen, though it may be a matter of wisdom after the event, long after. But how else, accepting the logic of the entire complex, could things now transpire except through this silent walk to the ring where her only magic lay, through what happened there and what I was prepared to have happen? The working lights were on still, and a couple of clowns argued metatheology over the last flatness of the champagne. The mammals had gone to their rest, but the birds were awake and preening. Aderyn said to the clowns:

— There is a thing my boy and I must rehearse here.

— Finsen is as unsound on that point as Onagros was. Onagros was, as I've perhaps said too often, a very tame ass. Eh, eh? Yes, dear lady, yes. Just going.

This zany still had nose and big flapperfeet on. He left with his colleague, who was German and knew all about Strauss and the Romantic School: part of his costume was a pair of exaggeratedly patched levis. I said:

— Plenty of intellectual life in this fucking circus, mam. Dr Fonanta sets the pattern like. And then there's you and your passage from fucking pure to fucking applied horny theology.

— You come now out into the open, boy. Your bolt is shot. What have you done with my son?

— Your son is going through a passage, mam. A married man now, see. And growing up in other ways too.

— You, Aderyn said, are Miles Faber. That girl is your sister. You have committed the most deadly sin, and it must be only to cover up the twin of that sin, which is murder.

She had dropped the Welshiness but was ready now for the *hwyl* of the small town Calvinistic Methodist preacher.

— Fucking nonsense, mam, and you know it.

— My son did many wrong things and was often threatened in town after town. I feared for him here and asked the police to keep watch on him and apologized also for any wrong he might already have done. And the police said my son had given the name of Miles Faber.

— And isn't it right sometimes to give a false name? And if I gave the surname of the girl I loved it was because the name was like a tune in my fucking brain, mam.

— This will not do, none of it. I can guess at what must have happened, although I am fearful of guessing. I would rather you were my son, alive and well and now married into a good family. You have lived a bad life, if you are truly my son, but I have loved you through it. And your start was so good. Good from the very day of your birth, which was the best of days, being no other than *Nadolig*. But they do say the Big Black Jesus too was born on that day, so he may have fought with the White One above your cradle and scratched you deep before he was sent raging off. If you are my son, if if if –

Clichés: my head reeled, etc. From the whole junkshop of old iron that was hurled at me I caught in midair a rusty poker and prepared to hurl it back. I said:

– *If* is a right word, mam. I might talk about *if you are my mother*. I might talk about a matter of adoption and long years of pretence. For it came out when you said about my father not being really my father only the other day. You were coming close to truth but not close enough, for it was yourself you meant, not him.

If all this sounds histrionic, remember that it took place in a circus ring and that the participants were naturally exhibitionistic and one of them was Welsh and the other pretending to be. Aderyn's response to my words was of a violence appropriate to crude entertainment. She staggered against her cage of hunters to say:

– Who has been talking to you, boy? Is it Dr Fonanta?

– Dr Fonanta was with me and my bride-to-be earlier today, yes, but he said nothing of this. I've been thinking a bit, mam, see, thinking. But as you mention Dr Fonanta, which isn't his right name, of that I'm fucking sure, I'll bet he had something to do with you getting me in the first place, when you were already a mature like woman with a husband that you left or a fancy man would be more fucking like it, and no kids of your own and wanting a kid. And that's about it, see, I fucking reckon.

– And whose son are you then, if you're not mine, if you *are* my son that is, Llew that is –

She was becoming nicely confused all the time things were becoming horribly clear to me, twincest, and me the older by an hour or so, and environment a great deal more important than heredity. I said:

– That's not important. What is important is me being a man with a wife and a life beginning and not the son of particular parents. But I'll say something about the name, oh yes, the name, mam –

– You're not him, I can tell all the time you're not, what with the voice and the hands and the words you're using –

– The name, mam. Would it have been Noel for Christmas

turned back to become Leon, a sort of a lion, or Nowell like in The First Nowell which goes back to give you Llew and there's the *no* cut out which I'm going to get from you loud and clear as from now, but very unconvincing, mam, and Llewelyn and Leon are the same name really and Llewelyn Llewelyn will do very nicely for the boy, yes yes yes, mam?

– No. No. No.

She almost propelled the cage towards the exit with the desperateness of her leaning on it for support.

– Just the word I'd said I'd get from you. And the same word is the last word from me to you, a word of what they call rejection. For I'm going off now, mam.

She took in a few calming breaths, deeply, professionally, right from the diaphragm. She was still in her ring robe and her false hair and her henna makeup. Impressive, no doubt, very. She said:

– Love is love, *bachgen*, even if sometimes it is only another word for possession. Sit down on that chair, *bach*, just for a minute before you go.

I had known, of course, that the scene couldn't end with my waving a fierce hand and walking off, *no* echoing like a final band chord. She needed more than words, and perhaps I needed it too. I sat down on one of the chairs left over from the wedding party. I waited. She said:

– All those things are not important, you're right there. But it is important to me to know whether my son is sitting down here before me, even though he is a changed son who talks of going off for ever.

– Marriage was my idea, mam, but a marriage as soon as possible was yours. Mistrust. Mistrust is a bad thing in a mother.

– I could ask if you remembered Alwyn Probert in Cardiff who went to sea and fell overboard. I could ask about the Misses Hogan who sold syrup of figs from a big bottle in the corner shop. I could ask many things about our past life together. But one thing will suffice and it will prove all.

– Proof and love. It won't do, mam. I can see you're going to put me through some kind of fucking fiery furnace to see whether I'm the loved thing you know is leaving you anyway.

Your senses and your reason ought to be enough. This is really the end.

– If you are not my boy then I shall start looking for my boy. But you will be punished first.

With that she opened the cage of hawks and, with her admirable skill, warbled them out in order – merloun, gerfalcon, falcon gentle, falcon of the rock, falcon peregrine, bastard, sacre, lanner, merlin, hobby, goshawk, tiercel, sparrowhawk, kestrel. The lovely creatures, with their frowning eyes that meant no enmity and their cruel flukes that would tear without malice, in a multiple whisper of wings soared, towered, looked down for the familiar castered perch that was not there, and were kept on the wing, circling, circling, soothed into the empty action by a new warbling from their mistress's throat. Aderyn opened the other cage and, rather like a housewife looking for the right package in a kitchen cupboard, searched with her hurt eyes and her gentle hand for the bird she wanted. Her wrist emerged with a snowy cockatoo that cocked its head at me as though, which was true, there were to be relations between us, though it would only be a relationship of a man and a machine. The hawks whirred above, a ring concentric to a ring. I said:

– This will be a riddle, won't it, mam? And the riddle will have come straight out of Dr Fonanta's Book of Versified Riddles available only to the trade, whatever the trade is. I've been learning a lot, see, mam.

– You remember the night in Norman, Oklahoma, she said, stroking the cockatoo's feathers. There was a kind of jeering professor, you remember, who laughed when some of the birds did not do well. They were nervous and it was an audience with very little sympathy in it, remember. So I had him up on the stage – you were there, you saw from the wings – and this riddle was asked him. And the consequence of him getting it wrong was that he was made very frightened and thought his eyes would be pecked out. If you are my son, you will know the answer. If you are not my son, you will be punished for your crimes, and one of these crimes is the crime of pretence.

– You're mad, mam, I said, putting my right hand in my,

Llew'sjacket pocket. If they all wanted a game they could have a game.

But she was coaxing the cockatoo with whispered cue-words. She said:

– Come now. *Who was the who was the.*

The bird preened, cocked, cleared its throat and squawked its riddle:

> Who was the final final, say,
> That was put back but had his day?

The Fonanta touch was in it. Stalling, I said:

– An owl should be asking, an owl.

For I remembered that dream in the Algonquin bedroom. But she said:

– An owl could say *Who?* Imagine an owl is saying it. And God help you now, boy, for the hawks are hovering.

The horror was that there were two answers, both perfectly valid. But two answers would not do. I could not get the riddle wrong but I could never, with such a riddle-mistress, get it right either. I said:

– I never properly heard, mam, whether he said God or the Devil. Because a dog has his day, and if you've had your day you've lived.

– Choose.

I chose, and I made the wrong choice. She cried out a strange word and the hunters swooped. The eyes the eyes. It was once common training to teach hawks to tear out the eyes of sheep. I fought off the whirring snapping phalanx with my left hand and with my right I brought my talisman from Llew's pocket. If they wanted a game they could have a game, complete with referee's whistle. I fumbled the silver cylinder to my lips and pierced a swathe through the whirling snappers with a great clean blast. I blasted and blasted and they were maddened and confused. The talking birds in their cage were confused into a response of maniacal multiple recitation, and the effect was, a segment of my brain was just about able to admit, not unlike Sib Legeru. I blasted, and the hawks knew they had to attack what my poor twin, my extrapolated id really perhaps, had Shakespeareanly called jellies, human ones, but none where that maddening shriek obstructed their right of attack. I blasted away still, and I knew that my right answer was not to the riddle but to the fear I should be feeling. In my panic of a childhood dream I should be calling *Mam mam I'm frightened take them away mam*. She would have known then: she would have called off the bogeybirds. But now she was fighting for her own eyes, though some of the lesser hawks had found a target in the cockatoo. He, squawking *Had his day had his day*, found his way back to his caged companions and safety, and Aderyn faced the entire army. It was she who cried *Stop it stop them Llew Llew*, and compassion drew my lips away. The birds woke from their violent trance and would have, in rational sobriety, turned on me who had tormented them, but she warbled desperately and rallied and called them to a flock and then to a caged flock and I said:

— I couldn't be a little boy again, mam. It's all different from now on.

As I left (and my first task must be to get Llew's passport from her handbag in the trailer and destroy it without reading it) she called for me to come back, but she seemed pretty sure it was her son she was calling, or the boy she called her son. She would be all right. She would get over it. In a day or so she would be talking of the consolation of her art, such as it was.

19

The Sunday bells were jubilant all over the capital, but nearby, perhaps in some heretic chapel or other tolerated pocket of dissent, a single bell tolled and tolled. That would do for Llew, wherever his body was. I had spent the remainder of the night in the attic of the house on Indovinella Street, dead asleep, undisturbed by Catherine and Miss Emmett, who kept vigil among their packed bags and must have been off in a taxi shortly after dawn. It was probably the noise of the banging front door that woke me and, after curiously painful micturition, sent me downstairs to find a note in the livingroom, a key holding it from the Caribbean wind that freshened from the window: *Give to Cunsummatu & Son Agent on Habis Road*. Nothing else.

I was not surprised to find that the body of Llew had disappeared from the outhouse. I would rest in the obscurity of Dr Fonanta's purpose while taking his power for granted. A revelation of sorts would come. Meanwhile I transported, under the joyous chaos of the bells, the works of Sib Legeru, or most of them, into the livingroom, more appropriate than the outhouse. I was astonished to find that he had composed music as well as created literature and pictures. There was an orchestral score headed *Sinfonietta* with parts for such instruments as chimburu blocks and Tibetan nosehorn. I could not at that time read music, though I have learnt very thoroughly since, and I was not able to judge of the work's merit, but I did not doubt it was great. There were no signs of any sculpture, but some boxes, most of them too heavy to handle, probably had stone and metal groups and figurines in them. But, for the time being, there was enough to be getting on with in the canvases and typescripts and notebooks.

I was struck, reading some elegiac hexameters over a mug

of tea with no sugar, by the sudden problem of how to get these things to America. I still had no money but I could wire for some and thus pay for airfreighting. But the danger of hijacking was considerable at that time – men with guns and much hair suddenly emerging from among docile air passengers and demanding that the plane be diverted from its true course and be flown to such places as Havana. The purpose of the hijacking was never really clear, but I think it was a kind of protest, like my own yummy campus affair. No no no, shut that out, for the time being anyway. Memo: *Ask Fonanta*. If a hijacked plane crash had killed my father, planes in general were not good for Sib Legeru. It seemed to me that the best thing to do was to convey the better part of his work tenderly in the *Zagadka II*, if those faggots would agree. I took time off from my reading to cross over to the Yo Ho Me Lads to see if at least drunken Aspinwall was there. He was, with a nearly full bottle of Azzopardi's special white rum in front of him. Safe then till, say, tomorrow. He called:

– Bastard's gone off again. Screw him. Have drink.
– Later. Order another bottle.
– Manuel Manuel Manuel!

I left, well satisfied, and was crossing the road when the shining monster of Dr Fonanta drove up, Umberto at the wheel affecting not to recognize me. Dr Fonanta was, in cloak and wide hat, very much the jelyf man; his baldness was chiefly for Manhattan. But he came into the house on his crutches, sat in the livingroom, beamed, then screwed his nose at the sight of the works of his artistic superior.

– Well, I said.

– *Well* meaning *Llew*. That poor boy is wiped out of the world now. There was never a more unnecessary birth than his, so no regrets. Umberto carried him off in a sack during the night, very Verdian. Verdi. That music you have there doesn't make sense. You can't have five crotchets in a bar when the time signature is three-four. A lot of nonsense. Look – that bassoon part goes down to F-sharp below the stave. Impossible.

– You know it all, don't you?

– And don't start talking about freedom of expression. The bassoonist is not free to play that F-sharp. Except of course in the mind in the mind in the mind. Berkeleyen, Gonzian, a lot of nonsense.

– You knew Gonzi well, did you?

– He sought philosophical adjustment from me, *he*, a philosopher. I wrote a little conundrum on his name. For some reason it gave him a sense of power.

– And what sort of a conundrum would you write on *your* name?

– It would go best in music, he smiled. Then he sang to *lah* four notes, in intervals which I have since learnt to designate as a major third, a whole tone, a fourth, adding: The last letter of the name can't be sphynxified, but R in Tudor notation stood for a rest.

– And your relationship to me, if any?

– Grandfather.

I stared at him for five seconds, long enough to sing F A B E with a rest after, and was nearly fool enough to ask jauntily: *maternal or paternal?* Instead I pretended that this was no great revelation and said:

– Have I, besides you and my sister, any other relatives?

– You had a brief supererogatory twin, of course. But I think you can be quite certain that your sister and myself and yourself represent the total remnant of a once large and flourishing family.

There was something I couldn't understand. I took out the almost pulped picture of Carlotta and showed it him. He squinted at it frowning. I said:

– Are you sure that's not my mother?

– Quite sure. You caught the word *tukang* last night, eh? I myself learned the word from the charming proprietress of the Batavia Hotel. Quite a coincidence, I admit.

– Really a coincidence?

– One could do nothing without the help of coincidence. This lady novelist's original name was, I believe, Ramphastos, but that did not sound much like a popular novelist's name. She tried Toucan, but that was too obviously ornithological. Tukang had a spicy Oriental ring about it. If you wish to know how I know all this –

– I don't, not really.

– I got Mr Loewe in New York to do some quick research. Guest book at the Lord Cumberland Inn in Riverhead, Massachusetts, newspaper files, the usual thing. I was concerned, you see. Something of great moment was about to begin.

– And is this bird woman any relation of Aderyn?

– You do seem to have relationships on the brain, don't you? Surprising in one who professes such an admiration for all this relationless nonsense mouldering here. No, no relation.

– What do you know about the Maltese language?

– Dear me, you do dart about. Nothing, except that it's a Northern Arabic dialect with Italian loanwords and that it's had a written form for a little over a century.

So I'd given the wrong answer. Plausible, but wrong. That Elizabethan play that had been titularly gold? Something lost, probably: *Midas and Hys Goulden Touche*; *A Girl Worth Gold* (but I seemed to remember that was later than 1596); *A Peece of Gold Good my Maisters*; *The Returne of the Golden Age, or Gloriana's Triumphs*; *Goldfinger and Silverskin*. I was satisfied about that, then. I said:

– Why is your accent French if you were so patently brought up in the Anglo-Saxon tradition?

– Anglo-Saxon tradition?

– Roast pork and apple sauce. Synchronic sweet and savoury. Not at all French.

– Clever. I have always found the Gallic approach to life sympathetic. A fair tradition of liberty and equality. Fraternity doesn't matter quite so much, does it? In America, when you consider what has to be considered, my French accent has been a help. A token, too, of rational and humane and revolutionary principles mostly now, alas, lost. But your mention of the Anglo-Saxon tradition is apropos. I have studied the language. I know what the name Sib Legeru means.

– And I know what the name Miles Faber means.

– True, but pseudonyms, of which Sib Legeru is one, carry a privy message. Perhaps my own main pseudonym has too general a signification. Z. Fonanta, *zoon phonanta*, the talking animal, man.

– Do you market a product called Jellif?

– I once suggested the name to a marketing organization in New York. May I say how glad I am to see you looking for connections, tightening bolts that aren't there, soldiering on despite your manifest weariness, hammering away at structures.

– Why should you have anything to do with a circus?

– Why not? Circuses cross national boundaries with comparative ease. I began by making use of other men's circuses, I ended by establishing my own. You see, my boy, I started with gross disadvantages. Crippled, no money behind me, full of incestuous guilt –

– God, you too?

– It runs in the family, I'm afraid. But you have exorcized the curse. That was your purpose in coming here. There'll be no more incest in the Faber family.

– Who was was –

– My own mother. The gods punished me with exemplary speed. I was run over by a tramcar in Lille. It has never prevented me from loving France. But back to my point. I had no trade, despite our family name, and I needed to make money quickly. Fate and the community denied me the opportunities I sought. I decided to conduct a business of illegal imports and exports.

– Using circuses?

– The floor of a lion's cage is left severely alone by the customs officers. Valuable objects can be lodged in the crops of birds. Circuses are innocent, complex, and highly mobile. Our present age is hungry for the passage of illegal commodities – drugs chiefly. But I've made the Faber fortune, I do little now. I have leisure for scholarship. But even there I have not been endowed with the singleminded capacity for specialization I would have wished. Dabble dabble dabble. My medical degree I obtained in late middle age from a disreputable university I shored up with a longterm interest-free loan. I wanted to specialize in the psychology of incest, but the scope is surprisingly limited. So I dabble still – music, literature, light philosophy. Art, I believe, will prove man's salvation, but not. This. Kind. Of. Pseudo. Art.

On these last emphatic words he beat his chairarm petulantly with his ceramic hand, wrinkling, puffing, beetling, looking old. I said:

– Who was Sib Legeru?

– Who? *Who?* *What* would be a more appropriate interrogative. Consider first the name. In a famous sermon delivered by Bishop Wulfstan at the end of the first Christian millennium, a time when Antichrist in the shape of the Danes seemed likely to corrupt, rend and liquidate Anglo-Saxon civilization, the word *siblegeru* appears. It means legging or ligging or lying with one's own sib, it means *incest*.

– No.

– You deny that is the meaning?

– No. No.

– You think of freedom of artistic expression as being wonderfully incarnated in these works, no doubt. No doubt, no doubt, you are *young*. Liberation even from the dungeon of unconscious obsessions. The death of the syntax of the old men. No more solar or lunar crudities of sharp light – instead, the glamour of the eclipse. What utter nonsense. These works are as rigidly encased in the iron waistcoat of imposed form as, say, that autumn sonnet of mine which the wrinkling of your nose indicated you found so jejune and distasteful, so oldmannish, so *unfree*. Look at that picture there. Its elements are derived from a children's page word transformation puzzle: *bread broad brood blood*. That companion picture yields *blood blond bland*. And there, with that blasphemous parody of the Droeshout portrait, you have another kiddy teaser: *book boot boat coat coal*. The pseudoliterary *works* are based on the meanest and most irrelevant of taxonomies, they derive their structures from the alphabetic arrangements of encyclopaedias and dictionaries. Try it, my boy; anybody can do it. Why, I can, as I sit here now, extemporize any number of *deathless* Sib Legeru lines. Like this:

Cased armadillo, snuffling gorger of ants,
Cruel cross between hyena and civet
Chew St John's whiskers, crunch great mullein,
    privet,
Goldenrod, all manner of plants,
While the deadmeatbird tears at the African sky
Above the sackbacked Arabs in the headwind's
    thrust,
And the balls are clicked on the wires in digital
    lust
Down to the limits of hell, where the long lost
    cry.

– Better, I said, than all the works of Swart Smythe put
together. Though that last line has too much of the ring of
Robert W. Service.

– An improvisation only. And I've barely tapped the first
column of the first page of any English dictionary you care to
name. Don't be taken in, my boy. Bad though my later
poems may be, they are at least honest. They deal with the
normal processes of human life – love, friendship, the changing seasons –

– Oh, Jesus.

– Jesus, yes, the consolations of faith, the desire for a happy
death, the living of a helpful and harmless life, the seasons,
friendship –

– You're repeating yourself.

– A boy should treat his grandfather with respect, but
never mind. One can expect little from the young. But to
revert. Those *works* of Sib Legeru exhibit the nastiest aspects
of incest – and I use the term in its widest sense to signify the
breakdown of order, the collapse of communication, the
irresponsible cultivation of chaos. In them are combined an
absence of meaning and a sniggering boyscout codishness. It
is man's job to impose manifest order on the universe, not to
yearn for Chapter Zero of the Book of Genesis.

– Are you, were you –

– Sib Legeru? Oh yes, I and others, patients chiefly. Your
father wrote a ridiculous epic poem about Laman and Rosh,
impossible spineless jelyfs. It was a kind of therapeutic ex-

periment. A spurious joy in spurious creation, followed by the salutory horror of seeing how mad and bad and *filthy* the pseudoworks were. The victims of incest too, the unwilling participators in the killing of communication. There is a poem there, I see, written by your own sister.

That poem, *that*? I read it again:

> And caged Cardinal Mabinogion
> Though M is NN copied slack
> A freehand onestroke perfect round
> Took that bony face aback!

– Oh no, I said, no.

– That's very nearly your only utterance today, dear boy. I trust you are saying *no* to *no*, negating negation. I notice, by the way, that one work is missing from this collection. It must still be in that outhouse. My nose tells me it is not here. I don't know how to describe it. Art takes the raw material of the world about us and attempts to shape it into signification. Antiart takes that same material and seeks insignification. I mean, of course (poor Dr Gonzi!), phenomena, sense data whether primary or secondary. Did you notice a certain smell in that shed?

– Yes.

– There's a little box labelled *Olfact Number One*. Open it at your leisure. Do you propose shipping this *junk* to America, or shall it remain on this unregarded island, a cynosure to the young and misguided who think God was not clever enough not to want to fashion a cosmos?

– I'll think about it.

– Think about it. Go back to civilization, my boy, run the great business founded on my circus money, marry cleanly, beget clean children.

– But I'm not clean myself.

– Meaning not free, not wholly free. But nobody is. Don't blame everything on myself and your father.

When he had left I went to the outhouse and was directed by that stench I had noticed before to a small wooden box hidden among old earthcaked trowels. *Olfact Number One*. It was fastened with a metal clasp. I opened up and nearly fainted. The work was a masterpiece of bad smells. It was not possible to tell what the substances were that were blended to give off so complex a horror – old meat, cheese, fragments of dogmerd announced themselves, but the appearance was of a brown trenched terrain in miniature. I closed it up quickly and wondered whether I ought to parcel it and send it anonymously to some enemy or other. But most of my enemies were public, and the stenches would never get past an undersecretary. It was, when I came to think of it, the sort of thing that Llew would have liked to carry about in his pocket. Be the life and soul of the party with *Olfact Number One.*

20

The *tramontana* is raging like Antichrist this last summer of the second Christian millennium. Lake Bracciano breaks on its shores like the North Sea, and from the cleared dining table on which I write I can watch the heads of foam racing in. All last night an unsecured windowshutter kept crashing, and though I got up three times to force it back to the wall and hold it with the iron *cicogna*, the gust freed it twenty minutes or so after I got back into bed beside Ethel. This morning Lupo Sassone, the garbage collector and oddjobman who lives next door, climbed out on to the parapet to make more acute the angle of the jut of the *cicogna* while the *tramontana* tore at him. I gave him a five-thousand-lire note, one thousand for each second of his work. Prices are high here in Bracciano, but I get a good rate of exchange for my dollars.

This house on the Piazza Padella is small, quite unlike our steel mansion in Stamford, Connecticut, or Ethel's family's palace in Kowloon. It lies under the wall of the castle. The castle, according to the local guidebook, *serves as an example of military architecture of the XV century and it is well preserved even if its vicissitudes were not amongst the most peaceful. It was object of many fights amongst which that between the Orsini and the Colonna families.* We have come here partly so that, in noisy Italian peace and far away from the increasing stresses of New York, I can write this chronicle of a few days in my early life, partly so that we can visit Romolo, who teaches economics in Siena, and so that Bruna, who was recently divorced by her American architect husband, can come in occasionally from Rome and visit *us*. These are two of our adopted children, the Italian ones. There are others, of varying colours and nationalities. We have no children of our own. When Ethel was of childbearing age I frequently begged her to consider being impregnated by some other man, so strong was my desire for a child of her loins. But she has never allowed her ancestral moral principles to be impaired either by the Western permissive ethos or by my own what she considers extravagant desire for her ivory beauty to be transmitted to the future by any means other than the celebration of my verses or of the paintings by Cespite, Manina and Tizzone. She is not really sorry, she says, that we have no children of her own: miscegenation is a fine humane political ideal but its aesthetic results are often undesirable. She believes this to be especially true of the genetic blending of her race and my own.

The verses of Miles Faber have been published by the firm of Stearns and Loomis in London. It was good of my poetic grandfather not to pre-empt that name and to publish instead under the pseudonym of Swart Smythe: it was as though he knew. He is long dead and buried in the Freethinkers' Cemetery outside Grencijta, with the legend M.F., nothing more, on the simple granite. My only other surviving relative, Catherine, is virtually in charge of Anna Sewell (*Black is Beauty*) – appropriate in two modes, unfitting in another, since she is far from beautiful herself. She has had her offers, nevertheless, but remains unmarried: once, she says, is enough. Miss Emmett died recently at the age of ninety in a diabetic coma, far from help and sugar.

The Braccianesi, though naturally polite and accustomed to foreign visitors, still stare at Ethel and myself as we stroll to the Grand' Italia to make a telephone call and wait for it to come through over coffee and Sambuca *con la mosca*. We're a striking couple, I suppose, though middleaged and running a little to fat, as they say. We're both tall, and we represent two totally opposed ethnic types. The sleekhaired louts up in Tolfa, mothercoddled, smug, untravelled, stare more boldly than their counterparts in Bracciano. They would stare less if Ethel were with Miss Emmett or Mr Dunkel or Pine Chandeleur or Aspinwall. But, like Tiger Bay Aderyn and Talking Animal, I am black. A Chinese woman with a black man is a sight for them to drink in slowly, like a three-thousand-lire Coco-Coho.

The story I've told is more true than plausible; at least I admit that the veridicality can, so to speak, be viewed relatively. The main structure is solidly true, but would it matter much if it weren't? Those Sinjantin cigarettes have least of all to do with the structure, yet in a sense they're the truest thing about the whole narrative. I liked them and still do. Ethel's father has friends in high Korean places and sends me cartloads of them. They do me no good, of course, but if you can reach the age of fifty with little more than pangs in the perineum, toothache, fitful dyspnoea and the like, forty Sinjantin a day aren't going to kill you, meaning me. As I said, the main structure is solidly true.

Don't try distilling a message from it, not even an espresso cupful of meaningful epitome or a Sambuca glass of abridgement, *con la mosca*. Communication has been the whatness of the communication. For separable meaning go to the professors, whose job it is to make a meaning out of anything. Professor Keteki, for instance, with his *Volitional Solecisms in Melville*. He, incidentally, had met my grandfather at Columbia and stayed with him briefly in Castita. He was not only a man of learning, he was a sort of a prophet, for he went to jail in 1980 for trying to keep pederasty in the family. He thought highly, you will remember, of Sib Legeru. As far as I know, Sir James Pismire thought little of him, or of any literature or art later than 1920. He had spent his youth in New South Wales and probably his favourite book was Norman Lindsay's *The Magic Pudding*. But he had negotiated a small and awkward loan with my grandfather and was only too ready to have part of the repayment written off in exchange for the use of an outhouse.

If you hunger for an alembicated moral, take one. Take several. Help yourself. Such as that my race, or your race, must start thinking in terms of the human totality and cease weaving its own fancied achievements or miseries into a banner. Black is Beauty, yes, BUT ONLY WITH ANNA SEWELL PRODUCTS. Carlotta, incidentally, commercialized for us on stereotel: Yum Eyestick, Figleaf Manegloss.

Her father, despite his Greek name, was a very black man, and why not? Melanchthon was a blond beast.

Such as that a mania for total liberty is really a mania for prison, and you'll get there by way of incest. Such as that the more they make you try not to commit incest (that poor Greek kid hanging from a tree by a twig thrust through his foot!) the more you're likely to do it (courtesy of Pants Reith). Such as that a good aim in life is to try to be able to afford Higher Games. Such as any damned nonsense you happen to fancy.

My daughter Bruna has, she tells us, been seeing rather a lot of my son Romolo lately. At least he's been coming down to Rome from Siena at weekends to ask her out to dinner and the latest movie of Fellazione or some other old master. I'd be delighted for any daughter of mine to marry any son of mine. I enjoy the movement of life – kids falling in love, performing birds (there was an article on Aderyn the Blind Bird Queen in a popular periodical just after she died), new *gelato* flavours, ceremonies, anthills, poetry, loins, lions, the music of the eight tuned Chinese pipes suspended from an economically carved and highly stylized owl head at our window facing the lake maddened into the sweetest cacophony by a *tramontana* that will not abate its passion, the woman below calling her son in (his name is Orlando and she says his father will be *furioso*), the *ombrellone* on our roof terrace blown out of its metal plinth, the spitted *faraone* for dinner tonight with a bottle of Menicocci, anything in fact that's unincestuous.